The bronze giant, who with his five aides became world famous, whose name was as well known in the far regions of China and the jungles of Africa as in the skyscrapers of New York.

There were stories of Doc Savage's almost incredible strength; of his amazing scientific discoveries of strange weapons and dangerous exploits.

Doc had dedicated his life to aiding those faced by dangers with which they could not cope.

His name brought fear to those who sought to prey upon the unsuspecting. His name was praised by thousands he had saved.

## DOC SAVAGE'S AMAZING CREW

**"Ham," Brigadier General Theodore Marley Brooks,** was never without his ominous, black sword cane.

**"Monk," Lieutenant Colonel Andrew Blodgett Mayfair,** just over five feet tall, yet over 260 pounds. His brutish exterior concealed the mind of a great scientist.

**"Renny," Colonel John Renwick,** his favorite sport was pounding his massive fists through heavy, paneled doors.

**"Long Tom," Major Thomas J. Roberts,** was the physical weakling of the crowd, but a genius at electricity.

**"Johnny," William Harper Littlejohn,** the scientist and greatest living expert on geology and archaeology.

**WITH THEIR LEADER, THEY WOULD
GO ANYWHERE, FIGHT ANYONE,
DARE EVERYTHING—SEEKING
EXCITEMENT AND PERILOUS
ADVENTURE!**

Coming in March 1983 a double volume of
*The Green Eagle* and *The Devil's Playground*

Two Complete Adventures in One Volume

# THE TALKING DEVIL
## and
# THE TEN TON SNAKES

### Kenneth Robeson

BANTAM BOOKS
TORONTO · NEW YORK · LONDON · SYDNEY

THE TALKING DEVIL
THE TEN TON SNAKES

*A Bantam Book / published by arrangement with
The Condé Nast Publications Inc.*

PRINTING HISTORY

The Talking Devil *was originally published in* Doc Savage *magazine,
May 1943. Copyright 1943 by Street & Smith Publications, Inc.
Copyright © renewed 1971 by The Condé Nast Publications Inc.*

The Ten Ton Snakes *was originally published in* Doc Savage *magazine
March 1945. Copyright 1945 by Street & Smith Publications, Inc.
Copyright © renewed 1973 by The Condé Nast Publications Inc.*

*Bantam edition / December 1982*

ISBN 0-553-22755-6

*Published simultaneously in the United States and Canada*

---

*Bantam Books are published by Bantam Books, Inc. Its trademark,
consisting of the words "Bantam Books" and the portrayal of a rooster,
is Registered in U.S. Patent and Trademark Office and in other
countries. Marca Registrada. Bantam Books, Inc., 666 Fifth Avenue,
New York, New York 10103.*

---

PRINTED IN THE UNITED STATES OF AMERICA

O    0 9 8 7 6 5 4 3 2 1

# Contents

# THE TALKING DEVIL

# Chapter I
## THE DEVIL AND COMPANY

Renny Renwick, the engineer, and Long Tom Roberts, the electrical expert, were on hand to meet Doc Savage when he brought his plane down on the Hudson River. Doc taxied the craft, managing it expertly on the wind-whipped river surface, into the big hangar which was disguised as a warehouse on the river front, almost in the shadow of New York's midtown skyscrapers. Renny and Long Tom were a little breathless as they met Doc Savage.

"It's a devil," said Renny.

"It talks," said Long Tom.

"A little statuette of a satan, or a devil, not much more than a foot high," Renny said. "It is made out of bronze or brass or some similar metal."

"It has a deep voice," Long Tom said.

"But only one man hears it talk."

"One man. Nobody else."

"His name is Joseph. Sam Joseph."

"The man who hears it, we mean," Long Tom explained.

Doc Savage listened to them patiently. Patience was one of Doc Savage's accomplishments, being one of the things that had been hammered into him as a part of the strange training which he had received in his youth—when, at diaper age, he had been placed in the hands of scientists to be subjected, over a course of almost twenty years, to an intensive program which was intended to fit him for one specific and rather strange career. Unlike many persons given an arbitrary training before they were old enough to know what it was all about, or speak for themselves, he had elected to follow the career for which he had been trained. It was an unusual career. It consisted, literally, of making other people's business his own. Or at least their troubles.

For some time now, Doc Savage had been taking it on himself to right wrongs and punish evildoers, traveling to the far corners of the earth to do so. He had five associates who worked with him. Renny Renwick and Long Tom Roberts were two members of this group of five.

"A devil," Doc Savage said, getting it straight. "And it talks. But only one man can hear it."

"That's right," Long Tom said. "Sam Joseph."

2

"There are more details," Renny said.

"But they won't make it sound less silly," Long Tom declared.

Renny took Doc's arm. "Come on," he said. "We will take you to talk to Montague Ogden."

"Who is Montague Ogden?"

"He hasn't any connection at all with the devil, or so he claims," said Renny Renwick. "But he is the employer of Sam Joseph, the man who has been hearing the devil speak."

The impressive Ogden building was new, just barely prewar, and the lobby was all black and gold and apparently designed by an architect who had fallen on his head when small. But it was utterly expensive. The elevators were gold and black and also utterly expensive, and the elevator operators were girls with shapes that also looked expensive.

"I would like to have the money it cost to think about building this place," said Renny Renwick, who was an engineer and knew what it had cost.

"I would rather have the elevator operators," said Monk Mayfair. Monk was a remarkably homely fellow with a remarkable eye for a well-turned ankle.

The elevator let them out in a corridor which was ankle-deep in rich carpet. Office building halls are ordinarily not even carpeted.

"What kind of a place *is* this?" remarked Monk.

"Wait," said Renny Renwick, "until you see the master of the establishment."

They walked into a reception room that might have been lifted from a spectacular motion picture. The carpet was even deeper, the colors even richer, the furniture more extreme. The blonde at the desk looked as if she had been manufactured with a magazine cover in mind.

"Mr. Ogden," she told them, bells in her voice, "is expecting you."

Then they walked into a log cabin. Or so it would have seemed, had not the big glass windows offered views of some of the financial district's more impressive buildings. Everything was rustic, extremely rustic, even to the logs blazing in the fieldstone fireplace and the two large dogs lying on the hearth. The dogs lifted their heads and barked.

"I am Montague Ogden," the man behind the desk said. He sounded as if he was accustomed to the name meaning something.

He was smooth. That was the first impression you got of him. As smooth as a polished rock. He was forty-five or fifty years old, well-preserved, and he was dressed in country tweeds and moccasins, so that he blended with his log-cabin inner office.

The general effect of Montague Ogden was a little ridiculous. Unless, of course, you were impressed by the obvious evidences of money.

There were conversational preliminaries, introductions mostly.

Then Montague Ogden got around to making what he evidently intended to be the outstanding statement of the conference.

"I am a very wealthy man," he said.

Doc Savage, with just a trace of the general feeling of distaste that the overly flamboyant office building, this office suite and the spectacle effect of the man himself had aroused, said, "At the moment we are more interested in a man named Sam Joseph, who is said to be hearing a small statue of the devil speak aloud to him."

"Exactly," said Montague Ogden. "Exactly."

"I understand you can supply details."

"Exactly," said Montague Ogden. "I am a very wealthy man, and I want nothing spared to straighten out poor Sam. Poor Sam is my office manager, my trusted employee. He is even, I may say, more than that. He is the real working head, the manager, of my rather wide enterprises. I owe Sam a great deal. Sam is paid an excellent salary, it is true, but his value to me extends far beyond that. Sam is . . . is—" He groped for words, found them. "Sam is like a part of my own heart," he finished.

Doc Savage asked quietly, "What do you mean by straightening out poor Sam?"

Montague Ogden blinked. He had blue eyes, very pale-blue eyes.

"Why, find out his trouble," he said.

"Just what has happened?" Doc Savage asked patiently.

Ogden spread his hands with the palms up. "Poor Sam has this statue of a devil—"

"Where did he get it?"

"I gave it to him," Montague Ogden said. "I frankly admit that."

"Where did you get the statue?" Doc asked.

"From a Chinaman," Ogden explained. "From an old China-man named Chi Sui. Poor Chi Sui was a very elderly Oriental who for a long time had operated a shop in Mott Street dealing in knickknacks, the trash that tourists buy in Chinatown. But old Chi Sui wanted to close up his business and go to China to help

Chiang against the Japanese, and he had very little money, but he did have this statue, which was realistic. I bought it from Chi Sui —ah—in spite of the rather hair-lifting story he told me about it."

Doc said, "So the former owner of the devil statue had a story to tell about it?"

"Yes."

"What was the nature of the story?"

Montague Ogden blinked, smiled sheepishly, said, "A ridiculous story, of course. One in which I placed no stock. Not a bit of belief, not for a minute."

"Suppose you tell it to us, anyway," Doc invited.

Ogden nodded. "It was a rather simple story. It seems that this Chinese statue was molded by Co Suan, a friend of the original Buddha, and that the spirit of Buddha captured a portion of the spirit of the King of Evil, and imprisoned it in this statuette. That was to give the little statue life, because Co Suan, the sculptor, was a great friend of Buddha, and the All-Mighty One wished to give his friend fame and fortune deserving of such a kind and goodly fellow. Therefore Buddha imprisoned the spirit of the devil in the statue in order to give the little thing of brass a life and realism which no other sculptor could ever equal."

"That is all of the story?"

"Yes. It's ridiculous, of course." Montague Ogden smiled at them. "I want you to understand, of course, that I do not credit for a minute the belief that the statue is actually talking to poor Sam Joseph."

"You have not heard the statue speak?" Doc asked.

"No."

"Anyone but Sam Joseph heard it?"

"No."

"What else do you know?" Doc Savage asked.

"Nothing. Nothing more."

"In that case," Doc Savage said, "we had better see Sam Joseph."

They surrounded Sam Joseph where he lay on a bed, a great chromium-and-green bed, in the penthouse on top of the flamboyant Ogden building. The decorating theme of the penthouse was chromium and other colors, broken up with large and vital flowers of bright coloration. The penthouse was not in quite as bad taste as the rest of the building.

"My personal apartment," said Montague Ogden of the penthouse layout. "I had poor Sam brought here."

Sam Joseph was obviously not himself. He was a man large

enough to make quite a hump on the bed, under the silken covers. He had gray hair, a not inconsiderable shock of it, and an angelic, peaceful, completely honest-looking face.

Sam Joseph had the kind of a face you would expect a man-angel to have. It was so entirely benign and innocent.

"Good evening, gentlemen," he said. "Or, rather, good afternoon. It is afternoon, isn't it?"

"Don't you know whether or not it is afternoon?" Doc Savage asked.

Sam Joseph seemed somewhat confused. "I guess so," he said. "That is, I was watching the snow, and the bluebirds singing in the snow. It only snows in the afternoon, does it not, or is it only on Wednesday, the first of June?"

Doc Savage asked Montague Ogden, "How long has he been talking like that?"

"Gracious, I never heard him speak like that before," Montague Ogden said. "I really haven't."

"His conversation hitherto has been rational?"

"Oh, yes. It really has."

Sam Joseph said, "I came out of the hill and it was very dark, but there was the fish in the sand, with the ice all around it. We sat down there, the fish and I, and we had fine steaks and caviar, but the fish wouldn't eat the caviar because he was not a cannibal, he told me. When the fish said he was not a cannibal he had a very deep voice."

Monk Mayfair, Doc Savage's assistant, looked at Doc thoughtfully. Monk put the end of a forefinger against his own right temple and made a motion as if he was winding up something.

"Like the things you pull corks with," Monk said.

Doc Savage studied Sam Joseph for a while. The man was smiling, but it was a vacantly empty smile, a smile without intelligence or even much feeling behind it.

Doc turned back to Montague Ogden again.

"The devil statue," Doc said. "Where is it?"

Montague Ogden seemed startled. "Oh, the devil. It is around somewhere, I suppose."

"Get it."

"But now you can see that poor Sam Joseph is—"

"The devil," Doc said. "The devil that talked. We want to see it."

Montague Ogden now seemed distressed, and also his brow wrinkled as if he was trying to think where the statue was, and he scratched his head.

"Oh, how silly of me," he said. "How really silly. Of course, I remember now. In my den. I'll get it. I placed the statue in my den and I will get it now."

He turned away.

Doc said, "Monk, go with him."

"Me?" Monk was surprised.

"Yes, you," Doc said.

"But—"

Monk stopped, and turned and followed Montague Ogden. Monk had remembered that when you argued with Doc you usually found yourself exceedingly in the wrong.

They walked down corridors, Monk and Montague Ogden. And Ogden examined Monk out of the corner of his eye, as if amazed at Monk's homeliness, and amused by it.

Monk's homeliness had amazed and amused many people, but he was not ashamed of it. There was a pleasantness about his homeliness and a fascination. Monk would not have to be seen in a very thick fog to be mistaken for something just out of the ape house in the zoo. His arms were as long as his legs, and he was coated with reddish hair that was close cousin to rusted shingle nails. Monk was even rather pleased with his clock-stopping looks because he had found that they exerted a hypnotic power over girls, and the prettier the girl, the greater the hypnotic capacity.

Montague Ogden opened a door, said, "This is my den, Mr. Mayfair."

The den was inhabited by the stuffed heads of animals, at least half a hundred of them, which hung on the walls and leered, stared, snarled, or showed gap-fanged jaws at anyone in the den.

There was a man already in the den.

"Aren't you afraid of staying in here?" Monk asked the man.

He was a timid-looking young man, quite pale and lean and soft. The very picture of a timid soul.

"Beg pardon?" the man said. He sounded frightened, nervous, embarrassed.

"This is Butch," said Montague Ogden.

"Butch, eh?" Monk said, and tried not to grin at the timid soul.

Montague Ogden remarked, "Butch, we have come after the devil statue."

"Oh," Butch said. He looked scared. "Oh! I haven't—that is —well, it's over there, but—"

"Never mind," Montague Ogden told him. "We'll take it with us. You can go ahead with your work, Butch."

Montague Ogden picked up the devil statue.

The statue was about what Monk expected to see, being not much over a foot high, rather fat, and made of brass that was tarnished, or bronze, wearing some sort of ceremonial robe, and holding a sword in one hand. This devil had a pronounced Chinese cast on his evil little face.

"I'll carry it," Monk said.

"But—"

"I'll carry it," Monk repeated.

Montague Ogden smiled and his, "Very well, if you wish," was the soul of politeness.

They left the den and Monk was glad to get out of sight of all the leering, staring or snarling stuffed animals. He wondered how Butch managed to stand it in there with all those man-hungry-looking trophies, and he wondered if that was what was making Butch look frightened.

"Who's Butch?" Monk asked. "What's he do, I mean?"

"His work?"

"Yes."

"Butch is my big-game hunting guide and my jujitsu instructor," Montague Ogden explained. "He also teaches me wrestling and the art of knife-throwing, in which I am interested as a hobby."

Monk laughed. He thought he was being kidded.

They went down a hall that was majestic in a futuristic modern fashion, with high walls and great pictures in gaunt plain frames, and lighting that was so subdued that it was difficult to tell from where it came.

Monk walked along thinking of the timid soul who was named Butch, and how funny it was that Ogden had jokingly said Butch was his hunting guide and instructor in the more robust manly arts. Ordinarily that would not have been funny, but after you had seen Butch it was quite humorous.

"We can go through this way," Montague Ogden said. "It is shorter."

He turned to the left and opened a door and went through it.

Monk was following behind Ogden and watching Ogden's back when something hit Monk's head. It hit hard, whatever it was, and there was only a slight sound, a slight grinding, just before the impact landed. It took Monk on top of the head, slightly to the right-hand side, so that there was the grisly sensation of the blow sliding down toward the right ear and taking off the whole side of his head as it went. In the middle of this awful feeling it got very black and remained that way.

## Chapter II
## THE GREAT MISTAKE

Monk accomplished the feat of opening his eyes, but did it with some difficulty, after which he stared at Montague Ogden. Monk had the feeling that some time had passed, and did not dare move his body for fear his head would fall off it. There was a gouging pain in the small of his back.

Soon his ears recovered their ability to hear.

"That nasty picture!" Montague Ogden was saying. "Oh, that nasty picture! I told the interior decorator when he hung it over the door that something like this would happen! I told him it would be just my luck to have the picture fall down and brain somebody sometime."

Monk tried out his voice with a groan and found his vocal chords satisfactory. "I'm brained, all right," he said.

"Oh!" gasped Ogden. "He's conscious! He has recovered!"

Monk felt a hell of a long way from complete recovery and said so. "What hit me?" he demanded.

"A picture hanging over the door fell down as you went through," explained Montague Ogden. "It was one of those freak accidents."

Monk grimaced at Ogden.

"It's a good thing you were walking ahead of me when it happened," Monk said. "Or I would have thought you beaned me."

Montague Ogden laughed deprecatingly. Doc Savage, Renny Renwick and Long Tom Roberts were standing around Monk, looking relieved that he had recovered. Monk wondered if he *had* recovered, or if there was going to be complications.

The gouging pain in the small of his back was awful. He investigated and found it to be the devil statuette.

"I must have fallen on the thing," Monk complained. "I wonder how many ribs it broke."

"That the devil statue which speaks?" Doc Savage asked.

"That's it," Monk said.

Montague Ogden said uncomfortably, "Of course, you gentlemen do not for a minute believe that the statue can speak?"

Doc Savage made no comment. He suggested that Renny Renwick find the building superintendent, and obtain a hacksaw and a cold chisel and hammer, in order that they might perform a dissection on the brass devil.

Fifteen minutes later they had the devil lying in half a dozen pieces on a table, and there was obviously nothing inside it but brass.

"That is that," Doc admitted. "The thing hardly seemed to have a conversational nature."

"Of course you knew it hadn't," Montague Ogden said.

Monk Mayfair explained to Ogden, "When you've been in the kind of a business we're in for a while, you get so you don't go around taking things at face value."

Doc Savage said, "We will examine Sam Joseph now."

The bronze man spent nearly an hour with Sam Joseph, doing the things a doctor does.

"According to all indications," Doc said, "the man has an advanced cerebral fibroma."

The bronze man then asked Monk to telephone the hospital and arrange for reception of the patient.

Doc told Montague Ogden, "I am going to call in other brain specialists for consultation. Do you have any particular doctors you would like to have pass an opinion?"

Ogden stared.

"I thought you were supposed to be the world's leading brain surgeon," he said.

Doc passed up the compliment, explained, "In a matter as serious as this we prefer to have a consensus of opinion."

Montague Ogden nodded. He seemed to be surprised, but to consider the matter reasonable now that he thought of it.

"Could I bring in Dr. Nedden?" he asked. "He is my private surgeon."

Doc Savage nodded. He had not heard of Dr. Nedden, but that did not mean the man could not be good.

"Certainly," the bronze man said. "Call Dr. Nedden."

They transferred Sam Joseph to the hospital, a small but wonderfully equipped hospital uptown, which specialized in brain cases, and which was largely supported by Doc Savage. He did most of his work there. Doc did not, as a matter of fact, do a great deal of surgery for surgery's sake, his specialty being stubborn and unusual cases upon which he could apply new and experimental technique.

Dr. Nedden appeared. He was a stocky man, face reddened by the outdoors sun, clothes immaculate, who seemed to know what he was doing.

"I have examined the patient previously," he explained. "The unusual cerebropsychosis aroused my interest, and I was fairly sure it was cerebral fibroma. I made a thorough examination with a cerebroscope and found nothing to support any other diagnosis."

Doc Savage called in two more specialists, and their diagnosis was the same.

"Cerebral fibroma."

Monk asked, "What the heck's a cerebral fibroma, anyway?"

"A brain tumor. A fibrous type. That makes it very difficult to remove," Doc Savage explained.

"Why don't doctors use words you can understand?" Monk wanted to know.

"For the same reason that chemists do not use small ones," Doc told him.

Monk had to grin at that. There was nothing more incomprehensible to a layman than a chemical formula, even when you simplified it and used the symbols. But if you took one of those chemicals and tried to explain what it was by using small words, it would run into an afternoon's work.

Doc Savage found Montague Ogden.

"Your office manager, Sam Joseph, has a brain tumor," Doc told Ogden. "An operation is the only answer."

"He will not die?"

"There is no such thing as a minor or a completely safe operation," Doc told him frankly. "But he should pull through."

"Oh, I want him to. Sam means a lot to me. He has always practically run everything for me."

Doc said, "Dr. C. B. Sticken would be a good man to do the surgery."

"Yes, I—" Ogden's eyes flew wide. "What did you say?"

"I recommend C. B. Sticken for the surgery."

Montague Ogden looked as if he was going to faint.

"But *you* must do it!" he gasped.

Doc Savage explained patiently, "This is not a sufficiently unusual or difficult case to warrant my doing the surgery, and, furthermore, Dr. Sticken is fully qualified."

Montague Ogden seemed horrified at the idea.

"I insist on *you* doing it!" he cried. "Why, I wouldn't think of anyone else! I'll pay any fee."

"It just happens," Doc Savage said, "that I do not work for a fee."

"What? Oh, yes, I remember. You get your funds from some unknown source. Well, then, I'll donate any sum you name to any organization you wish if you will do the operation."*

"That will not be necessary. Dr. Sticken is capable—"

"I'll donate a hundred thousand dollars," said Montague Ogden, "if you will do this operation."

Doc Savage studied the man. "That is not necessary."

"I mean it. A hundred thousand, Mr. Savage. To any charity, or army or navy relief group you care to name." The man was so earnest he was pale.

"All right," Doc Savage said finally.

Doc Savage did the operation in the special amphitheater pit at the brain clinic. It was a cup-shaped arena surrounded by the most transparent type of glass. Beyond the glass were seats for witnessing surgeons. The lighting was fluorescent and brilliant.

As was always the case when Doc Savage was operating, the amphitheater was crowded. There were very few students among the witnesses, the majority being brain surgeons of established name and reputation, some of them men who had hurriedly caught airplanes and flown halfway across the continent in order to watch a master at work.

Doc Savage made the scalp incision, laid back the scalp, then used a special electrical bone knife of his own invention, a device which would cut without shock, having the property of rendering bone and nerve more insensible to shock in the area near the cutting head.

The operation progressed with brilliance up to the point where Doc reached the spot where the tumor should be.

There was no tumor.

The thing was so astounding that Doc was stunned. He stood there rigid and speechless, then after a few moments made the small trilling sound which was his unconscious habit in moments of intense mental stress. The trilling was low, exotic, might have been the product of an eerie wayward breeze in a naked forest. It

---

* Doc Savage's mysterious source of fabulous wealth is located in a remote lost valley in Central America, an enormous golden treasure guarded over by a clan of descendants of ancient Maya.

had a ventriloqual quality, seeming to come from everywhere rather than any definite spot in the operating room.

There was certainly no tumor, either a fibroma or otherwise.

There was only one thing Doc could say, and he said it.

"I have made a mistake," he said.


## Chapter III
## A PLAN ROLLING

Dr. Nedden, the man who had been introduced into the case as Montague Ogden's private doctor, was one of the spectators in the arena above the operating pit.

He got out of there in a hurry.

He found a cab. "Across town," he ordered. "And hurry!"

Dr. Nedden leaned back in the cab. He seemed to have been holding himself in, and now he relaxed. As men sometimes do after they have been under terrific strain and try to relax, he started going to pieces.

He trembled and twitched. He pounded his knees wildly with his fists.

"Hurry, you fool!" he screamed at the driver.

He got out at an ordinary-looking brick apartment house west of Central Park and stumbled inside. He was so weak he had to hold to the hand rail in the elevator while riding up.

In the sixteenth-floor hall a man met him. The man who met him was the timid-looking soul called Butch.

"Goodness, doctor," Butch said. "What is wrong?"

"Nothing's wrong," said Dr. Nedden. "I'm just having a nervous reaction, that's all. I'll be all right as soon as I can take a sedative."

Butch nodded. "Here," he said. He handed Dr. Nedden a bundle. "Put these on." Butch had an identical bundle. "We can put them on in the inner reception room," he added.

They went to a door.

A legend on the door, in discreet lettering, said:

DR. MORGAN
PRIVATE HOSPITAL

They tried the door. It was locked.

"One of the others in there masking," Butch said. "Let's try another room."

There were half a dozen doors in the hall, all bearing the same legend. They found one which was unlocked and it admitted them to a bare room fitted with two white chairs, a white desk, a stool behind the desk, and a telephone on the desk itself.

Dr. Nedden and Butch unwrapped their bundles, which proved to hold ordinary white surgical robes, surgical hoods, and the gauze antiseptic masks which operating-room personnel wear.

When they had donned these their identities were thoroughly concealed.

Dr. Nedden led the way into another and much larger room after unlocking the hall door of the room where they had dressed.

There were seven men already seated in the room. All were enveloped in the surgical robes and masks.

Dr. Nedden was still shaking. Butch had had to tie the strings of Nedden's robe.

Nedden hurried to a cabinet containing medicines, got out a few pills out of a bottle, and swallowed them with water.

The other masked men watched him intently.

Dr. Nedden faced them.

"Gentlemen," he said. "It worked. Doc Savage is trapped."

Dr. Nedden then sat down and explained, "I am suffering from nervous shock. The strain has been very great on me, gentlemen. If you will wait a few minutes, please."

They waited patiently. Judging from the eyes visible above the surgical masks, all of them were vastly relieved. Even elated.

The sedative took effect on Dr. Nedden. His agitation subsided and he arose and drank more water. He added a hooker of whiskey.

He faced the men.

"It was an incredibly difficult and ticklish business," he said. "Doc Savage is unquestionably the world's greatest general surgeon, and probably the greatest brain surgeon. To pull this we had to deceive him at his own business.

"Fortunately, mental difficulties are the most uncertain to diagnose," continued Dr. Nedden. "By the use of drugs, largely types of barbiturates in overdoses, I was able to produce fake mental symptoms in Sam Joseph. A number of very cunning devices were resorted to in order to deceive Doc Savage, but I will not take up your time describing them, and you would not understand them anyway, not being doctors yourselves."

A man interrupted, "What about the devil-statue mix-up?"

Dr. Nedden shrugged.

"We had a narrow escape there," he said. "A devil statue containing a small loud-speaker and radio had been used to fool Sam Joseph into thinking the little statue was talking to him. Through an oversight, this statue was still in Montague Ogden's den when Doc Savage wished to see it."

"I heard," said the other, "that you had to knock out one of Doc Savage's men, that fellow they call Monk, and swap a harmless statue for the trick one."

"We did that," admitted Dr. Nedden. "We pulled it without a hitch."

Butch said, "I pulled it. I popped him one on the head. Then Ogden made him think a picture had fallen off the wall just as he was going under it, and conked him."

"That was a goofy explanation to give him."

"Its goofiness made it good," Butch declared.

They seemed satisfied.

One said, "That fixes everything so we can go ahead with the next step of the plan."

"Not everything," reminded Dr. Nedden. "There is still the Harrison matter."

A man growled, "I'd call it the Duster Jones matter."

Butch spoke up smugly.

"That will be taken care of," he said. "The thing to do is let this operation have its repercussions."

"Savage may think there is something strange about it."

"Too late now, if he does."

"All right, but murder isn't something to make mistakes with," one of the men said.

## Chapter IV
## THE INDIGNANT MAN

It was a bright crisp morning, the sunlight crisp out of an utterly clear sky, and the air a thing like wine which you noticed in a way that you do not ordinarily notice air, when Ham Brooks came into Doc Savage's offices in a midtown skyscraper.

Ham looked concerned. Ham was another Doc Savage assistant, another member of the group of five. He was a man of medium height with good shoulders and a thin waist, and clothing which had made him notable as one of the country's best-dressed men. He was the law expert of the group.

"Doc," Ham said, "I'm worried about something."

"Yes?"

"You know that operation on Sam Joseph?"

"What about it?"

"The news is all over town, in the surgical profession, that you pulled a bloomer. You operated on a man who did not have the slightest trace of what you were operating for."

Doc Savage was not worried. "Just gossip within the profession," he said. "Maybe it is not very nice of us, but it is a very human trait to get a kick out of seeing a big shot make a mistake. We all make them. It just goes to prove he is human, and that we are human to talk about it."

Ham shook his head. "I know. I discounted it at first, thinking it was that kind of talk. But it's more."

"What more?"

"There is some ugly talk about malpractice."

"That is ridiculous."

"The definition of malpractice," Ham said, "is wrong or injurious treatment. At least that's the way the medical dictionaries give it."

"You need not have gone to the bother of looking it up," Doc told him. "This is just gossip. I have it coming to me because I did make a mistake."

"All right," Ham said. "I just wanted to mention it and tell you that, legally, no one can hang anything on you."

Doc Savage smiled. "That is fine, Ham. But you are making a mountain out of a molehill."

"I hope so," Ham said. "But I don't like the way this malpractice talk is going around through the profession. It looks as if someone might be spreading it."

Mr. Montague Ogden was more blunt about it. He came into Doc Savage's headquarters with his jaw out and his hands made into fists, and he was accompanied by two gentlemen who carried brief cases and looked like bulldogs.

"Mr. Savage," Ogden said, "I am not at all satisfied with the thing you did to poor Sam Joseph."

"Just what do you mean, Ogden?" Doc Savage asked.

"Why did you perform that brain operation on Sam Joseph?"

"For the same reason that you operate for an appendix," Doc said. "It seemed to be the thing to do. The man's symptoms indicated brain tumor."

"So *you* said."

The most outstanding of Doc Savage's features was probably

his unusual eyes, like pools of flake gold always stirred by tiny winds. These took on a rather cold light now.

"You will recall," he said, "that Dr. Nedden and two other brain specialists agreed with me on the diagnosis."

Montague Ogden drew himself up.

"They have admitted," he snapped, "that they took your word for it. As a matter of truth they were so overawed by your—ah —reputation—that they did not wish to disagree with you."

Doc decided this was rather unprofessional behavior on the part of the three doctors, but he made no comment on that, saying instead:

"I am sorry it happened," he said. "There is no denying I made a mistake."

"Sorry," said Ogden, "isn't enough."

"What do you mean?"

"I demand," snapped Ogden, "that you make a cash settlement of five hundred thousand dollars on Sam Joseph by way of reimbursing him for the peril to which you subjected his life. I also demand that you publish a half-page advertisement in all New York newspapers admitting that you made an error in diagnosis."

Ham Brooks, who was present, jumped to his feet.

Doc waved Ham back. He digested Montague Ogden's demand.

"That is ridiculous, of course," he said.

"I'll show you how ridiculous it is!" Montague Ogden bellowed. He waved to his two bulldog-faced companions. "These are my lawyers, Flack and Morrow. They'll show you how ridiculous it is."

This was too much for Ham. He shot to his feet.

"Get out of here!" Ham yelled. "I know these two shysters, Flack and Morrow. They're crooks of the first water. The only thing different about them is that they are big thieves!"

"We'll sue you for slander!" bellowed a lawyer.

"Who ever heard of one lawyer calling another lawyer a crook being slander?" Ham snarled.

Ham habitually carried an innocent-looking black cane, and almost everyone in the legal profession knew this was a sword cane, the tip of which was coated with a chemical producing quick unconsciousness.

"Get out of here!" Ham roared, and flourished his cane as he made a rush for Ogden and his lawyers.

Ogden and his attorneys took flight.

As he ran, Ogden shouted, "You can't shut us up this way!

We're going to get at the truth about your strange brain operations! We'll unmask your devilish scheme!"

Then they ran for their lives from Ham, got into the elevator and escaped.

"Doc," Ham said, "something isn't up-and-up about this."

The fight on the speaker's platform at the big Army Relief rally at Madison Square Garden got a great deal more publicity.

It was not much of a fight. Montague Ogden merely popped out of the crowd, dashed across the speaker's platform in full view of the audience of many thousands and tried to assault Doc Savage with his fists.

The police soon hauled Ogden away.

But everyone in the audience heard the words Montague Ogden shrieked at the bronze man. The public-address microphones picked them up and made them loud in the great auditorium.

"There's something devilish behind your brain operations!"* Ogden screamed. "What are you doing to those men? You're a monster!"

The thing got in the newspapers. Montague Ogden was reputedly one of the rich men of the nation, and Doc Savage had a worldwide name. So it could hardly have kept out of the newspapers.

---

* Early in his career, Doc Savage recognized the need of some permanently effective, but at the same time humane, method of treatment for criminals which he captured. The numbers of these criminals as time went on would be considerable. So, out of his skill as a brain surgeon, and his understanding of human psychology, Doc evolved a method of permanently curing criminals of crime. He established an institution in a remote section of upstate New York, the mountainous area which is surprisingly one of the most deserted sections of the United States. Here he installed brain specialists which he had trained. When he sends a criminal to the "College," the routine does not vary greatly. First the "student" undergoes a brain operation which Doc perfected, and which wipes out all memory of past. The criminal, having lost all vicious effects of environment, is then trained to make a useful and comfortable living at some worthy occupation. The results of Doc's experiment have been remarkable. It was his dream, and still is, to have such a method of criminal treatment widely accepted and practiced, for he feels it is one of the few sure cures for habitual criminality. However, the treatment is far too drastic for public acceptance. It is a hundred or two hundred years ahead of its time, probably, like other things which the bronze man uses regularly.

Also, Doc Savage was not a man who sought publicity, and items about him were scarce, so, accordingly, their news value was greater.

Doc Savage, as a matter of fact, had antagonized some of the newspapers at various times by refusing to give out information concerning his activities. One paper in particular, the *Morning Blade*, a blaring tabloid which featured a stable of columnists who were unreliable sensationalists, did not have a great love for Doc Savage.

It was the *Morning Blade* in which the black-type editorial said:

We know all about the laws of libel and slander. Sometimes we wonder if these laws don't protect people who shouldn't be protected.

Is it libel and slander to ask some questions?

Question one: Why is this fellow Doc Savage so secretive about himself that he is known as the Man of Mystery? What has he to hide?

Question two: What does Doc Savage do with the men he seizes, the men he says are criminals. (He alone says they are criminals; isn't it the right of our courts to judge those things?) What happens to these men? They disappear. Their old friends never see them again.

Question three: What is this mysterious "college" which Doc Savage maintains, of which rumors are sometimes heard? Has it horrors to hide?

Ham Brooks came in with this in his hands, a scowl on his face, and said, "Blast them! I think we could stick them for libel and slander on the strength of that. Doc, shall we try it?"

Doc Savage shook his head, but he was thoughtful. On the big inlaid table which was one of the principal articles of furniture in the reception room of his eighty-sixth floor headquarters, lay the other metropolitan newspapers, all of which contained items about what had happened last night at Madison Square Garden.

"Ham," Doc said quietly, "it seems I made two mistakes."

"One of them when you operated on Sam Joseph?"

"Yes."

"What was the other one?"

"When I overlooked your suggestion that something might not be on the up-and-up about this thing," Doc said.

Ham grinned. "We better get to looking into it, eh?"

Doc nodded.

"We better," he said.

Another interested reader of the newspapers that day was Butch, the timid-looking soul. He read them and rubbed his hands together in glee.

He carried his newspapers and his delight to Dr. Nedden.

"It's beginning to roll," Butch said. "You think we ought to have another meeting?"

Dr. Nedden was worried. He had not been sleeping well and was losing weight. He was getting peevish.

"Call a meeting?" he said, and sneered. "Are you forgetting it is the man we work for who calls the meetings?"

Butch grinned. "That's right. O. K., then. I just got too happy over this. But it's sure rolling now, ain't it?"

Dr. Nedden looked at the newspapers, wet his lips and admitted, "It's rolling, all right."

"What are you afraid of, doctor? You look like a singed cat."

"It's trying to perpetrate a thing like this on a man like Doc Savage," muttered Dr. Nedden.

"Hell, it's so big it can't fail."

"Savage will start investigating before long."

"It'll be built up too much for him to stop it by then. And he doesn't know what is behind it. He'll never guess. The thing is so unexpected that it would be the last thing in the world he would look for."

Dr. Nedden nodded. "The murder doesn't help my sleep," he confessed.

"Murder? Oh, that." Butch laughed. "Didn't you know the Harrisons were going to be taken care of tonight?"

"More murders?"

Butch grinned. "Ever hear of fighting fire with fire, doctor?"

"Where will it be done?"

"Kansas City," Butch told him. "Our man is waiting at the airport there now."

# Chapter V
## MURDER AND KANSAS CITY

R. J. Harrison had been christened Ranzo John Harrison in his cradle, and he had come to hate the name "Ranzo" and the nickname "Randy" so thoroughly that he never told anyone his two christened names if he could help it. He was now called, and had been called for years, Rotary Harrison. Strangely enough, he did not object to Rotary. He was even proud of it.

The name came from the so-called rotary method of drilling oil wells, as opposed to the cable tool method. Rotary Harrison had been a pioneer in the mid-continent oil fields in the use of rotary drilling.

Rotary Harrison was a big man physically, a hard-hammered giant of a fellow, now a little more thin than he had once been, but with the hard, solid look of a frontiersman in his blue eyes and the same quality in his fists.

He had made and lost ten or a dozen fortunes, and they had been oilmen's fortunes. Anything less than five or ten million dollars is not considered much of a fortune in the oil business. The fortunes Rotary Harrison had made and lost had been big ones. He had another big one now, and again he was on the verge of losing it.

He was a spectacular old reprobate. His private airplanes, for example, were always the fastest and most luxurious.

The one he was flying now was a sample.

His daughter, Sister Harrison, was sitting back in the cabin.

Sis was holding a .250/3000-caliber rifle equipped with a telescopic sight.

Sis was on the spectacular side herself, being a long blond girl who won tennis cups, prizes for riding horses in rodeos, and once, a complimentary squib from a Broadway columnist for knocking a leering stew bum into the middle of next week with a left. These were accomplishments enough, but she was also with mentality, as the saying goes, being the possessor of various scholarship keys which were not given for having oil millions, as well as two books and a play she had written, and clippings of many pointed letters she had sent the Tulsa *World*, her favorite newspaper, concerning what she thought about the oil situation, and its probable effect on the national economy. Assuredly with brains.

Rotary Harrison said, "Sis, there's a river down there. I think it's the Kaw."

"In that case we may make it," Sis said.

"Maybe so. We should hit the Kaw close to Kansas City."

Sis put down the rifle and picked up a pair of good binoculars. She focused these on the sky behind the ship and searched intently for a while.

She eventually located the winged speck that was the plane following them. It was about where it had been during most of the trip.

"We still got our gadfly?" asked Rotary.

"Still got it," Sis agreed.

"Yonder's Kansas City," said Rotary Harrison. "When we get there we'll see what luck we have pulling a shenanigan."

The plane which had followed the Harrisons had, they believed, picked up their trail sometime after they left the municipal airport at Tulsa. Because no plane had followed them off the municipal airport at Tulsa, they surmised the other ship had been at another airport nearby and had been notified when they left the ground.

They knew the other plane was following them. They had made sure of that by detouring slightly in the direction of Oil Hill, Kansas, where Rotary Harrison had once opened a field of gushers —that was his third fortune in the making—and the plane behind had trailed them on the detour. The other ship had always remained some miles back, practically out of sight in the distance.

Rotary Harrison's face had become rocklike when he knew they were being followed.

"Poor old Duster Jones," he said once.

Then Rotary had leaned back, letting the plane fly herself, and had remembered Duster Jones.

Duster Jones had come out of Ohio or Pennsylvania or some such place forty years ago and he had brought his hard luck with him. It had been a kind of inexhaustible hard luck, good for all the years of Duster Jones' life. Fate was particularly cruel, because she hit her blows of hard luck with platinum and diamond hammers. He made such ungodly rich strikes and he always lost them. Duster Jones had the golden touch of Midas, but his hands were greased. He never quite got hold of the riches, but always it was almost. Duster Jones became a legend in the oil fields.

Duster Jones liked Rotary Harrison. They were opposites, in a way, because it seemed that Rotary had only to turn a hand to make a fortune, while Duster could turn handsprings and wind up as poor as a mouse.

They had been very, very close friends for years. Neither of them ever did a thing, ever had hardly a thought, that the other did not know about.

Rotary believed he knew why Duster Jones had been shot between the eyes with a .22-caliber bullet.

Rotary Harrison set his plane down at the Kansas City airport. He taxied back along the edge of the runway toward the office and hangars, letting the ship move slowly.

He watched the other plane, the ship that had been following him, come out of the southwest.

He was not surprised when it did not land. Nor was he puzzled when the craft roared overhead and dropped first one wing then the other in a series of measured maneuvers.

"Signal," he said. "They got somebody here at the airport waitin' for us."

He looked back at his daughter then. He was oppressed by the feeling of danger around them, of poor old Duster Jones' death, and of mystery. He studied Sis' face. They had been through a lot together, through more than most fathers and daughters. But he found himself wishing, suddenly, that Sis was somewhere where it was safe.

"Scared, Sis?" he asked.

"Sure," she admitted. "But don't let it bother you."

Rotary grinned. "Nothing is gonna bother us. *We're* gonna do the bothering."

He parked his plane on the line where civilian aircraft were supposed to park. He went into the office and filled out the arrival forms and applied for the permission which the army required civilians to obtain before they could fly on to New York.

"Want to leave in about half an hour," he said. "See that my plane is refueled."

"Half an hour?" the C. A. A. man said. "Be night before you get into New York. You experienced in night flying?"

"Sure," said Rotary. "Here's my license with instrument rating."

Rotary and Sis got a cab, acting as if nothing out of the way was transpiring, except that Sis carried the rifle, which made her a slightly odd spectacle.

When the cab was crossing the Missouri River bridge into Kansas City, Rotary asked, "Got him spotted?"

"Second cab back of us," Sis said.

"Little man, dark hair, dark skin, blue pin-stripe suit?"

"That's the one," Sis agreed.

"All right," Rotary said. "Pretty soon we surprise him."

They rolled down off the bridge through the shabby commercial district, then started to climb the hill. They topped the rise and rolled down Grand Avenue. Traffic was thick around them now.

Their cab halted for a red light, a big truck on their right. "Pull in ahead of that truck a little," Rotary ordered. Their driver obeyed.

Rotary got out. The truck screened him from the machine behind.

"Go right ahead," he told Sis.

The pursuing cab drew alongside the truck, passing it.

Rotary Harrison jumped out from around the side of the truck. He got an arm around the door post of the cab—its windows were down—wrenched the cab door open and was inside.

Rotary showed the occupant of the cab the six-shooter he had inherited from his Indian-fighting dad.

"Don't jump, hop, skip or reach," Rotary said. "Just sit."

He used the kind of a tone he used when he had just lost a string of tools in a six-thousand-foot oil well. It was a tone that would curl wire.

"Follow that second cab ahead," he told the driver.

The driver looked around. He seemed undecided.

Rotary showed him the six-gun and said, "When I shoot a rabbit with this thing, all they generally find is one ear."

The driver followed orders.

They turned left and found a street where there was no traffic. Sis got out of the cab ahead and came back.

"Got him, eh?" She examined the man. "Never saw him before."

The man would have looked suave enough ordinarily perhaps, but now he was scared.

"Go back to the airport," Rotary told their driver.

The cab chauffeur, more than anxious to get rid of his passengers and wash his hands of the whole thing, lost no time in driving back across the river to the airport.

Rotary told his prisoner, "You know what happened to Duster Jones?"

The man said nothing, but more fear swam in his eyes. He knew what had happened to Duster Jones, all right, and apparently that was the big thing now in his mind.

"The same thing will happen to you," Rotary told him, "if you make one bleat or one jump."

They got out at the airport. The Harrison plane was refueled, ready for the air.

Rotary put the captive in the cabin, indicating that Sis should watch the fellow.

"I'll go get my papers for the New York flight," Rotary explained. "Getting papers every time you turn around in an airplane is a danged nuisance, but on account of the war I guess you gotta do it."

He went away and came back. "All set," he explained. He took over the controls, started the motor and warmed it, checked both magnetos, then swung the tail around, got out on the runway and fed it the gun when he got the O. K. from the control tower.

The plane was soon slanting up into the sky.

Rotary Harrison turned to their captive.

"I didn't include you in my cargo when I checked out," he said. "You know what that means?"

The man got white.

"That's right," Rotary told him. "I can't have you along when we land." He turned to his daughter. "Sis, plot a course that will take us over one of the Great Lakes. And haven't we got a fishing tool back in the cabin that will do as a sinker for this hombre's body?"

## Chapter VI
## DEATH IN THE SKY

They flew north, left the Missouri River behind, climbed until the concrete ribbon of Highway 69 was a vague thread below and behind. Rotary turned the controls over to Sis, whispering, "Don't get excited, but you can act as if you are. I'm fooling about killing this bird."

"I knew you were," Sis said.

Rotary went back. He stood looking at the prisoner, who was sprawled in a seat and gripping the seat arms.

"Got a name?" Rotary asked.

"Smith," the man said.

"John Smith?" asked Rotary.

"Yeah."

Rotary hit him, drove two quick blows like lightning. The man lifted up in the seat, then flopped back. He turned slightly blue and his tongue stuck out and he breathed nosily.

"That's for John Smithing me," said Rotary. "I don't guess there's any need of fooling with you."

Rotary then fell upon the man, yanked him into the aisle, hit him again. That blow produced unconsciousness, but it was brief.

When the man awakened it was in time to find Rotary just finishing tying his ankles to his wrists, and both of these to an oil-well fishing tool, a piece of steel which weighed possibly forty pounds.

Rotary noted the man was awake. He made a gesture as if to hit him again, then changed his mind.

"What the hell," Rotary said. "What yelling you do on the way down won't hurt anything."

Rotary dragged him to the plane door and forced the door open against the propeller wash.

"See, we're over the Missouri River," Rotary pointed out. "Changed our minds about the Great Lakes. Too far away."

Rotary then picked the man up, and—the fellow struggled horribly but ineffectively—heaved him out of the plane door.

The man's screams were ghastly.

Rotary seemed to encounter an accident. The loose end of the rope—it was a cowboy lariat—with which the man was tied, became tangled, apparently, with one of the seat supports. The man was stopped and dangled helplessly just outside the plane door.

"Danged rope got caught!" Rotary bellowed.

He fought as if to free the rope. He did not succeed.

"Got a knife, Sis?" he yelled. "Gotta cut this hombre loose."

The screaming of the man dangling outside the plane, the propeller wash smashing against him with cold horror, became articulate words.

"Please!" he screeched. "Don't! I'll do anything! Anything!"

Rotary sneered at him.

"Brother, you'd just tell me more lies," he said. "Sis, hand me that knife."

The man blubbered and screeched that he hoped to die if he was lying. He was about as scared as a man could become and remain rational.

"Oh, all right," Rotary said with seeming reluctance.

He yanked the prisoner back inside.

"Just one little fib and out you go," he warned the man.

The plot—the terrorized captive told Rotary Harrison—was a large thing, and it probably extended into foreign countries. There were millions of dollars involved, and there had been one murder executed and others were planned.

"The killing of old Duster Jones was that murder?" asked Rotary grimly.

It was. But that one had been done by a man called Butch, who had been sent out from New York City for the job. Butch was a fellow who looked as meek as a rabbit, a regular milksop man in appearance, but a fiend who had the bloodthirsty instincts of a weasel.

"Why was Duster killed?" asked Rotary fiercely.

"He found out too much," the man explained. "Or at least I gathered that was what it was. It seems Duster was in a honkatonk one night and heard two men talking. He bought the men drinks and got them tight. He got their tongues loose and went riding with them in the night, and at the end of the ride he had learned enough to be dangerous to the plan."

Rotary scowled and demanded, "Why are they trying to knock off me and Sis?"

"Because," the man explained, "they are afraid you know too much."

"What makes them think that?"

"Your decision to go to New York."

Rotary Harrison was astonished. He was going to New York, as a matter of truth, on what he believed in his heart would be a fruitless attempt to raise money. He had to have the money, because without it the whole structure of his oil enterprises would collapse.

"Why am I going to New York, do they think?" he asked the prisoner.

"To see Doc Savage. To tell him what you know."

Rotary hid his amazement. "So they think that," he said.

He had nearly asked who Doc Savage was, but he caught himself in time. And now, probing in his mind, he decided who Doc Savage must be. He had heard of a rather mysterious man with headquarters in New York by that name. For some reason or other, Rotary recalled, many men in the oil fields had heard of Savage, but he did not know exactly why. He did remember that crooks were supposed to be afraid of Savage, if that meant anything.

Rotary listened to the prisoner talk. The man was getting sickly worried as he watched the hard look on Rotary's face.

He was really a small fry, the prisoner explained. Just a hired hand. He had been dishonorably discharged from the army for assaulting an officer, had served a term in Leavenworth, and had lately been released from prison. He was under bond in a theft case in Missouri, and had sought to pick himself up a bit of lawyer money by taking on this job. A friend, another crook, had recommended him for the job. He had been ordered to seize Rotary and Sis, and hold or kill them, whichever was convenient.

"I don't even know who the head guys are," he insisted.

"But you know some of the small fry?"

"Yes. That Butch, and three or four others."

Rotary asked ominously, "What about Doc Savage?"

The man knew something about that. Evidently he and Butch, or someone else, had talked about it.

"They have a big scheme whereby Doc Savage is going to be made to take the blame for the whole thing," the prisoner explained.

"Why pick on Savage?"

The man said, "That's the first question that occurred to me, too. But Savage is made for the part. He is a mysterious figure. Then, there's all these brain operations he has performed, and the men who disappear after he gets his hands on them."

"Men who disappear when Savage gets hold of them?" Rotary echoed, and his surprise got in his voice.

"Crooks."

"Oh."

The thing as a whole did not make much sense to Rotary Harrison.

He didn't have the real explanation behind it all, he felt.

He was convinced, though, that this hireling he had captured did not know the real answer.

Rotary sank in the seat beside Sis. He told her, pretty much as the prisoner had given it, what he had learned. "Make sense to you?" he finished.

Sis was thoughtful. "Looks to me as if our trouble is just part and parcel of a great mess of trouble that's cooking for a lot of folks," she decided.

"Sis," said Rotary, "this makes me look at our own trouble in a new light."

"Just how?"

"This is our situation: Six months ago we borrowed a mess of money from a New York outfit owned by a man named Montague Ogden. But Ogden himself didn't handle the deal. It was handled by Sam Joseph, who was Ogden's office manager, and seemed to run everything for Ogden."

Rotary Harrison made a grim jaw for a moment.

"Our deal with Sam Joseph was witnessed by Duster Jones," he continued. "The deal included an agreement that the loan was to be renewed on our request in six months, and it was a written agreement. Duster Jones witnessed it. We had a copy, and Sam Joseph had a copy."

His scowl darkened.

"Now Sam Joseph wires us there was no such agreement," he growled. "Our copy of it disappears—stolen probably. And poor Duster Jones, the only man who could prove there was an agreement for me, is killed. That means this Sam Joseph can demand full payment of the loan in three weeks. I haven't got the money. I have got no more chance than a rabbit of getting it. He'll foreclose, ruin me, and grab control of my company. As soon as word gets around I can't meet my obligations—and he'll see that the word gets around—the stock of my company will go to hell for cheap."

Sis was also grim.

She said, "Dad, I wonder if they could have killed Duster Jones because he witnessed that agreement."

"Probably," Rotary agreed.

"What about this Doc Savage, the man they're trying to hang it all onto?" Sis asked.

"He might want to know what's goin' on," Rotary said. "So we better hightail it into New York and give him the news."

Rotary went back and tied the prisoner in a somewhat more comfortable position. He talked with the man for some time and the fellow poured out all he knew with frightened eagerness, but it was nothing more than he had already said.

"Ever hear of a man named Sam Joseph?" Rotary demanded.

The prisoner had.

"He the big boss?" Rotary asked.

The other didn't know. The killer named Butch had just mentioned Sam Joseph, but the prisoner couldn't remember in what connection.

In order to fly over the Missouri River and frighten the prisoner, they had flown south from the route laid out for them as a permissible course by the army authorities. Sis turned the plane north and got on the course again. It was the regular airways route, Kansas City to Chicago, part of the distance.

Rotary consulted the map. "Here's a place named Millard," he said. "There's a civil airways radio station there."

He got out a notebook and scribbled on it, tore out the page on which he had written, and folded it around a five-dollar bill. Then he tied them both around a monkey wrench with a piece of string.

Rotary said, "O. K., fly low over the radio station. Make the engine sound as if we're in trouble."

Sis followed instructions. A man, probably an operator, came out and stood watching them.

Rotary tossed the paper and the bill, tied to the monkey wrench, overside. The man below began walking toward the falling object.

"What was the idea?" Sis asked.

"Just a piece of insurance," Rotary explained. "Cautious in my old age. That's me."

It could not have been more than three minutes later when a plane came piling out of a cloud a little ahead of them. It was fast. It bored toward them.

"Look," Sis gasped. "That's the same plane that followed us from Tulsa to Kansas City!"

"This is the regular route the army assigns to civilian planes," Rotary said grimly. "So he just flew up here and waited around for us. Where's that rifle?"

He yanked open the cabin windows. Motor thunder and inrushing wind was a roar.

"Careful of the propeller!" Sis warned.

The plane ahead was coming at them straight-on now. The pilot must know they couldn't shoot through the propeller, and was keeping ahead of it.

Sis said, "I'll do a flat skid to the right. Be ready."

She sent the plane into the skid, presenting Rotary with the other ship as a target. But the plane ahead was ready for that. It skidded also.

Rotary's rifle banged. Then there was a terrific racket, thudding jars, as machine-gun bullets stormed into their ship. The metal framing was hit at least a dozen times. Bullets slashed their fuel tank. The tank was located between the cockpit and the engine, and suddenly high-octane gas was flooding back into the cockpit and cabin.

The planes thundered past each other and apart.

Rotary growled, "Must be losin' my eye." He hadn't, as far as he could tell, hit anything effectively.

"See if you can keep them back," Sis said. She hauled the hand throttle as far open as it would go.

Rotary nodded. He climbed back into the cabin, noting that their prisoner was white-faced, but apparently unhurt as yet. "Your pals!" Rotary told him. "Maybe you'd been better off if I had tossed you overboard."

He leaned out of the cabin window from time to time, aiming carefully with his rifle and firing. He was not a particularly good shot. Not expert as modern marksmen go, although he could hold his own with any man on a quail hunt, or shooting jackrabbits from a moving car. He emptied the clip. He had no idea a plane would be so hard to bring down.

The other ship gained on them rapidly and flew below and behind so that it was almost impossible for him to hit it or even catch sight of it. Time seemed to go swiftly. But actually only twenty minutes had passed.

Because the Mississippi River, broad and darkly turgid in the afternoon sun, was below them when they caught fire. The leaking gas tank did it, of course. They were tempting providence to try to fly. But there had been no place where they could land, and still protect themselves after they were down. And, suddenly, Sis screamed, and the plane was full of bundling flames.

They were low, trying to get the plane behind them out of the blind spot. The river was snaking below no more than two hundred feet.

"We'll have to take to the water," Sis said. She had cut the motor and her voice was astonishingly loud.

They hit almost at once. There was not much of it. Not much more roughness than a seaplane landing.

Rotary slashed their prisoner loose. Then he went out through the plane cabin door. Sis was ahead of him. Water was pouring in, their ship beginning to stand on its nose as it sank.

Rotary and Sis swam clear. The water was fairly cold. Fifty yards away, low and glistening in the sun, was a sandbar. It was more than half a mile long, looked smooth, and was completely bare of vegetation. The plane which had brought them down was floating in for a landing on the sandbar. Everywhere else, it seemed to them, there was water.

"They got us," Rotary Harrison said.

# Chapter VII
## MIDWEST TRAIL

The telegram had just come. Doc Savage gave it a second reading.

"Renny," Doc said.

Renny Renwick appeared.

Doc handed him the telegram, explaining, "It just came."

Renny examined the message, then turned it thoughtfully in his big hands. "Telephoned to Kirksville, Missouri, from a place called Millard, Missouri, where there is an airways radio station," he said gravely. "Operator of the airways radio says a plane flew over, apparently with engine trouble, and dropped a message to be telegraphed to you."

"Notice the content of the message," Doc said.

" 'You are being framed to take the rap in scheme involving murder and no telling what else. Coming to give you story.' And it's signed by Rotary Harrison. Do you know a Rotary Harrison?"

"The name is not familiar," Doc admitted. "Get copies of national business directories and Who's Who, and see if we find anything."

Renny's search got results.

"Holy cow!" he said, his great, rumbling voice fully impressed. "Rotary Harrison is an oil man. Got a financial record like a jack-in-the-box. Up and down. Right now, seems to be up, but in a shaky way. Like a man sitting on a stack of packing cases."

Doc Savage said, "Check on this plane Rotary Harrison was flying. Get Monk and Ham to help you, and Long Tom. Keep track of the ship, once you find it."

Renny got on a telephone.

Ham Brooks came in, said, "Doc, this thing isn't shaping up so good from a legal angle."

"You mean that Montague Ogden is still threatening to sue me because of the error in operating on Sam Joseph?"

"He's more than threatening. He's filed suit." Ham spread his hands. "Ogden claims that he has lost the services of Sam Joseph and is therefore entitled to damages."

"That is a fragile basis for a lawsuit."

Ham shrugged. "Ordinarily, yes. But the letter of the written law is not always the law that prevails. Other connected circumstances are usually taken into consideration, whether they should be or not."

"You mean, Ham, that the unpleasant publicity we are getting in the newspapers will weight the scales against us?"

"That," Ham said, "is what I mean."

"I see."

"And, furthermore, I think somebody is behind that publicity campaign against you."

"Our investigation has not turned up a deliberate plot," Doc reminded.

"They're too slick. Too smooth to be caught."

Doc said, "Montague Ogden is certainly doing all he can to discredit me. But you can say one thing about Ogden—he stands right out in the open and beats his drum."

Ham admitted, "He does that," grudgingly. "But the thing is spreading like wildfire. I don't see how one man could stir up all that stink."

Renny came in to report on the results of his search for the plane of Rotary Harrison.

"The ship is down somewhere," Renny said. "Here's a report from a place called Keokuk, on the Mississippi River right at the border of Missouri and Iowa. A plane answering the description of Rotary Harrison's ship passed over that town closely pursued by another plane about two hours ago. That would make it right after the telegram was sent from Millard."

Doc Savage nodded. "Are you getting one of our planes ready?"

"It'll be fueled by the time we get there," Renny said. "Monk and Ham are down there now."

Doc Savage did not take off for the Midwest immediately. He got Long Tom and Renny aside.

"You two stay here," Doc directed, "and begin a general investigation of the situation."

"Just what," asked Renny, "would you suggest was a general investigation?"

"Go to a lot of trouble," Doc said, "to find out whether this campaign against us is the work of an organization."

"I see. Apparently it is the work of Montague Ogden. But you want to know whether there is a gang behind it."

"Another thing," Doc said, "is an investigation of Montague Ogden. I want the history of the man, a complete picture of his life from the beginning up to now."

"Montague's life story. O. K."

"I want a complete report on his financial condition."

"The low-down on Montague Ogden. Right."

"I want a full report on Dr. Nedden."

"The low-down on the Ogden private physician."

"He thoroughly agreed with me that a cerebral fibroma was Sam Joseph's trouble," Doc said.

"So did two other doctors," Renny reminded.

"I want the low-down on them, too."

Renny nodded. "All right. We'll do the best we can."

"Good. We will return as soon as we look into this matter of a man named Rotary Harrison, who has disappeared in the Midwest."

"I take it," Renny said, "that you know how serious this thing can get."

"I have an inkling."

"I'm talking about our college," Renny said.

Doc Savage's face was suddenly solemn, with a trace of strain. Plainly, Renny had touched on the worry uppermost in his mind.

"I think you have hit the nail on the head."

"I thought I had," Renny said.

"If the public gets one single inkling of the kind of an institution we maintain up there, there will be a terrific uproar."

Renny nodded. "We'll be lucky if they only hang us."

"You understand everything you are to do?"

"I'm to get all the dope possible on Montague Ogden and his business interests, find out if there is an organization behind this newspaper campaign against us, and check up on Dr. Nedden and the other doctors who concurred in the diagnosis which said Sam Joseph had a cerebral fibroma. Is that all?"

"Add Sam Joseph to your list. Find out all about him."

"Sure," Renny said. "I can see where Long Tom and I are going to be as busy as one-armed paperhangers."

"You better hire two or three good detective agencies to help you."

"That wouldn't be a bad idea," Renny agreed. "We'll handle it, Doc. Are you leaving for the Midwest now?"

"Right away."

"I hope you find Rotary Harrison," Renny said. "I have a hunch he is the first proof we've had that this thing is a lot bigger than anybody dreamed."

Doc Savage took off from the Hudson River with Monk and Ham. They used one of Doc's small planes, a craft which could handle five passengers at the very most, a ship which was mostly motor. It was an experimental army pursuit-type job which had been constructed on Doc's specifications, and which had proved too "hot" to be handled by the average run of pursuit pilots. Considering how "hot" the pursuit ships now used by the army were, this plane became something of a freak. It held a little over four hours' gas supply, and they had to detour by St. Louis to find a runway long enough to accommodate them. But the trip required very little time. Monk insisted he hardly had time to spit.

They were in the air again when Ham, who was wearing the telephone headset, said, "Here is Renny in New York on the air. Voice. He wants you."

Doc plugged in his headset, picked up the microphone, said, "Yes?"

Renny's deep voice said, "Another telegram just came in from that place in Missouri, Millard. You want it?"

"Go ahead," Doc said.

"It says that Rotary Harrison's plane has landed there and that he and his daughter are waiting to see you if you can fly there to meet them," Renny explained.

"All right," Doc said. "Thanks." He consulted a chart and the wind-velocity information he had gotten from the St. Louis airport. He changed his course.

Alarmed, Ham Brooks consulted the logged data concerning the Millard field, the runway length. "They've got a hard-surfaced runway north and south," he said. "The wind is north and fairly strong. We may be able to set this bumblebee down there."

Monk Mayfair was less concerned about their landing.

"Rotary Harrison and daughter, eh?" he remarked. "I wonder what kind of a daughter."

Ham frowned. "I thought you were cured?"

"Cured of what?"

"Making a yassack out of yourself every time a pretty girl goes past."

Monk grinned. "The only time I feel like a fool," he said, "is when I let one get past me."

Doc Savage said, "Millard Field coming up."

"In this thing," Ham said, "you no more than put your finger on a place than you are there."

They made the usual traffic circle of the field, came in low over the fence and already stalling. The airspeed indicator when they touched said better than a hundred and fifty miles an hour. That was plenty "hot," and as the ship slowed so that the abbreviated control surfaces no longer had much effect, it took expert brake controlling to keep them on the runway and out of the fence at the other end.

When their ground speed was down to twenty miles an hour, Doc braked the right wheel, sent the ship toward the small cottage of an airways radio station with its windmill-like tower for the anemometer and wind sock.

They were not fifty yards from the cottage when a storm of lead hit their ship.

All of the bullets—and no one but Doc noticed this, and he certainly did not discuss it then—hit back in the cabin section where Monk and Ham were riding. None of them hit near the cockpit where Doc was seated in plain view.

## Chapter VIII
## MAN LOST

It was a machine gun. A heavy military-type gun operating on a tripod. It had been set up on the ground and covered with a large canvas, and gun and canvas had been behind a car where it had not been noticed—or more probably the setting up of it had not been noticed—by the operators in the radio station. The car drove forward a few yards, the canvas was yanked away, and the gun began shaking a red-lipped snout.

The effect on Doc's ship was terrific. The machine-gun bullets, .30-caliber with a hitting energy of around twenty-nine hundred foot-pounds, seemed about to turn the plane over. They raked the ship from stern to propeller and took about a fourth off one propeller blade, so that vibration of the unbalanced prop helped shake the ship.

Then everything was silent. The motor had stopped.

Finally Monk spoke.

"That's a nice Missouri reception," he said. "What if this hadn't been an army experimental job with an armored cabin?"

A man appeared in the radio cottage door. One of the operators. Someone shot at him. He jumped, high and wide, and began to run. He did not jump back into the cottage, which would have seemed natural, but took out across the field toward some orange hangars, labeled as the property of a flying service, on the other side of the field. He was a long thin man who ran as probably he had never run before.

"He's a little excited," Monk said mildly.

The words were hardly out of Monk's mouth when a grenade exploded directly under their ship. It might have been a home-made bomb of dynamite. It lifted the plane, Monk said forty feet but ten was probably closer, and snapped off both wings, ripped open the armored cabin compartment, and dumped the wreckage over on its side.

Monk, always ready with a wisecrack, for once was speechless. They were dazed. Their ears had stopped working for the moment.

Doc Savage dug into his clothing. When he was operating, his clothes were invariably a mine of gadgets. He came up with a smoke bomb, a little egg of a thing, which he flipped toward the machine gun.

The smoke bomb hit the ground, ripened, made a cloud of smoke so black that it looked solid like a large and spreading mushroom of tar. It shut off view of car and machine gun.

"Run!" Doc rapped. "They may use another bomb."

Ham piled out of a rip in the cabin. Doc followed, then Monk. Doc and Ham ran, heading for the radio shack, which had a good concrete foundation that should stop lead.

Monk was bellowing. He liked to bellow in a fight, and he jumped around, half of a mind to rush through the smoke and try his luck on the gun crew behind it.

Then an object came gyrating out of the smoke, hit the ground, rolled and stopped near Monk's feet. It was another bomb, homemade, fifteen or so sticks of dynamite and a fizzing, smoking fuse. Monk popped his eyes at it. He let out a howl much louder than any previous effort and started running, not seeming to touch the ground.

Doc Savage scooped up the bomb and threw it back into the smoke on the theory that he could get it away from them faster than they could get away from it. Monk had often claimed that Doc Savage had a mind which could stop and reason such things out under such circumstances. Monk maintained this put Doc on a practically abnormal plane.

The bomb made a noise that a Fourth of July never heard and immediately there was some satisfactory howling.

"Run," Doc said.

They followed Monk, who already had reached the radio cottage. Monk went inside, through the open door where the operator had been standing when shot at.

Doc and Ham followed, except that they did not go inside, but circled the end of the building and went down behind the foundation. "Keep down!" Doc warned. He had seen that the explosion had merely ruffled their enemies.

There seemed to be at least five of the foe, two handling the machine gun, the others with rifles.

The rifles began making the crisp, violent reports that gelatined nitrocellulose powders make, and the bullets went entirely through the radio cottage in most cases. A few were stopped by generators and other solid apparatus inside.

Monk came out through a window, landed beside them. He had discovered bullets would go through the cottage.

"Why don't somebody tell me them things," he complained.

Doc Savage stepped back a few paces, threw another smoke grenade. Then another, and a third. He was spacing them carefully. They made the noises of firecrackers that had fizzled.

To Monk and Ham, Doc said, "Pay no attention to the yelling I do now."

In a much louder voice, a bellow, Doc howled, *"Monk, Ham, make a break for it! Run! We've got to get away. We want to reach the Harrisons. Let these fellows go!"*

He waited for that to soak in. Then he repeated it, almost exactly the same words.

After which he dashed out around the corner of the radio cottage, back toward his mangled plane. The smoke pall had now spread enough to envelop the entire vicinity. He could hear the assailants saying things, mostly profanity, in the pall. Doc got into the hulk of his plane largely by the sense of touch and found an equipment case. This was intact and he got it open, took out two metal flasks.

He returned with both flasks to Monk. He gave one to the homely chemist.

"They have a plane," Doc said. "It is undoubtedly over by the hangars, so get over there and put this stuff in the fuel tank."

Monk knew what was in the flasks. He had helped concoct the stuff.

"Sure," he said.

Doc made his voice loud again and bellowed, *"Get away! Don't take any chances on being shot. Our job is to get the Harrisons!"*

Then the bronze man ran back into the smoke pall again. He went cautiously now. He heard a man swearing and made for the fellow, found him and struck with a fist, simultaneously grabbing the man by the throat to throttle an outcry. The fist blow he sent to the stomach. It was not very successful for the man was wearing an armored vest. One of the plate-type commercial armored vests which sell for about seventy-five dollars. It stopped most of the effect of Doc's fist blow. The man squirmed, fought. Doc hit him again and the fellow subsided.

Doc took the man's coat and hat. Strangely, the hat was harder to remove than the coat; the man had yanked it down over his ears so he wouldn't lose it in the uproar.

*"Use gas on them!"* Doc shouted, using his own voice and making it loud.

He then hauled on the coat, which fit him better than expected, and yanked the hat over his own ears, splitting it at the band in the operation.

He found the criminals' car. There was no one behind the wheel. He got in, started the motor, made it moan and race.

Thrusting his head out of the car, he yelled, imitating one of the voices which he had heard, "Gas! Gas! Come on! Let's get out of here!"

There was no gas, of course. But the black stuff thrown off by the smoke bombs had an acrid odor that was distinctive enough to give the imagination a good start.

They thought there was gas. They were not prepared with masks evidently. And the roaring, racing car engine was like a magnet. None of them wanted to be left behind. They converged on the machine in a wild rush.

Doc added to the confusion—it was intensely black there in the smoke pall, impossible to see an arm length—by honking the car horn steadily and bellowing, "Come on! Gas! Gas!"

When he knew they were aboard he meshed gears, let out the clutch and gave the machine plenty of gas. He drove blindly until he was out of the smoke. Then he wheeled to the right, went over a driveway curbing with a flying bump and out through the airport gate onto a graveled road.

Doc drove fast. The men in the car leaned out of windows and fired back into the smoke cloud. Two were clinging to the outside, and one of these tried to fire, but almost fell off and lost his rifle.

So far the hat and coat Doc was wearing had fooled them.

But he did not want to get them too far away from the airport. Not so far away but that they would try to go back and get their plane.

He went over a railroad crossing. It was rough, so rough that only the solid top of the car kept some of them from flying out.

Then there was a sharp turn onto another highway, a concrete one, and that did not ease the situation.

Doc Savage drove two hundred yards more, saw a cornfield at the roadside. The growing corn was about the right height for his purpose.

He jammed on the brakes hard, gave the wheel just the right treatment and got the car on its side in the ditch in a cloud of dust, the door on his side open.

He got out, feet pounding in grass, went over a low barbed-wire fence into the corn. By stooping, the corn tassels were well over his head. The corn, fortunately, had not been check-planted, so that its rows ran in only one direction, which was parallel to the road. They could not look down a corn row and see him.

"That ain't Bill!" one of the men bellowed.

There was some more shooting then, but not as bad as it had been back at the radio cottage.

Doc Savage kept going and circled widely, coming back to the road. Once there he was very cautious once more. But it was not needed.

The men had deserted their car. They had crossed the railroad and were running across the airport toward the hangars on the opposite side. They all were there except the one Doc had slugged. That one had recovered his senses and was sprinting across the field, also headed for the hangars.

Ham Brooks, at the radio shack, began shooting. Ham seemed to have found a double-barreled shotgun inside the radio cottage. He unloaded both barrels with a terrific report. He was kicked backward through the radio-shack door. The running man only ran faster.

Doc went to the railroad tracks. There was a culvert close by, a small one, and he sat down there. He waited calmly.

He was pleased. His plan was working as smoothly as if it had been rehearsed. They did not always go this well.

The running men, just crossing the airport, were staggering with fatigue. They did some wild shooting at the hangars, the bullets causing a general rush for cover on the part of a number of young men, evidently Civilian Pilot Training students.

The plane setting in front of the hangars was a black cabin job, one large motor, low-wing. One of the expensive ships built for the rich private trade before the war, and not taken over by the government because of an overly large number of hours on motor and ship. But airworthy and fast. A ship large enough to take all the men off the ground.

They piled into the craft. It had an electric starter, and this whipped the prop over. Dust picked up behind the ship and whirled away in clouds.

The plane tore across the airport, ignoring the paved runway, quartering into the wind. It got its wheels off, and immediately the pilot began to slip a little into the wind to keep away from the fence corners.

A small man, a very indignant small man, came out of one of the hangars and began to pop away with a revolver at the fleeing plane. Monk appeared hastily, said something to the small man. He stopped shooting, then he and Monk ran into the hangar.

The plane with the criminals in it got a hundred and fifty feet of altitude, banked quickly, came back. It was obvious they were after Ham, at the radio shack. And maybe the radio shack, too, if they had more of those dynamite bombs.

Doc Savage showed himself. He made as much of a spectacle as he could, jumping around and waving his arms, seizing a short piece of plank and going through the motions of aiming it, as if it was a gun.

The plane wheeled, came boring toward him. Out of the cabin windows, came fire and noise.

Doc went into the culvert. The machine-gun bullets jarred the ground around the mouth of the culvert. The plane whooped overhead. Doc waited. Soon there was a terrific concussion and sticks, dust and leaves flew into the culvert. They'd had another dynamite bomb, all right.

Doc waited awhile, crawled out. He looked around for another bomb instantly, but located none. Then he eyed the plane. It was heading into the east. It had the purposeful aim of a definite place to go.

Doc ran across the field to the hangars.

Monk and the small man—the latter was swearing really wonderful profanity and not asking questions—were wheeling a neat-looking blue biplane out of the big hangar.

Monk said, "I knew you'd want to follow them right away, Doc."

Doc Savage glanced over the ship. It was faster than the cabin job which had just left the field.

Ham had appeared at the radio shack again, was doing something around the wreckage of their bomb-ripped plane.

Doc made a hand funnel, yelled, "Get the scanner!"

Ham, shouting back faintly, said, "I'm getting it."

He disappeared into the plane ruin, came out and ran toward them. He had a case about the size of a typewriter case, and a longer and heavier box of metal.

Doc climbed into the biplane. It was an open-cockpit job.

The small man stopped swearing long enough to say, "That's my C. P. T. advanced trainer. You guys bust up that ship and it won't be healthy for you. They're getting hard to get."

Monk said, "Keep your shirt on. Has anybody some goggles?"

Two young men, wearing the C. P. T. wing emblems on their blouses, had goggles. They parted with them—for about twice what they were worth, cash.

Ham arrived.

"You and Monk ride in the back," Doc said, "with the gadget."

Ham said, "It'll be a trial riding with that goon." He got in the cockpit with the homely Monk and the two cases. They were very crowded. And they were quarreling when Doc gave the hand throttle a steady pull and sent the ship across the tarmac.

Doc lifted the ship off and sent it into the east on the trail of the other plane. The latter was now out of sight, had been out of sight for some minutes.

The plane, being a trainer, was equipped with gosports, the speaking-tube-headset device used in training student fliers. Doc indicated Monk should put on the headset, said, "Get the scanner working."

Monk nodded violently and went to work with the apparatus.

Ham watched, puzzled. He understood only part of this. Doc's unorthodox conduct of the fight back at the airport had been aimed at scaring the enemy into flight, or, more specifically, into flight to wherever they were holding the Harrisons.

Also, the fight had been arranged so that Monk could introduce something into the gas tank of the plane ahead. Some chemical, Ham surmised.

"What kind of mumbo-jumbo is this?" Ham yelled at Monk.

"Keep your hair on," Monk shouted back, "until I get this thing percolating."

Of the two parts of the apparatus, the metal case seemed to contain a large collection of batteries of the "B" radio type, batteries delivering a sizable voltage. In addition there were coils and vacuum tubes, arranged so that they did not make sense to Ham. But it was certainly not a radio.

The second box contained a device into which Monk proceeded to thrust his face, after plugging it into the other apparatus. The thing was about a foot and a half long. At the end opposite Monk's face was a large lens, and Monk stared at the surrounding sky through this.

"North, Doc," Monk shouted. "They swung north right ahead. Guess they figured they were out of sight of the airport. And they're climbing fast."

Ham bellowed, "How do you know where that other plane went?"

"Look," Monk said. He thrust the gadget into Ham's hands. "Look through it."

Ham stared into the thing. At first he saw nothing but a deep-purple darkness and he said so.

"Look to the north you overdressed shyster," Monk ordered.

Ham did so. Immediately and astonishingly he saw a faintly silver-colored thread of what looked like smoke. Smoke from a tracer bullet, but very vague. He told Monk what he saw.

"That's it," Monk said. "That's the trail of the other plane."

Ham jerked the thing away from his eyes. "You're crazy!"

"You're the crazy one!" Monk roared at him. "Doc and I have worked for months on this thing."

"How does it work?"

"Simple, like all great things," Monk snapped. "You introduce a chemical in the gasoline which a plane burns. After it burns and passes out of the exhaust stacks, it is a vapor that hangs quiescent in the air. It will hang there for hours. Of course it drifts with the wind currents, but it's there anyway, marking a plain trail."

Ham objected, "But I can't see it with the naked eye."

"That's what makes it good," Monk assured him. "You can only see it with this gadget here."

"How does it work?"

"That would take two hours to explain, plus about four years of chemical education for you so you would know enough to understand the explanation," Monk assured him. "But it works with both ultraviolet and infrared wave lengths of light from both ends of the so-called visible spectrum."*

---

* Doc Savage's researches into light have been extensive, his employment of it varied. As regular readers of Doc Savage magazine will surely have noticed, in almost every new adventure, Doc Savage manages to introduce one or more surprises in the shape of a scientific gadget. What readers of a scientific bent will also have noted is that it is the policy of the author of the Doc Savage material to have Doc employ only methods and

"All right, all right, you don't have to be sarcastic, you ape," Ham said.

He was satisfied.

The plane flew north, got above an extended bank of clouds. Then it turned east again. And, eventually, when the cloud bank widened it angled southward. Compared to the terrific speed of the plane in which they had come out from New York, they seemed to be crawling.

Ham had been silent, thinking about the gadget they were using. He was fascinated. He began to see possibilities in the thing.

"Say," Ham yelled. The roar of air in the open cockpit made it hard to talk. "Say, why wouldn't this be a good gadget for the American army or navy to use on the enemy?"

Monk sneered at him. "What do you think we developed it for?"

"Has it already been tried?"

"Europe and Asia," Monk said, "are full of English and American agents busy introducing quantities of that chemical into the gasoline supplies of the enemy."

"Is there any way of them licking it?"

"Sure. They can work out some chemical to nullify the effect of this stuff. But that will take weeks or months, and in the meantime their planes can be tracked back to their airdromes by our ships. There won't be any such thing as a concealed enemy airdrome."

Ham grinned. Particularly in crowded Europe did bombers operate from secret bases. This trailing method would be death on such bases. You would follow the trail, and if there was wind, allow for wind drift. On still-air days, the stuff should be marvelous.

As time went on Ham was beginning to understand why both the army and navy had refused active service to Doc Savage and his associates as well. The explanation then had been that they

---

devices which have been developed, or which other scientists have accomplished at least on a laboratory scale. Since the first Doc Savage novel appeared in 1933, many of the mechanical devices employed by Doc Savage, which seemed completely fantastic at the time, have been placed in every-day use. These range from simple devices, such as a generator-operated type of flashlight, which are now so common they can be bought in toy stores for children or in expensive deluxe models for blackout use, to the method lately employed of introducing a gas into the fuel tanks of military pursuit planes to make the gasoline vapor non-explosive when the tanks are hit by the incendiary bullets from enemy guns. This, however, is the first time the device for trailing planes has been employed by Doc.

could do more good for the war effort by going on as they had been. That had seemed a thin argument to Doc and the rest of them at the time. Certainly it was not satisfactory.

Because in the final analysis their main thirst was for excitement and adventure, and that even included Doc himself. The war was a great show, probably the greatest show of the century, and they hated to miss it. Or at least fool around in the cheering section, only now and then getting a finger into it. But the army and navy simply wouldn't have them. They had been tossed out on their collective ears. Not once, either. Just about weekly.

## Chapter IX
## RIVER FIGHT

Doc Savage's voice was quiet in the gosport when he said, "All right, there they are!"

The river was a width of gray corduroy below them, and in it lay the white scar of a long sandbar. At the north end the bar thrust an arm out toward the shore, and the water there seemed to be wading depth mostly, except for a narrow channel. In fact, at the far side of the channel, very near to the river bank, was a paddle-wheel steamer which was obviously a derelict, a hulk which had been there many years.

On the sandbar, however, and in motion, was the black plane which they had followed from the Millard airport. The pilot had seen them, was taking off.

Tiny figures were sprinting along the sandbar toward the derelict steamer. Doc counted them. Four. That meant the pilot was alone in the craft that was leaving the bar.

That plane and this one were so closely matched in climbing rate and maneuverability that the presence of even one added passenger would be too much of a handicap.

Doc said, "Two of us have to go over."

There were two chutes in the plane. They were regulation parachutes for the C. P. T. students, so they would be all right. Seat-pack type.

Ham said, "I'll fly her. I'm the lightest one, anyway."

There was no argument. He was right. And Ham was a good combat pilot.

Doc directed, "Dive her. Get her about a hundred yards north of the old boat."

Ham nodded.

To Monk, Doc said, "Hold off cracking your 'chute until you're almost in the trees."

"You're telling me," Monk yelled. "I hope none of those guys are wing shots."

Doc watched the river surface, the position of the plane, judging the wind velocity—which would influence their parachute drift very little, but nevertheless somewhat—from the condition of the river waves.

Direction of the wind, of course, was easy to judge from the unruffled surface of the water next to the bank over which the wind was blowing.

He went over. He got a bad start, slipping on the cockpit rim, and began to turn over and over. He stopped that by violent kicking at the right moments. The earth came rushing up at him. He kept his eyes on it. A long fall and a break-out of the 'chute as low as he intended to crack this one was not something to fool with. You fell fifty feet in no time at all; fifty feet misjudgment could kill you.

He was being shot at. He could hear the fiddle-string-break sounds of the bullets passing. He did not take his eyes off the ground, which was magnifying enormously. He hauled on the ripcord.

He was a little ashamed of what he did then. He threw the steel ripcord away in his excitement, something parachute jumpers in the army and navy were taught never to do. The ripcords cost nearly five dollars apiece.

The next instant he was jarred solidly, then he was in trees. The trees were willows and they cushioned his fall, tore clothing, took off hide, planted a few splinters.

With a flourishing of willows and a painful grunting, Monk was down a moment later. He was not over fifty feet away. Doc got out of the harness, left the chute there, and ran to Monk.

Monk said, "These danged willows ain't as soft as they look from the air." He was not seriously damaged.

"Come on," Doc said. "They must have the Harrisons on that old boat."

They ran toward the boat. The ruin of it projected above the willows, higher than would have been possible if the old derelict was resting in the water. It must be grounded, planted high and dry by some flood years ago, perhaps far out of the river channel, and now the river had channeled almost to the boat.

Doc saw water through the willows, slowed his pace, and

located the sandbar. The four running men were off the big bar, were in the deeper channel which separated it from the grounded derelict. Two of them were wading while the other two were swimming, making slightly better time.

Doc drew back, made for the boat. Monk was close behind him. Monk had picked up a club, a small oak fence post, a most impressive shillalah. "An Irishman's toothpick," Monk explained, waving the post.

Doc picked up two tomato cans as he ran. Fishermen must have brought them here to carry worms; now they were full of sand, and made good missiles.

Feet had trampled the bank near the old boat. There was a crude gangplank, a tree trunk which had been felled from the bank to the derelict.

A man was coming down the gangplank, walking sidewise, using his rifle for a balancing stick. He must have seen the two parachutes come down, had decided to get ashore and do his fighting bushwhack style.

Doc threw one of the sand-filled tomato cans.

The man on the log squawked, lost his rifle, fell down and wrapped his arms around the log. He remained there, dazed.

Doc pegged a smoke bomb onto the deck of the sidewheeler, let it burst, then went out on the log. He ran lightly, hardly seeming to slacken speed while on the log.

Monk followed but paused to give the man clinging to the log a wallop with his club, with the result that he nearly fell off the log. The clinging man, stunned still more, lost his grip with his legs. But he still hung to the log by his hands. Monk trampled on his fingers for a while, poked with the club. The man remained there, crying, "I can't swim!" in an awful voice.

"You've got a fine chance to learn," Monk assured him, and kicked him loose.

It was about fifteen feet down to the water, and the water was not waist-deep.

Monk ran on, entered the smoke from Doc's grenade, which was spreading.

"Monk," said Doc's voice in the black pall.

"Yeah?"

"You've got to be less reckless," Doc warned. "You take too many chances."

"O. K.," Monk agreed, and grinned. A fight, he figured, was the place to be reckless.

The men fording across from the sandbar were shouting excitedly, howling warnings about the parachutes to the boat.

Overhead there was tense moaning from the two airplanes.

Doc lifted his voice, shouted, "Harrison! Rotary Harrison! This is Doc Savage. Where are you?"

Over the plane-motor noise, over the yelling of the men coming from the bar, and the anxious squalling of the man Monk had kicked off the log and who was trying to drown in waist-deep water, there was an answer. It was a response in a bellowing voice. From the boat somewhere. Deep inside. The voice made no words, just anger and noise.

Monk said, "That sounds about like I figured Rotary Harrison would sound."

"Monk, come on," Doc said. "We have got to find the Harrisons and get them out of here, safely. That is the first job."

Monk thought of the four men in the river and decided to misunderstand Doc's order. Now and then Monk permitted himself to do something like that, usually when to follow instructions meant missing a fight.

"Sure, I'll get 'em, Doc," Monk yelled, and made off up the deck.

There was enough noise, what with the planes and the yelling, that he figured he could get away with that.

He wanted a fight. The men trying to board the derelict would be just about what he considered suitable odds.

He made for the bow, which was where he surmised the men would try to board the old boat. Almost at once he fell through to his armpits in a hole in the deck. The boards did not seem to be rotten; someone had merely removed them.

He got out of the smoke, made better time. He reached the rail, heard the men splashing alongside. He put his head over the rail quickly.

The men, waist-deep in mud and sand, were working along the side of the derelict. Their heads were not more than six feet below. Wonderful targets for Monk's long club, he decided. Like playing golf.

He drew back quickly, got a grip on the very end of the club. He leaned over the rail.

Two of the men below were ready. They had an old piece of rusted wire hawser about a dozen feet long. Each had an end.

They came up and over with the hawser, swinging it as if it was a skip rope. It came down on the back of Monk's neck. They yanked. Monk did a one-and-a-half turn over the rail and lit standing up in the mud beside them.

It occurred to Monk, a little too late, that they could have seen his shadow when he appeared at the rail the first time.

They were on him instantly, all of them. And Monk had his fight. He knew immediately it was the nastiest fight he had ever had, which was saying a great deal. Two of them had double fistfuls of mud, which they at once slapped into his eyes.

Someone hit him with something a little later. It felt like a rifle stock when he clutched it helplessly, going down. He was dazed.

They got on him with their feet, trampled him deep into the mud.

He never heard one of them say, "Don't do him clear in! We can use one of them alive, the big boss says."

Doc Savage crouched at the edge of a hatch, listening. The voice that undoubtedly belonged to Rotary Harrison was howling steadily below. It was close.

Overhead, the two planes were circling, sparring. From time to time gun clatter joined the noise of their motors. Ham seemed to be the better flier. At least he was holding his own. But the other pilot had an automatic rifle. And Ham, who was used to a ship with an armored cockpit, with fuel tanks treated so they would not leak, was handicapped. Like Monk, he was inclined to be reckless, too.

Doc looked down into the hatch. The hold planking had long ago been ripped out; there were only the naked beams of the old sidewheeler's internal frame.

But there was, lurking down there somewhere, a guard. Probably a man with a gun. It was tobacco smoke that told the bronze man this, not the smoke itself, but the pungent odor from the clothes of a man who smoked a pipe a great deal.

Doc picked up a long stick, a fragment of fishpole someone had left on deck, and sent it away from him like a spear. The pole hit, skittered down through another hatch, made a clatter.

Instantly, Doc swung down through the hatch where he was crouching. He landed on a crosspiece, leaped to the right, got behind a timber.

At one time the hold of the derelict had drifted full of mud and sand. But of late years the hull at the stern—Doc was now near the stern—had fallen apart, and the mud and sand had washed out again when the river was at flood stage. So the central section of the derelict was still piled high with a sandbank.

Doc searched carefully, located the guard. The man was standing behind a timber himself, only the muzzle of his gun showing.

Doc worked toward him and managed to get closer and closer.

The two figures lying bound on the sandbank did not stir and made no sound. A man and a girl. The girl even turned once, quickly, as if she heard some small sound in the direction opposite Doc, which was clever.

Doc got the guard, reaching around the beam to take him. He tried to make the fellow unconscious silently. He did that all right, but the man's gun was on cock, and it exploded, the blast ear-rending in the confines of the place. Immediately another guard, one stationed farther toward the bow, but inside the boat, howled an alarmed demand.

Not knowing how many more there were, Doc shouted, "Run! The place is full of cops!"

The cavelike acoustics of the place, he hoped, would make his voice sound like anybody's voice.

He dropped the guard, ran to the Harrisons and freed them, slashing with a knife at their ropes.

"Run," he ordered. "Get ashore!"

They had been tied too long and couldn't run. The effort they made was agonizing.

Doc gathered them up, one with each arm, and carried them.

The guard toward the bow hadn't been fooled. He was coming back, and cautiously. Once he fired at them, the bullet scooping rotten wood off a timber.

Carrying the Harrisons, Doc got to a burst hull planking, and worked through it. They fell out into river mud. Carrying two people was incredibly difficult in the stuff. But he worked toward the bank, which was steep, and got up onto the sunbaked mud, then climbed more rapidly. He piled into the willows that furred the top without being shot in the back.

He dropped the Harrisons.

"Keep crawling away from here," he said.

The noise of the planes overhead had changed. He looked up. It was bad news. The motor of Ham's plane had gone dead and he was slanting off to the east for a motor-off landing somewhere. He evidently figured he was high enough to reach some of the oat-stubble fields that were back half a mile or so from the river.

The second plane—for some reason or other, the pilot was not pursuing Ham to finish him off—was spiraling down toward the sandbar.

The ship landed on the sandbar.

There was some shouting when the plane stopped. Doc moved to a position where he could see the ship.

Three men were hauling a fourth toward the plane. The man they hauled was Monk. Monk seemed to be unconscious.

Then, three more men appeared, wading to the sandbar. They were the two guards who had been in the derelict, and the man Monk had kicked off the log gangplank.

Monk was dumped into the plane. The others climbed in. The plane went flogging down the long sandbar. The sand seemed to be packed as hard as a runway, otherwise the ship would never have taken the air with that load.

But it got off.

They flew straight up the river, slowly gathering altitude. The plane was hardly above the level of the river-bank treetops when it was out of sight and out of sound.

"Harrison!" Doc called.

Rotary Harrison and the girl appeared, coated with mud and dust, twigs and grass, from head to foot. They walked stiffly, staggering because of stiffened muscles.

"This is my daughter, Sis," Rotary Harrison said quietly. "They got away, huh?"

Doc Savage nodded.

"They not only got away," he said grimly. "They escaped with one of my best men."

Doc Savage went back aboard the derelict river steamer alone. He searched the ruin from stem to rudder post, from keel to passenger deck.

There was nothing to show that the men had used the wreck for anything but a very temporary hide-out.

Doc spent some time measuring footprints, storing the measurements in his mind, using a mental-impression memory system which he had developed.*

He decided that the river steamer had been wrecked here originally through the misfortune of having its boilers blow up.

---

* The remarkable memory ability which Doc Savage possesses is not, as his other traits are not, particularly freakish. Really amazing memories, as experts on psychology know, are usually the result of the use, consciously or subconsciously, of various systems, association or otherwise, of filing a fact in the brain tissue along with various labels by which it can be found.

But there was nothing of real value.

After a while, Ham Brooks came stumbling through the willow thickets.

"A blasted lucky shot brought me down," he complained. "The only bullet that hit the plane, I think. It shorted out one mag, and the other was out of order. Just one of those freaks."

Doc Savage said, "They got away with Monk."

Ham did not say anything. But his face was fixed, and afterward it lost color. He could not have been tortured into admitting it, but Monk was probably closer to Ham than any other person.

## Chapter X
## THE DEMENTED TRAIL

It was not yet daylight the next morning when Doc Savage walked into his headquarters with Rotary Harrison and Sis.

Renny Renwick and Long Tom Roberts were at work, surrounded with telephones, scratch pads, pencils, and half-consumed sandwiches.

The big-fisted engineer, Renny, said, "Holy cow! Where's Ham? Monk was seized by those guys; we knew that. But where is Ham?"

Doc explained, "Ham stayed behind to look for Monk."

"He got any clues?"

"Only that the black plane which carried Monk away was a type of ship which probably did not have a large fuel capacity, and therefore it had to land three or four hundred miles from where they got Monk."

Renny nodded. "Long Tom and I have been as busy as jumping beans. But we've checked up on Montague Ogden and his company. We've looked into that newspaper campaign against you, and we've checked up on the doctors who concurred in the diagnosis which led to the operation on Sam Joseph. And we have looked up Sam Joseph."

"Take the last first," Doc Savage suggested, "and begin with Sam Joseph."

Rotary Harrison and Sis crowded close. "Yeah," said Rotary. "I think I got me a big personal interest in that hombre."

"This is Miss Sister Harrison, and her father, Mr. Ranzo John Harrison," Doc Savage explained. "Colonel John Renwick and

Major Thomas J. Roberts. Better known as Renny and Long Tom."

"Call me Sis," Sis said, smiling.

"And call me Rotary," Rotary Harrison rumbled, "if you want me to be happy."

Renny nodded.

"Here's the report on Sam Joseph," the big-fisted engineer rumbled. "Birthplace, parents, nationality, early environment unknown."

Renny stopped speaking, looked at them expectantly.

"Unknown?" said Doc. "What do you mean, unknown?"

"Sam Joseph," said Renny, "is a victim of permanent early amnesia, or so he claims. He knows nothing about what happened to him before he was about twenty-five years old. He claims that he is one of those men who wake up in hospitals, not knowing who he is. He claims he still does not know."

"What about the rest of his life?"

"His business career has been about the usual career of an executive in a business organization. He has worked for three different firms, a bond house, a mail-order concern, and the Ogden outfit. Good record."

"You mean he ain't a crook?" Rotary demanded, disgusted.

"There is no evidence of his being crooked," Renny said.

"He's just too slick for you then. He's got it all covered up."

"If he covered anything up, he *is* slick," Renny rumbled. "We've done everything but look at the roots of his teeth. No, we even did that! One of the detectives we hired brought in X-ray films of Sam Joseph's teeth. Got them from his dentist."

Rotary Harrison smashed a fist into a palm. "Sam Joseph is a crook!" he declared. "And I think he's a murderer, too, or at least hired murder done."

Renny was interested. "What makes you say a thing like that? That's a pretty harsh statement."

"Six months ago I borrowed a large sum of money from Sam Joseph and we signed an agreement to renew the loan in six months. Now I can't pay. Somebody stole the written agreement to renew, and Sam Joseph say there wasn't any. The only witness I had to the agreement was an old friend, Duster Jones. He was murdered. A man named Butch killed him."

Renny jumped. "Butch! There's a man working for Montague Ogden named Butch."

"Working for Sam Joseph, you mean, don't you?" demanded Rotary.

"No, for Odgen. But maybe—" Renny scratched his head.

Doc said, "The thing to do seems to be to talk to Sam Joseph. Renny, do you know where we can find him?"

"He's back at Montague Ogden's place, as far as we know."

They rode downtown in a black limousine which was large but subdued, discreet, ordinary, giving no hint that it was actually a rolling fortress of armor plate and special bullet resistant glass and as formidable as a tank. Long Tom had remained behind to continue the investigation to which he and Renny had been assigned.

"Doc," Renny said thoughtfully.

"Yes?"

"You remember that thing which first got me and Long Tom so excited about this case?"

"The talking devil, you mean?"

"Yes."

"What about it?"

"It keeps cropping up in my thoughts. You suppose it had any peculiar significance?"

Doc Savage said, "The thing possibly was not what it seemed."

Rotary Harrison demanded, "What's this stuff about a talking devil?"

Renny gave him the story about Sam Joseph apparently hearing the small devil image speak. It was plain from the way Renny told the story that he had been giving it a good deal of thought and was still much intrigued by it, as well as far from convinced that the speaking satan was a figment of a disordered mind.

Sis Harrison also listened to the story, and she watched Doc Savage. She seemed to be noting the physical qualities of the bronze man and seemed quite impressed.

Sis said unexpectedly, "This whole thing hasn't made much sense so far, has it? If it is just a plot to steal the oil interests which dad and I have built up, it seems rather elaborate."

"My guess," Doc Savage told them, "is that we will find that a great deal more is involved. What happened in the Midwest shows we are up against a big organization."

"A cultus bunch of hombres," Rotary put in. "And they won't stop at nothin'."

A man in a butler's livery tried to prevent them entering the fantastically modernistic Ogden penthouse on top of the Ogden building. Rotary Harrison lost no time in elbowing the butler out of the way. Rotary had risen to a rage as he looked at the fabulous richness of the Ogden building, and had growled, "Probably got the dough for this by robbing other guys like me! Well, I'll put a quietus on that!" He slammed the butler one on the chest and said, "Don't argue with us, fancy britches!"

Dr. Nedden met them at the door of the room where Sam Joseph lay on a bed.

Dr. Nedden's manner was cold as he eyed Doc Savage. His greeting was brusque. "You are fully aware the patient should not have visitors yet," he snapped.

Doc made no comment on that. Instead, he said, "Dr. Nedden, is it true that you have stated that you did not actually diagnose Sam Joseph's trouble as cerebral fibroma?"

Dr. Nedden's face tightened. "I refuse to discuss the case with you."

"But you have so stated to the newspapers, have you not?"

"I—"

"When as a matter of truth you told me in plain words that you agreed your diagnosis was cerebral fibroma," Doc added.

Dr. Nedden swallowed.

"You can't see the patient," he snapped.

Rotary Harrison said, "Brother, where's your riot squad? You better have one when you tell us what we can't do."

Dr. Nedden backed away indignantly. "Remember," he snapped. "I haven't given my permission. This is on your own initiative, and against a surgeon's advice."

He wheeled and went away.

Rotary Harrison looked after Dr. Nedden and said, "When I was a kid I used to think I had a strange power where snakes were concerned. I thought I could *feel* when a snake was around me. Maybe it was imagination then. But I *feel* that way about that guy."

They went into the room.

Sam Joseph smiled at them pleasantly from the bed.

His color was good, although his head was swathed in bandages, and he was obviously quite weak. His voice, when he spoke, was low but healthy, quiet and quite sane-sounding.

"Good morning," he said. "I am very sorry to be the cause of all this trouble."

Rotary Harrison roared, "Good morning—hell! Listen, you dirty, black-faced crook, you—"

"Hold it, hold it," Doc Savage said. Although Doc did not lift his voice, Harrison went silent.

Sam Joseph examined Rotary Harrison, asked, "Who is this man? He seems familiar—"

"You oughta remember me, you snipe," said Rotary. "I'm Rotary Harrison."

"Oh, yes. Yes, indeed," said Sam Joseph. "I do remember you now. But you have changed a little."

"You loaned me a hundred and eighty thousand dollars," snapped Rotary.

"Yes, I recall. On your oil interests."

"And you signed an agreement to renew the loan in six months."

"I am sure you are mistaken," Sam Joseph said. "I would have remembered that. There was no such agreement."

"Why, you—"

Doc Savage got in front of Rotary, pushed him back. "You will have to keep that for later," Doc said. "This man underwent a major operation three days ago."

Sam Joseph smiled, said, "Thank you. But I am feeling better. Except at times, when I seem to fade off mentally and have rather strange dreams."

"What kind of dreams?" Doc inquired.

"I never seem to be able to recall the details," Sam Joseph said. "However, one strange thing happened. I heard that little devil statue speaking again."

"You heard the devil talk again?"

"Yes, I really heard it again."

Sis Harrison blurted, "But I thought the devil was supposed to have been destroy—"

Doc, interrupting, asked, "Where was the devil when it spoke?"

"On the table there, beside my bed."

The indicated table was a small modern metal one which bore a rather expensive-looking bedside reading lamp which gave a focused and controlled beam that could be changed from a switch on the end of a cord, which an occupant of the bed could use.

"It was the little brass devil statue?" Doc asked.

"Yes."

"What did it say?" Doc inquired. "Or did you understand the words?"

The bronze man's voice had not changed, had not taken on excitement. But there was an intense activity in his flake-gold eyes and tension in his jaw muscles.

"I understood the words," said Sam Joseph.

"What were they?"

"The devil said, *'Hello, hello, hello. We have to see you. That thing in Missouri turned out better than we expected. We have the short ugly one. What shall we do with him?'*"

Sam Joseph closed his eyes for a moment. "I am sure that is what the devil said," he continued. "I made a particular point to remember it. It was a rather long speech, but I kept repeating it to myself. I have a good memory, really."

Rotary Harrison growled, "If you have such a memory, it's funny that agreement—"

Doc interposed, "Mr. Joseph, had you been asleep just before you heard the devil talk?"

"Yes."

"One of the sleepy spells when you dream?"

"Well, yes. But my head was quite clear when I heard the statue talk."

Doc Savage nodded.

"What became of the devil after it spoke?" he asked.

"Oh, it disappeared. I don't know where it went."

"Do you have a nurrse?"

"Only Dr. Nedden. He has been staying here day and night. He seems very disturbed over what happened."

"Dr. Nedden does not leave your side?"

"Oh, I wouldn't say that. He goes away frequently, but for short times only. Never for more than five minutes at a time."

That ended the discussion because Long Tom Roberts burst into the place."

"Get out of here, Doc!" Long Tom yelled. "The police are on their way here to arrest you!"

Long Tom did not get that excited without reason. Doc wheeled, made for the door. The Harrisons, father and daughter, seemed undecided, then followed him, running. They lost no time getting into an elevator and down to the street.

Long Tom had a car waiting. They piled into that. Long Tom yanked the machine into traffic, said, "You better get down out of sight, Doc. They'll have prowl cars looking for you."

Rotary Harrison swore.

"I thought you were a special policeman yourself," he said.*

Doc made no reply.

---

* Doc Savage has held, through most of his career, honorary police commissions, usually of high ranking. From time to time, due to one misunderstanding or another arising out of the bronze man's unusual activities, these have been revoked and restored.

Long Tom said, "Special commission or not, Doc, you are in plenty of trouble."

Doc said, "It must have developed suddenly."

Long Tom popped a hand down on the steering wheel.

"Like that!" he said. "Like lightning. Out of a clear sky. Bang! But we should have seen it coming."

Doc said, "It has been building up, all right."

Long Tom, startled, eyed him and demanded, "You mean to say you have seen it coming?"

Doc nodded.

"When did the police appear?" he asked.

"Not very long after you left to come down to examine Sam Joseph," Long Tom explained. "The commissioner himself came in, with the head of the detective bureau, the head of the frauds investigation bureau, and some other big shots. So I knew it was bad. I tried to stall them. Said I didn't know exactly where you were, which was true in a way."

"And then?"

"They got a telephone call. It was a tip-off about where you were. So they lit out. And I lit out faster, because I beat them down here."

Renny Renwick emitted a rumble of anger. "That Dr. Nedden! He tipped them off!"

The sound of a police siren came at them so suddenly that it was surprising. The car, a white radio prowl, whisked past with two grim officers leaning forward on the seat. The machine was headed for the Ogden building.

"I didn't beat them by much," Long Tom said.

Rotary Harrison emitted a growl of disgust. "Do you guys do everything backward?"

"What you mean?" Long Tom asked.

"What're they tryin' to arrest Savage for?" Rotary demanded. "Why? You haven't said."

Long Tom stared at him, then at Doc Savage. "Doc," Long Tom asked, "do you want to discuss it in front of these people?"

Doc Savage spoke then in Mayan. The language of ancient Maya was one they had learned in the course of their first really great adventure together. Although simple, it was spoken, as far as they knew, by no one in the civilized world but themselves.

"Has the existence and location of our College actually been disclosed to the police?" Doc asked in Mayan.

"Apparently not," Long Tom replied, also in Mayan. "But they are convinced there is such a place."

"Then, in our discussions, avoid admitting there is such a place," Doc directed.

"O. K.," Long Tom said in English. He added, "What do you say we go to my laboratory? The police don't know where it is, and we'll be safe there."

Doc nodded.

## Chapter XI
## THE DEVIL'S WORK

Long Tom Roberts was a man who was noted for two things, the first being his ability with electricity, for it was conceded that he was one of the great contemporary men of electrical science; and, secondly, he was known for his ability to look as if he was so unhealthy that he was going to collapse with his next step. Undertakers invariably looked at him with hope. Monk Mayfair claimed Long Tom's complexion was one a mushroom would consider anæmic.

Long Tom had gotten the complexion by spending some time in his laboratory, judging by the looks of the place. It was in a basement, in a neighborhood which was so tough that the cops walked in pairs in the middle of the street. There was no vestige of natural light in the place, and apparently no fresh air ever entered either.

But the array of electrical machinery was impressive, actually frightening.

"Great grief!" said Rotary Harrison in awe.

Long Tom brushed pliers, wire and gadgets off chairs and seated them.

"Doc," he said, "you want to know the whole situation?"

"All of it," the bronze man said.

"All right," Long Tom told him. "First, I'll begin with this stuff against you that appeared in the newspapers. I'm talking about stories like that one which appeared in the *Morning Blade*. That was a typical example. Just a lot of innuendo. That story in the *Morning Blade* was typical, although some of the other newspapers were not that blunt."

Long Tom picked up a piece of copper wire and began to twist it absent-mindedly.

"That newspaper campaign," he said, "was the work of an organization."

Doc asked, "You are sure of that?"

Long Tom shoved out his jaw and nodded. "That's the first real piece of information Renny and I dug up. It was a campaign, all right."

"How was it managed?" Doc inquired.

"In the crudest and most effective way. Money. Bribes. This thing wasn't hatched in an evening over a glass of beer. Whoever cooked it up spent plenty of time and has plenty of money to back it and get it going. But the money that is spent will probably be only a sneeze in the bucket to the final take."

Doc said, "You were explaining how this newspaper campaign against me was put in operation."

"By bribing one or two guys on each paper," Long Tom said. "They just bought off a reporter here and there. Not on every paper, mind. Just where they could find a soft man. We got this information from reporters they had planned to bribe and couldn't."

"Did one man do the bribing?"

"One man; that's right."

"Who," Doc asked, "was he?"

"Butch," Long Tom said. "The fellow they call Butch."

Rotary Harrison, frowning heavily, said, "I don't see how newspaper stories could start the police looking for you. Or is there something behind the stories?"

"Yes, what is the rest of it?" Doc asked.

"We," Long Tom said, "have investigated the Montague Ogden business enterprises, and found the whole institution about to collapse. Accountants haven't finished going over the books yet —there hasn't been time. But it seems that Montague Ogden, who thought he was a rich man, is without a cent, or maybe even in debt. Suspicions are that the firm has been looted. It has had the money sucked out of it like a weasel sucks the blood out of a chicken."

"The weasel," bellowed Rotary, "was Sam Joseph, I bet."

"Right," said Long Tom. "Sam Joseph, a man who—and mark this, because it is the important part—a man who does not have any memory of his early life. A man who cannot recall where he spent his youth, or anything about his early environment or existence."

Doc Savage was suddenly showing the most intense interest.

"Go on," he said.

"Sam Joseph is No. 1," Long Tom said.

"Yes?"

"There are at least ten others." Long Tom looked at Doc gravely. "And every one of them is a man who does not remember what happened during the early part of his life."

Rotary Harrison frowned. "This is a crazy thing. First, a brass devil that talks. Then men who have lost their memories."

"Not lost their memories," Long Tom corrected. "Men who have simply had all memory of their early lives erased from their brains."

There was now the strangest expression on Doc Savage's metallic features.

"Name some of those men," he directed.

Long Tom said, "Charles Moore, T. B. Moresco, Dan Taylor, Reynold Rice Doyle—"

"That is enough," Doc Savage said.

The bronze man almost never showed emotion. But now there was stark amazement on his face, shock and stunned amazement.

"What's the matter with you?" Rotary asked.

Doc was silent.

He could not very well answer.

The men Long Tom had named were men who had once been criminals, men whom Doc Savage had captured in the course of his strange career of righting wrongs and punishing evildoers!

"Name the rest of them," Doc said suddenly.

Long Tom named them.

Doc nodded grimly. They were successful graduates of his College—all of them.

"What have they done?" Doc asked.

"Every one of those men," Long Tom said pointedly, "has become a crook, robbed his concern of enormous sums of money."

Doc Savage stood erect slowly and walked into another room. He sank in a chair and sat there. Long Tom Roberts glanced at the Harrisons and indicated they should remain where they were. Then Long Tom followed Doc. He closed the door behind him and stood studying the big bronze man. He had never seen Doc look as deeply affected.

"It's an awful thing to happen, Doc," Long Tom said finally.

"Very bad," Doc agreed.

"I don't understand it at all. None of the graduates from our College have ever turned back to crooked ways before. How come a whole bunch of them do it now, all at once?"

"Dirty work," Doc said.

Long Tom rubbed his jaw thoughtfully. "It must be. You figure it is all tied in with the talking devil and Sam Joseph."

"Apparently."

"Sam Joseph was never in the College."

"No. But all the others were."

Doc Savage came up out of the chair. He seemed to have reached some kind of a conclusion, a decision.

He said, "The particularly terrible aspect of this thing is that the whereabouts of our College, and proof that it actually exists, may get into the hands of the police and the public when they are unfriendly. We have always known that our method of treating criminals is too drastic for the public to accept, and probably will be too drastic for another fifty or a hundred years." He paused and shook his head grimly.

"I had hoped," Doc continued, "to keep the College in operation, and perhaps in the future evolve some way of quietly bringing the method of treating criminals to the attention of the public. Present it in a favorable light, so that it would be seen as the only sure cure for criminal minds. Then, with that accomplished, if we could present a sound groundwork of many cases of criminals cured and made into upright citizens by our treatment, we could get our method accepted. It would mean the elimination of the most troublesome type of criminal of all, the confirmed criminal.

"But," Doc concluded, "if our plans are wrecked now it can well take another century or more for such a thing to be developed and accepted by the public. That is the really grim thing about this. You and I believe in this thing, and we know how it works, and what a benefit it will be to mankind. We know how tragic losing it would be."

"Doc, there is one thing the police haven't been tipped. They haven't been told where our College is located."

"We have got to stop this thing before they are informed."

"If we knew where to start," Long Tom complained.

Renny Renwick brought Doc Savage the newspaper. It was a copy of the *Morning Blade*, the paper which had attacked Doc Savage with the greatest violence.

"This just went on sale on the streets," Renny said. "Take a look at it."

Red ink for headlines went out of fashion years ago, even for the *Blade*. But this one was in red ink.

## DOC SAVAGE AID CONFESSES

The following is a true, signed statement made to representatives of *The Blade* this morning by Lieutenant Colonel Andrew Blodgett Monk Mayfair, for a long time aid and close confident of the notorious and monstrous Doc Savage.

Editor, *The Blade*,
And Whom It May Concern:

This is to inform you that I have just discovered the real nature of the incredible thing which Doc Savage has been doing to the brains of men. Accordingly, I have not only severed all relations with Doc Savage, but I shall do what I can to right this horrendous wrong.

I shall have in the hands of the *Morning Blade*, and all other newspapers and press associations, in time for publication tomorrow morning, a full and true signed statement concerning Doc Savage's so-called College and the hideous brain operations conducted there. My statement will include the location of the College in order that the poor wretches still there may be rescued. It will also include a full list of past graduates of the place, as nearly as my memory can supply the names of these poor victims.

(Signed) Monk Mayfair

Renny rumbled, "Holy cow! That's Monk's signature, too. And the document isn't a fake."

That was also Doc's opinion. The letter from Monk, or the statement, whichever it would be called, was not printed, but was a reproduction of a photograph of the letter itself. It was a good cut, quite large, full of detail, and there was no doubt that Monk had signed it. Furthermore, Monk's fingerprints were affixed.

Renny waved the paper angrily.

"How'd this happen?" he bellowed. "It's incredible! What the blazes has gotten into Monk?"

"They've bought him off," said Rotary Harrison.

Renny looked as if he was going to slam Harrison with one of his big fists.

"Don't be a fool," Renny growled. "They couldn't torture a thing like that out of Monk. How'd they get it?"

Then Renny stared at Doc Savage and his jaw fell, for the

bronze man's manner had changed. Doc looked alert, even relieved. The bronze man was on his feet.

Doc indicated the newspaper.

"They stubbed their toes," he said. "They went just one jump too far and gave it all away. Now we can go into action."

"Action," Renny said, "is what we can use some of."

"Get Ham Brooks," Doc Savage said. "Get him here at once."

## Chapter XII
## MAN-THEFT

Ham Brooks did not arrive at Long Tom Roberts' experimental laboratory, which was serving as Doc's headquarters, until early that night. He came in looking haggard, pouches under his eyes, lips cracked from wind.

"I got your message to come," he told Doc. "But I had a heck of a time dodging police. Did you know there's a police alarm all over the United States for you?"

Doc admitted he knew that, because he had been listening to shortwave radio police broadcasts. He led Ham into a room where they could be alone and closed the door.

"That thing Monk had in the newspapers—that incredible thing!" Ham exclaimed. "How'd they make Monk sign a thing like that? He must have been horribly tortured."

Doc said quietly, "Do not worry about Monk. He probably is still alive, and they probably have not tortured him."

"But—"

Doc indicated a chair. "Sit down," he said. "I have a job for you. It may be dangerous, but it is important. It requires a man of your build, a man who can act. That is why I called you in."

"I'll do it," Ham said. "Calling me in was all right, too. I hadn't found a single trace of poor Monk."

"Lean back in this chair," Doc said.

Twenty minutes later the bronze man opened the door and called in Rotary and Sis Harrison, and Long Tom. They came to the door and gasped in astonishment.

"Sam Joseph!" exclaimed Sis. "Where'd you get him? How—"

"Does he look like Sam Joseph to you?" Doc asked.

"Why, of course he does," Sis said. And Rotary nodded agreement.

Long Tom Roberts, however, grinned and said, "So that's why you wanted Ham. He *does* look a lot like Sam Joseph, at that."

The resemblance which Ham now bore to Sam Joseph, the victim of the wrongly diagnosed brain operation, was in fact startling. There had been a physical resemblance to begin with, and the disguise work Doc had done had enhanced the likeness.

Doc said, "All right, I just wanted to see how effective the disguise was. Will you leave us alone now."

"What's going on?" Rotary blurted.

Sis took his arm, said, "Come on, dad. It looks to me like we're going to get some action."

They went out, leaving Doc and Ham alone. Doc said, "Ham, his voice will be the tricky part. We are going to work on that now. It may take several hours. I will talk to you, using the nearest thing to Sam Joseph's voice and tone I can manage, and you will repeat the words after me."

The truck was large, painted a silver gray, and had a body like a metal box. It was labeled *Department of Sanitation,* and it had the usual mechanism at the rear into which the contents of an ash can could be dumped and loaded automatically into the dust and odor-proof body. There was nothing about it to indicate it was not a city sanitation-department truck of the type which called at downtown office buildings each morning before dawn for ashes and waste.

It did arrive a little early.

It stopped at the service entrance of the towering modern Ogden building, near the stack of ash cans which the janitors had already placed on the sidewalk, as was customary.

Two men came out of the Ogden building. They wore janitor's coveralls marked *Ogden Bldg.,* but they did not look like janitors, and the bulges in their pockets near which they kept their hands were obviously guns.

They stood and watched, a pair of sinister figures, very alert, in the rather thick gloom.

Two men piled out of the truck and began loading ashes. They worked methodically, as if they had done that work for years. Only twice did they seem to have a little trouble, grunting and banging large ash cans against the rear of the truck before they lowered them to the walk, replaced the lids and took the cans back to stand them along the wall just inside the service entrance of the building.

They got in the truck, drove to the next building and collected more ashes.

One of the two men wearing janitor coveralls laughed. "Some guys make it the hard way, don't they."

"We'd look more like janitors," said his companion, "if we got busy and rolled these empty ash cans back into the boiler room."

"You gone crazy?" the other demanded. "Hell with it."

They closed the service door, locked it, and walked away, discussing a bottle and a card game they had been forced to desert.

It was quiet in the passageway for two or three minutes after they had gone.

Then lids came off two of the ash cans. Doc got out of one. Ham Brooks, wearing his Sam Joseph disguise, with coveralls and a Cellophanelike hood to protect his clothing and the bandages from ash dust, appeared from the other can.

"Lucky we used a system to get in here," Ham said. "They've got the place under guard, all right."

Doc said, "Look for the stairway."

The only other guard they encountered was outside the door of Montague Ogden's penthouse. He was equipped with brush and pail, and apparently it was his job to look innocent by scrubbing at the parquet floor when the occasion required.

Doc used an anæsthetic bomb on him. The bomb was about the size of a bantam egg, consisted of a thin, glasslike plastic shell containing liquid. The shell burst when the bomb hit near the man, making hardly any noise, and the liquid splattered, evaporated.

The guard seemed to go to sleep. Actually, that was about what it amounted to. The anæsthetic gas, one of the most efficient gadgets ever developed by Doc Savage, took effect without causing sensation, and the man would awaken as one awakens from sleep, after half an hour or so.

Doc and Ham avoided effects of the gas by holding their breath. After about a minute the stuff lost its effectiveness, mingling with the air.

Doc carefully gathered up the glasslike plastic fragments and pocketed them, so no trace would remain.

There were no servants in the elaborate penthouse layout, which Ham considered a little strange.

"And I wonder where Montague Ogden himself is?" he added, whispering.

In the bedroom where Sam Joseph lay, Dr. Nedden was sitting. Nedden occupied a deep chair and he was reading. He had the lights on very bright, as if to keep himself awake.

Doc Savage tossed another of the anæsthetic grenades into the room, after easing the door open a fraction of an inch at a time. He and Ham held their breath, until Dr. Nedden's head sagged forward, and the book slipped out of his hands to the floor.

Doc Savage picked up the book Dr. Nedden had been reading. It was a technical tome, one on *medinals,* the monosodium salts of diethyl-barbituric acid.

The book title meant nothing to Ham, but he noted that Doc Savage seemed to think it significant, for the bronze man made, for a brief moment, a tiny trilling sound, a note that was almost inaudible. And yet it sounded satisfied.

Ham saw also that Doc picked up a small bottle on a table at Dr. Nedden's elbow. Evidently the man had been using the contents himself.

"Something to keep him awake," Ham remarked.

Sam Joseph was asleep. They awakened him. He knew them and smiled.

"We are going to take you out of here for a while," Doc Savage told him, "and leave Ham Brooks in your place."

"I do not see any sense in that," Sam Joseph said.

"There will be sense to it, we hope," Doc said.

The man seemed agreeable.

Ham took Sam Joseph's place in the bed.

"Be very careful," Doc warned him.

Ham nodded. "How long will I have to do this, do you suppose?"

"Let us hope, no longer than a few hours," Doc told him. "We will put the genuine patient back as soon as possible."

Ham said, "O. K., I'm game."

"There are some weapons you can use concealed in your head bandage," Doc said, "if it comes to that."

The bronze man got Sam Joseph out of the building without difficulty, without being discovered. He carried the patient to a car which Renny Renwick had waiting around the corner.

"Feel all right?" Doc inquired.

"Oh, yes, excellent," Sam Joseph said. "You know, it is strange. I feel very well at times, and then at other times I go off into those strange unconscious spells."

Doc Savage made no comment.

But Renny glanced at the patient, asked, "Heard that devil do any more talking?"

"No," Sam Joseph replied. "I guess you gentlemen think I am crazy, don't you?"

"Seen anything more of the devil?"

"No. You *do* think I'm crazy, don't you?"

Doc Savage said quietly, "You are as sane as any of the rest of us, and you can rest assured of that."

The bandages kept much expression from showing on Sam Joseph's face, but into his voice came almost pitiful relief when he spoke.

"I am so glad to hear you say that," he said eagerly. "So much has happened to make me doubt my—well—rationality."

"For example?"

"Well—those periods of coma, of unconsciousness, when my senses leave me—yet it is not sleep." Sam Joseph opened and closed his hands slowly, painfully. "That has been happening for many weeks, and always there has been growing a kind of premonition of something terribly wrong."

Doc put a comforting hand on his arm. "You have a very strong subconscious, Mr. Joseph."

"You mean something *is* wrong?"

"Very."

Long Tom Roberts helped them carry Sam Joseph into the electrical research laboratory in the dank basement when they arrived. Long Tom was somewhat sullen and scowled frequently at Rotary Harrison.

"Something wrong?" Doc asked.

"I don't see why the hell I can't get out and walk around the town," Rotary snapped. "It's not *me* the police are looking for."

Long Tom said, "I told him your orders were for everybody to stay out of sight, Doc. I practically had to hit him over the head with a chair to keep him here."

Rotary growled, "You try kissing me with a chair and it'll be the last guy you try it on."

"Now, dad!" Sis said. "He's right. The police probably know we are with Mr. Savage. We cannot do anyone any good in jail."

Long Tom, Renny, Sis and Rotary watched with interest, but with no immediate understanding, as Doc Savage went to work on Sam Joseph.

It first appeared that the bronze man was going to do nothing but give Sam Joseph another physical examination, including various blood tests. Then it was clear that the examination was of specialized nature.

Doc analyzed blood samples, tissue, saliva. It seemed to the others that he was making every possible analysis.

He spent some four hours at it.

Then he asked Sam Joseph questions.

"These periods of coma, or unconsciousness, to which you refer," Doc said. "Did they come on regularly?"

"No, not at all," Sam Joseph assured him. "There was an irregular interval of time between each one."

"I want you to think carefully," Doc said, "and tell me whether some of them came on after meals."

"Yes. Yes, after I had taken a cocktail sometimes. I thought it was the cocktails causing it, and I even stopped drinking."

"Who was with you when you had the cocktails?"

"Why . . . why, Dr. Nedden, now that I think of it."

Doc Savage was pleased.

"Have you ever heard of the monosodium salts of diethylbarbituric acid?" the bronze man asked.

Sam Joseph frowned. "No—except that I believe I have seen Dr. Nedden reading a scientific text concerning something like that."

Doc nodded.

"Your spells of coma," he said, "have been brought on by medinals and other drugs. My analysis is not complete, but there is unmistakable evidence of the presence of medinals and their continued administration."

"What is a medinal?"

"A hypnotic," Doc explained.

Renny gave a violent jump. "Holy cow! Hypnotics! You mean there's a drug that hypnotizes a person—"

"No, no," Doc corrected him. "The medical application of the term hypnotic simply means an agent producing sleep. But in the present case other drugs have been added to the barbituric group to produce physically a state of coma with apparently only the loss of the facility of memory and initiative."

Sam Joseph apparently understood it better than any of them.

"They drugged me!" he ejaculated. "And then they made me do whatever they wanted me to do, and I didn't remember."

Rotary Harrison seemed astounded. "That's why you don't remember the agreement you signed to renew my loan!"

"That must be it."

Doc Savage confronted Renny Renwick and Long Tom Roberts. He said, "There is one thing more we should do to make sure about this thing. That is to get hold of at least one of the graduates of our College who, according to the police, have turned crooked."

"Right now?" Renny asked.

"Right now," Doc said.

Renny and Long Tom left on the job.

Doc Savage went back to work testing and analyzing blood specimens from Sam Joseph. It was a job not made any easier by the fact that Long Tom's electrical laboratory was not equipped with medical type slides for the microscopes, nor proper chemicals. There was, however, a wonderful atomic microscope which made up for much that was lacking.

Sis Harrison waited patiently, employing her time in administering little comforts to Sam Joseph. Sis, it was evident, was admiring Doc Savage more and more.

"What will happen to Mr. Ham Brooks if they find he is not Sam Joseph?" she asked.

Doc said, "We had better cross our fingers and hope on that."

An hour later Renny and Long Tom came back. They had a man named Charles Moore, once a patient in the College.

"We got him," Long Tom explained dryly, "by highjacking him away from two police detectives who were taking him to talk to the district attorney."

Charles Moore was a smooth, brown, capable man, a little taller than the average, in good physical shape. Clean living had made his face pleasant, and there remained very little of the thin hardness that had once been there when he was a notorious criminal. He had once, as a matter of fact, very nearly succeeded in murdering Doc Savage. But that was before he had been captured, subjected to a brain operation that wiped out all knowledge of past, and trained as an accountant. He had been a successful, honest man in the field of accountancy, having risen to be vice president of his firm.

"They had arrested me," Charles Moore said. "I do not understand it at all. They say I have robbed my company of large sums of money. That is ridiculous."

He looked extremely worried.

Doc Savage asked, "How do they claim the robberies were executed?"

"As vice president of my concern, which deals in heavy industrial and oil-field machinery, I handled a lot of executive matters," Charles Moore explained. "There are many occasions where I could sign the wrong kind of a bill of sale, or lease, or other document, and steal a large sum. In the company files, they claim they have found a lot of such papers. One example is a bunch of receipts for money paid out, and no merchandise was received. The money went into my pocket, they claim. It does look logical. But I'm no crook. I hate crooks."

Doc Savage's voice was quiet, intended to restore the man's confidence in himself.

"How about those spells of coma, somewhat like sleep, from which you have suffered?" Doc asked.

Charles Moore stared at him in astonishment.

"How did you know about those?"

"You have had them?"

"Oh, yes."

"Do you know a man named Dr. Nedden?"

"Why, yes, I do."

"And do you have a drink with Dr. Nedden now and then?"

"Yes."

Renny Renwick leaped up and slammed a fist into a palm, bellowing, "This tears it! This tears it right up the middle! I see the guts of the thing now!"

"Sit down or they'll hear you in China," Long Tom snapped. "We all see it now."

Renny subsided. Charles Moore didn't know that he had once been a criminal; none of the graduates knew that about themselves. Charles Moore did not even know the purpose of the strange institution in upstate New York where he had received his training, nor did he know its exact location.

Charles Moore must not, Renny knew, be told of his past, or the unorthodox method that had been used to change him from a criminal to an honest man. It would do Charles Moore no good, and it might saddle his mind with a worry that would hamper him through the rest of his life.

Doc Savage told Charles Moore, "The thing for you to do is go back and give yourself up to the police. We are going to do our best to straighten out this mess."

"Shall I tell them about this meeting with you?"

Doc nodded. "It will do no harm. Yes, tell them. But do not tell them where the interview took place."

Charles Moore departed, not a little relieved.

"A devilish scheme," Renny said when they were alone. "That fiend, Dr. Nedden, somehow learned the identity of a group of the men we have made honest by brain operations. He worked on those men with drugs, got them to perpetrate crimes which they did not know they were doing. And now he is saddling the whole thing on us."

Long Tom looked at Doc, asked, "Doc, do you suppose Nedden is the brains behind it."

The bronze man did not seem to hear the question, which was a rather aggravating eccentricity of his when he did not wish to answer an inquiry. Renny and Long Tom had seen him do it many times before. They did not put the question again, knowing it would get no response.

Long Tom said finally, "We know how that letter from Monk came to happen, anyway. They drugged him. He signed it when he was drugged."

Renny nodded, agreed, "That is why they kept him alive."

"What about Ham? When do we put Sam Joseph back in his place?"

Doc Savage looked as if he was worried about Ham.

## Chapter XIII
## KILL ORDER

Ham Brooks was a little worried about himself. He had played the part of Sam Joseph, recuperating operation victim, with complete success for some hours now. The success was so complete that it was contributing to Ham's worry. Nothing had happened so that he could prove to himself that he could get away with it.

He did not like the looks of the medicine Dr. Nedden was mixing either. Medicine was something Ham didn't want.

Dr. Nedden approached. "Here's your little tonic for the day," he said.

"I don't feel as if I need anything," Ham said hurriedly.

"Oh, but you must build up your strength. This will just make you rest comfortably and sleep a little."

Ham felt more kindly toward the stuff. Sleep, eh? Well, if he was asleep it would be that much easier to get away with this thing.

He drank the stuff. It tasted as if they had drowned a cat in it about a month ago and forgot to remove the remains.

He was a little astonished at the speed with which he became sleepy. It was sure potent stuff. Not unpleasant, though. He remembered thinking that, and then he was able to think of no more.

Dr. Nedden bent over Ham and said, "Sam! Sam! Can you hear me?"

There was no response from the figure on the bed.

Dr. Nedden rolled back Ham's eyelids and examined the reaction of the eyes to the beam of a small flashlight which he splashed into them. He seemed satisfied.

"Fully under," he remarked.

Dr. Nedden then went into the kitchen of the elaborate penthouse layout, and from there into an excellent—and bizarre, considering that it was on top of a skyscraper—imitation of a French wine cellar. This was well stocked with imported wines and champagnes.

Selecting a wicker-covered jug labeled as a wine, Dr. Nedden separated this. The gut had been cut in the middle, the two halves fitting together inside the wicker covering.

He took a brass devil image out of this.

Having carried the thing back to the room where Ham lay, Dr. Nedden placed the image on the table, and turned on a thermal switch by holding a lighted match against the devil's left ear. The switch evidently operated as a thermostat functions.

There was a click and a radio apparatus began humming as it warmed up inside the thing.

Dr. Nedden took hold of the thing, pressed on a spot where there was a concealed button, said, "All right. You can come up now. And bring the papers."

"Be right up," the devil said, but with the voice of Butch, the meek-looking man.

Butch came in looking very subdued and sheeplike in blue suit, black shoes and a stiff collar. He had a brief case under an arm, and wore a pair of rimless spectacles. He was altogether benign.

"Good afternoon," he said gently. "You need new batteries in that devil, doctor. Your signal comes in very weak. You may want to contact someone at the other end of the city sometime, and they will not be able to hear you."

"Thanks," said Dr. Nedden shortly.

"Furthermore, I would suggest you dispose of the devil," added Butch. "The thing nearly got us into trouble once, when you insisted on having it talk to poor Sam Joseph to further convince him he was mentally unbalanced and needed a brain operation. Suppose Doc Savage had gotten the real statue containing the transceiver that day instead of the fake one which he did finally get? Savage's suspicions would have been aroused."

"Oh, stop harping on it," Dr. Nedden snapped. "Savage didn't get the real one, and he operated on Sam Joseph, and all those witnessing doctors saw that he had made a mistake, and that gave us the foothold we needed to start accusing him."

Butch shrugged and placed his brief case on the table. He removed several documents, together with a fountain pen. "Here they are," he said.

"That the last of them?" Dr. Nedden demanded.

"Sure. This finishes up cleaning out Montague Ogden. These papers prove that Sam Joseph bought, or rather pretended to buy, a large quantity of stock, which he proceeded to carry on the books of the concern. The stock, being actually nonexistent, will prove Sam Joseph shystered his boss out of a fortune. The checks, of course, have already been signed by Sam Joseph two weeks ago, when he was under the effects of the drug, and cashed. The boss has the money. All we need now is these few papers to help clinch the blame on Sam."

Dr. Nedden grinned, waved an arm. "There he is. Go to it."

Butch seated himself beside the bed. It was obvious that he had gone through the routine many times before, because he leaned forward, took Ham's hand and said, "Sam, Sam, hear me? Sam, do as you are told. Here is a fountain pen. Take it and hold it. Take the pen, Sam."

Ham's hand then moved vaguely, finally grasped the pen in writing position.

Butch said, "Write! Write, Sam. Sign your name. Sign it. Sam Joseph. S-a-m J-o-s-e-p-h."

Ham wrote the signature.

Butch repeated this painstakingly with the other documents, got all of them signed.

"Fine," he said. "Now you won't need to dope him up any more. We're all shaped up."

Dr. Nedden looked much relieved. "You think everything is fine then?"

Butch nodded. "Sure. All hunky. Savage hasn't made any progress whatever. We just hit him with everything and hit him so fast that he hasn't been able to get his head above water. He was tricked into that operation. That stunned him. We had him framed before he knew it."

Dr. Nedden said, "That operation on Sam Joseph here was risky. I still don't think it was worth the risk."

"You don't? Why, dammit, that was the crowning touch. That

was what will convict Doc Savage. That's what they'll electrocute him for."

"I don't understand."

Butch whipped out a paper which bore typed lines. "Look, here is what the morning newspapers will carry."

The typing said:

## WHY DID SAVAGE OPERATE ON SAM JOSEPH?

Sam Joseph is a man who was formerly an amnesia victim. He is a man who has no idea who he was in his youth. All the embezzlers in this case are the same. None of them remember back past a certain day. Did Doc Savage operate on the brains of all these men? Did he make them crooks? Did he take their loot from them? Did they work for him? Did Savage operate on Sam Joseph in an attempt to hide the crime he had committed in operating on the man's brain?

Dr. Nedden laughed and said, "I see it now. The operation is the one thing that implicates Doc Savage directly in the affair."

"Sure."

Butch, very satisfied with himself and the world, started to fold the documents which Ham had just signed, and place them with other papers in the brief case.

He froze. He eyed the papers. His eyes came out of their sockets a little.

"Look!" he croaked. "The signature ain't his!"

"What?"

"This signature ain't Sam Joseph's signature!" Butch yelled.

Dr. Nedden leaped to the bed and rubbed Ham's face vigorously, dislodging some of the wax make-up which Doc had applied as disguise.

"It's not Sam!" he gasped.

"It's Ham Brooks!" Butch said.

Dr. Nedden nearly went to pieces then. He wrung his hands, seemed wildly baffled, then suddenly snatched up his hat and headed for the door in frenzied flight.

Butch said, "None of that!" and produced a gun. Dr. Nedden came back. Butch ordered, "Help me take this guy along."

"But what—"

"Don't ask baboon questions!" Butch snarled. "Grab him!

We've got to get out of here with him. We may need a hostage, somebody we can knock off if they don't stay off our trail."

They got out of the building a great deal faster than it seemed possible they could have managed it. Butch warned the rest of the gang, the minor members, who served as guards around the place. All of them piled into cars from a nearby parking lot.

They went to the ordinary-looking brick apartment house west of Central Park. Butch ordered all of the men to wait outside, preferably in nearby bars, and to respond to a signal comprised of two short, one long and two short blasts of an automobile horn.

Butch and Dr. Nedden carried Ham, who was still unconscious, into the elevator. At the sixteenth floor they got out and packed Ham through one of the numerous doors marked:

DR. MORGAN
PRIVATE HOSPITAL

Two men only were there, and they were minor members of the gang, wearing white male-nurse suits—and at the moment in a fright, and carrying towels wrapped around pistols.

"Call a meeting!" Butch snarled at them. "Get everybody here!"

This seemed to be the general headquarters of the gang, the spot where conferences were held. And in ordering the summoning of *everybody*, Butch apparently meant only those who held positions of responsibility in the organization. Men who considered it important that the other members did not become too familiar with their faces.

They began arriving. They entered the outer reception rooms and changed to the surgical robes and masks which were their conference disguises.

Butch was impatient with this mumbo-jumbo.

"Rome is burning!" he snarled. "And you guys fiddle with your faces!"

The group was eventually gathered. Butch counted. Seven of them.

"And the boss makes eight," Butch said. "But the boss won't be here."

Butch produced the little statue of a devil, a devil with Chinese characteristics, and placed it on a white operating table. He switched the thing on, let the tubes warm, said into the microphone:

"Boss, come in. This is important."

He got no answer.

"That's what I was afraid of," he said. "And that doesn't make it look any better."

Butch apparently held no more position of authority than any of the others because a man growled, "Where do you get off, calling a meeting and giving orders?"

"Oh, shut up," Butch said. "Something has gone wrong."

He told them about the finding of Ham Brooks in place of Sam Joseph, and pointed out Ham's unconscious body as proof of the story.

He informed them he did not know just what the unexpected discovery might mean. But it was sure to be nothing healthy for them. It meant at the least that Doc Savage was a lot closer to arriving at the truth than any of them expected.

The boss, he reminded them, had made a provision for a case like this.

"If anything serious went wrong," he told them, "we were to make a break for the boss' southwestern ranch and stay there until the hounds quit howling. Until things blew over."

Butch tried to get an answer out of the radio transceiver concealed in the devil statue and failed.

"Get going," he directed. "You," he told Dr. Nedden, "will light out first with Ham Brooks here. We're taking him along as a hostage if we need him. Also, when he comes out from under the effect of that hypnotic, we're damned sure going to find out how much Doc Savage knows."

Dr. Nedden nodded. He and another man got a stretcher on which they placed Ham. They carried him to the elevator and rode down. They were alone, the other men being busy getting rid of their masks and surgical robes.

At the lobby floor they bent to pick up the stretcher.

"Oh!" gasped Dr. Nedden. His eyes got wide.

Montague Ogden was standing there. Ogden's feet were well apart, and his eyes narrow. He wore a topcoat, and from the way his hands rested in the pockets it was obvious they held guns.

"Oh!" repeated Dr. Nedden. "Uh—hello, boss!"

Montague Ogden said, "So you know who you take orders from?"

"I—yes, yes, of course." Dr. Nedden was uncomfortable. "After all it isn't much of a secret. And your . . . your ranch, of course. We all know about that. Know we are to go there and keep out of sight if the breaks get too tough."

"I see," Montague Ogden said. He did not seem angry. "And where are you going now?"

"To the ranch."

"Who gave those orders?"

"Butch," said Nedden maliciously. "Butch gave them. He's becoming very officious."

"I see. Officious, eh." Montague Ogden looked fierce. "Well, we'll see about that. Is everyone going to the ranch?"

"Yes. Everyone. Monk Mayfair is already being held there, of course. And we're taking this other fellow, Ham Brooks, as a hostage if we need one."

"Then what?"

"Then, if we don't need Monk or Ham, they can be killed."

Montague Ogden seemed to give the situation thought.

"You two will go with me and bring Ham," he said. "We will take my private plane. You can fly, can you not, Dr. Nedden?"

"Yes, I can fly."

"And you know where the ranch is?"

"Yes, yes, of course."

"Then get going," Montague Ogden snapped. "We will go together—you two, Ham Brooks and myself."

They got going. For a man who was in command of a situation, Montague Ogden seemed very strained, and he took only one or the other of his hands from his pockets at a time, never removing both hands.

## Chapter XIV
## KING AND JOKER

Doc Savage drove his ambulance with care and concentration. On the seat beside him, Sis Harrison sat and watched with admiration.

"You mean to tell me," she said, "that you built a radio set small enough to inclose in the bandages on Ham's head?"

From the back of the ambulance, Long Tom said, "Drive north awhile, Doc. And better put on more speed. The signal isn't too good."

Doc said, "Not a radio set. Just a transmitter. A little oscillator powered with concentrated flashlight batteries which puts out a simple wave that can be traced with a direction finder."

"It's marvelous!" Sis exclaimed.

The ambulance was one belonging to the hospital which Doc

Savage controlled, the one which he had employed in performing the unfortunate brain operation on Sam Joseph.

Sam Joseph was now back in that hospital to recuperate under an assumed name.

"We have used the device before," Doc said. "There is nothing stupendous about it. It will only work for a few hours. Not over a day. It is only good for horizon distance because the wave length is so short. It has several drawbacks."

"I think it's marvelous," Sis said.

Long Tom said, "Go east again, Doc. We're getting a little closer to it."

Rotary Harrison bellowed, "I hope we catch up with him soon! I'm getting tired of this chasing around. I want to get my hands on somebody. I want my hands on a throat."

"Quit bawling like a bull," Long Tom said. "You are worse than Monk."

Doc asked, "Long Tom, are you still in contact with Renny?"

"Yes. I can hear his carrier wave."

"Tell him to keep somewhere above us. But plenty high. High enough that he'll not be noticed."

"O. K. Renny is bothered. He says what if the Civil Air Patrol or an army plane orders him down?"

"That is a chance we have to take," Doc said. "A plane is the only way of following if they take Ham away in a plane."

Sis saw that the bronze man was under an intense strain. She understood his feelings. It was at his suggestion that Ham Brooks had undertaken the job of pretending to be Sam Joseph. Now Ham was in trouble, or everything pointed to it.

As soon as Ham had been moved—as indicated by the shift of the little radio transmitter—they had hurried to follow. They had gotten uptown a little too late to intercept Ham at the time he was stationary, somewhere near Central Park, and now they were trying to catch him.

Feeling a change of subject would do Doc good, Sis said, "You have five assistants, have you not? There are only four—Monk, Ham, Renny and Long Tom—working with you this time. But don't you have five?"

"Yes, five," Doc Savage said. "The other is Johnny—William Harper Littlejohn, the archæologist and geologist. He is in Alaska, where he is preparing some specimens."

Long Tom yelled in the back, "Doc! I think they've got Ham in a plane! I think they're just taking the air!"

The plane was a bright cabin job. They saw it flash overhead, climbing steeply, and caught a faint trace of its strong motor roar.

Doc Savage rapped, "Long Tom! Call Renny down with our plane. Quick!"

"I've already called him down," Long Tom said.

Doc Savage tramped on the brake, wheeled the car to the right, up a steeply rutted road into a field. The field was large and flat, a meadow. Nearby was a hangar, and a car parked in front of it. An elderly man in coveralls stood in front of the hangar, rolling a cigarette.

Doc braked the car to a halt before the man, demanded, "Who owns the field?"

"Reckon it's me," the man said easily. He looked honest.

"Whose plane just took off?"

"Private ship. Belongs to Montague Ogden, the financier. Keeps it here. Had three friends with him, one of them so sick he was on a stretcher. Head all bandaged."

"Know any of the friends?"

"One. Feller named Dr. Nedden. Family physician of Ogden's, I think."

Renny was down on the field now. He was flying a fast cabin plane that was far from being the freak of speed in which they had made their earlier flight into the Midwest. This ship could hold its own with Ogden's plane, however.

Renny taxied up in the ship. They loaded in. Renny fed the cylinders gas and they took off.

Long Tom had brought his direction finder and he was feverishly setting it up. This was the critical period and his manner showed it. The little transmitter concealed on Ham was weak, and if it got out of range now they were lost.

When he picked up the signal his yell of delight startled everyone.

"Got it!" he bellowed. "Head more south, Renny."

And fifteen minutes later Renny was saying, "I can see the ship now. What do we do? Overtake them?"

"Keep back far enough not to be seen," Doc Savage said. "We might as well find out where they are going."

Rotary Harrison looked disgusted at that. "Always followin'!" he snapped. "About time we was gettin' our hands on some necks, ain't it?"

Doc made no comment.

Long Tom remarked, "There is an old Chinese proverb that

says: 'Snake is small because he suck egg; fox is big because he wait and catch grown bird.' "

"What kind of an answer is that?" Rotary snarled.

It got dark and they followed the other plane several hours by radio alone, after which the other ship landed. They saw its landing lights streak out beams and these picked up a smooth field, and came to a stop on it.

"Over Georgia somewhere," Long Tom said. "Near the coast."

Doc Savage watched the plane lights below for a moment.

"Parachutes," he said. "One man with me. Either one of you."

Renny said, "Match you," to Long Tom. And then lost.

They went over the side together and cracked open their 'chutes at once. It was very dark, clouds above, and small chance of their being seen. And probably their plane motor had not been heard because they could see that the engine of the ship below was still idling over, and that would drown any sound from above.

Doc called softly, "Get out of the harness."

"Sure," Long Tom said.

They squirmed and strained and unfastened the parachute harness snaps. These were 'chutes from Doc's plane, so they were equipped with a gadget which Renny Renwick had worked out for use by American parachute troopers, a gadget for releasing themselves quickly from the encumbrance of a parachute harness.

So, when they hit the ground, they were instantly free and running.

They separated.

Luck was with them. The engine of Ogden's plane was still turning and its coughing had covered the noise of their hitting the earth.

Ogden and two men were standing in the glare of the plane landing light.

Ogden had a gun in each hand. The two men—one of them Dr. Nedden—slowly put up their hands.

Doc Savage did not carry a gun, never carried one if he could avoid it, believing to carry one made you rely too much on a firearm, and be lost without it. He waited. Long Tom had a gun, a small machine pistol with a tremendous rate of fire.

Long Tom walked into the glare of landing lights, presented the muzzle of his machine pistol, said, "This little gun puts out a million bullets a minute."

Montague Ogden turned slowly. He looked at Long Tom. He inspected Doc Savage.

"I've been a hell of a fool," Ogden said.

He tossed his guns on the ground.

"And I'm a very puzzled man," he added.

Doc said, "Puzzled?"

Ogden nodded. "For some reason or other, these three men seem to think I am their leader. I am nothing of the sort. It puzzles me."

No one said anything.

Finally, Ogden added, "I tricked them into bringing me down here from New York, thinking they would lead me to their headquarters."

He stared at them.

"I became scared," he finished. "I am very glad you came along."

While Renny landed the plane containing Rotary and Sis Harrison, Doc Savage tied Dr. Nedden and the other man. Then Doc examined Ham and found him unharmed but very groggy, able to mutter only that they had given him some kind of a damned shot of something. He sounded weakly indignant.

They listened to Ogden's story.

It was the story of a man who had been duped. A man who had inherited his wealth and had always had other men manage it for him. A man who knew little or nothing about business, but who liked to put on a big show, liked to impress people with his wealth. The flamboyant Ogden building was an example.

A man of close loyalties, of intense friendships. A man who would sacrifice for his friends, and liked to fight for them.

"I was intensely worried about Sam Joseph's mental troubles," said Montague Ogden. "It was Dr. Nedden, I realize now, who convinced me you would be the man to operate. And then you did operate, and there was no brain tumor. How did that happen, anyway?"

Doc Savage was uncomfortable in the darkness.

"I was outsmarted," Doc confessed, "at my own game. They had imitated the symptoms of cerebral fibroma so skillfully that I was completely taken in."

"That must have taken a clever doctor," Ogden said.

"It did. Nedden is clever. I think we will find he has other clever doctors working with him."

Montague Ogden sighed explosively.

"They are all clever," he said. "So much smarter than I am. But I became suspicious finally. Who wouldn't, after I found that Sam

Joseph apparently had been looting my company. I knew Sam would not do a thing like that. My true friends do not double-cross me. That is one wonderful fact I have learned about human nature.

"I became suspicious too late. My indignation, and it was righteous indignation I assure you, even if egged on by Dr. Nedden, about the operation mistake had already touched off the newspaper publicity. I made a terrible fool of myself there. But you must understand I did that because I thought Sam Joseph, my closest friend, had been wronged."

Doc Savage said, "You made that clear enough, and it was understandable under the circumstances."

Montague Ogden sounded grateful.

"I have been shadowing them," he explained. "Following them around. And that was how I happened to track them to an apartment house near Central Park. I was waiting downstairs, not knowing what to do, when Dr. Nedden and this man came out with the stretcher and what I thought was poor Sam Joseph on the stretcher. I confronted them. Imagine my astonishment when I found they thought I was their leader."

He sounded bewildered.

"They said they were going to *my* ranch," he said. "I haven't got a ranch. I own lots of things, but no place like that. But they landed here and I didn't know what to do. And then you landed and I'm glad."

He groaned.

"I imagine you thought I was the leader, too," he concluded. "You must have thought I was the king. And now you find I'm only a silly, gullible pawn, the joker. You are probably disgusted."

Doc Savage asked, "The ranch is near here?"

"Yes. I don't know exactly where, though."

"Is this the ranch flying field?"

"No," Montague Ogden said. "But there is one. I made Dr. Nedden land on this meadow, telling him I did not want the others to know we were here. I told him I wanted to sneak up on Butch, who has been becoming too officious."

"Nedden knows where the flying field and the ranch is?"

"Yes."

Without exchanging a word, Renny and Long Tom fell on Dr. Nedden, clubbed him to the ground and announced they were going to dispose of him then and there if he did not tell them where the ranch was located. There was nothing ridiculous about their performance, although they admitted later it should have been. They sounded so utterly convincing. They sold a bill of goods.

"Please!" Nedden gasped. "I'll tell you."

The ranch was about two miles and a half distant, along a country road which bordered one edge of this meadow.

"Far enough that they didn't hear us land, probably," Sis Harrison said with relief.

Rotary Harrison growled, "Let's get going! I want my hands on somebody's neck, and quick!"

"Just a moment," Doc Savage said.

The bronze man went to their plane, his own ship, the one which Renny had just landed. In the cabin there were equipment cases in special racks, and he selected one of these.

He carried the case to the others.

He exhibited the contents.

"A new type of grenade," he explained. "A new gas, one against which no mask is effective. Extremely potent. Acting almost instantaneously."

Renny looked at the grenades and seemed startled.

"Holy cow, Doc, but—"

"We are each going to take some," Doc explained, interrupting quickly. "Here, we will divide them."

"How d'you work the gadgets?" Rotary asked. "Pull this key out?"

"Twist the key," Doc Savage corrected. "You will find that it seems to wind like an alarm clock. Twist it up tight then get rid of it. Throw it as you would an ordinary grenade."

"What's the idea of the winding?"

"The peculiar internal construction which was necessary."

"Oh," Rotary said. "I see. Another one of your gadgets."

## Chapter XV
## SATAN'S RANCH

They left Dr. Nedden, Montague Ogden and the other crook behind. Doc Savage used a hypodermic needle on them and they were almost immediately asleep. They would remain that way for some time until noon the following day, at the least. Renny dragged them off in the tall weeds where they would not be likely to be found before then.

Montague Ogden did not object to being drugged and left

behind. "I expect you to suspect me," he said. "I see how you could not conceive of a man being as big a fool as I've been."

Walking away, Long Tom remarked, "You know, I halfway think he's innocent."

"Oh, hell!" snorted Rotary Harrison. "Next thing you'll be thinking toads have wings."

Ham Brooks went with them. He was rapidly regaining his equilibrium. He stripped off his bandages, which contained the little radiowave transmitter, and had salvaged the gadget. When Sis insisted she would like to have it as a souvenir of an incredibly fantastic adventure, Ham gave it to her, which somewhat irritated Long Tom. It was Long Tom's device.

Having covered about a mile, they heard a series of three planes approach from the north and land in the night far ahead of them. They saw, by looking up, the faint glow of landing lights reflected against the very low clouds.

"The gang arriving," Renny rumbled. "The way I understand it, the whole kit and kaboodle will be there. What a chance to make a roundup!"

They pushed forward more rapidly. Dust was thick on the country road, a soft pad for their footfalls.

Light appeared ahead. Electric glow around low buildings. The structures seemed to be made of logs and slabs, in keeping with the piny woods around them. And there was the excited barking of dogs which seemed to be confined to a fenced inclosure.

Doc Savage said, "We had better close in immediately while the dogs are still barking. Otherwise, the animals might give an alarm."

"Good idea," Rotary agreed. "What's the plan of campaign?"

"We will get a little closer," Doc said, "and look over the place."

Rotary stopped.

"Sis," he said, "you go back."

"But dad!" Sis objected. "I may be able to help."

"You're a girl, and—"

"But I'm not scared. At least I'm not going to go to pieces—"

Rotary was suddenly harsh. "You go back," he said. "I'm not going to have a daughter of mine mixed up in the kind of a thing this is going to be."

"I—"

"Better go back, Sis," Doc said. "Someone should be free and clear to go for help if we fail."

Sis finally consented. "All right, if you insist," she agreed.

They left her in the darkness and went on, moving with increasing care. Sis had been so disappointed at being left behind that they were silent.

They were quite close to the ranch buildings when Long Tom spoke in a whisper.

"Sis sure hated to miss out on this," he said.

Doc said, "It was necessary."

Rotary Harrison was suddenly confronting them.

"You bet it was necessary," he snarled.

He had a gun and a flashlight. He menaced them with the gun.

"Wouldn't do for her to know what a hell cat her old man is," Rotary said.

He splashed glare from the flashlight on them. Men came running from the ranch.

"Get Butch!" Rotary snarled at the man. "I don't want no more mistakes about who's boss of this thing!"

They took Doc Savage, Renny and Long Tom and Ham into a long low room with beamed ceilings and native fieldstone fire-places at each end. A room where saddles and bridles hung, ropes and spurs, steer horns and buffalo horns. All the stuff that goes into a phony ranch set-up.

"Get back, get back!" Rotary Harrison kept snarling at his men. "Don't get close to these hombres. No tellin' what they'll pull."

He pushed back his men bodily, and they made a large circle around the prisoners.

"Careful; they got more tricks than a centipede has legs," he warned. He bellowed out a laugh. "I oughta know. I been their shadow for two days."

Doc Savage said, "You went to a lot of trouble, Rotary."

Rotary Harrison laughed.

"Hell, yes, and why not?" he asked. "I've spent the best months of my life, to say nothing of what money I had left in the world, working this out. It was complete." He waved an arm, added, "It was complete, even to this little hide-out here, which I bought and recorded in Montague Ogden's name."

Doc said, "And while you were committing the robberies, you included yourself?"

"What could have been finer? Who would suspect a robbed man?"

"Particularly," Doc Savage said, "one who came to me for help."

"That's the idea."

"And one who has an innocent daughter," Doc suggested.

That hit Rotary Harrison where it hurt. The smirk slid off his face, the lips off his teeth.

"She don't know about it," he said. "That's why I didn't want her to come along."

It was still in the room. Light in the place came from electric bulbs in ox-yoke and old-fashioned lantern devices, and from a few false candles. The men stood tense. None of them looked at ease.

Running his gaze over them, Doc Savage picked out two men who were doctors. He knew they were doctors without recalling their names, but he'd seen their faces before. They were cerebrologists, or specialists on the human brain. They were not prominent men, yet skilled enough to help in perpetrating the gigantic hoax that had been pulled. They were crooks, certainly.

Doc looked at their leader, Rotary Harrison, said, "You could have saved a lot of your elaborate scheming."

Rotary stared. "Huh?"

"It was needless smoke screen," Doc said.

"What the hell do you mean? Mean you were wise to me?"

Doc said, "You made a few mistakes. First, when you were captured on the Mississippi River, you were not killed. You were kept alive. There was no reason whatever for you being kept alive, particularly when you insisted your friend, Duster Jones, had been killed because he knew too much. You had yourself seized to arouse my interest, and it did arouse my interest, particularly in the phony aspect of it.

"Again, your business of a loan renewal agreement with Sam Joseph was a false note. Sam Joseph recognized you, but he did not make any loan-renewal agreement with you in talking to you, which you said he did.

"And also," Doc continued, "you were in a position to know about all the companies and concerns which were robbed in the course of this thing. All of them were companies with which you would be familiar. Charles Moore's oil-field machinery concern, for example. You are an oilman. You would naturally know more about how to rob an oil-field machinery concern. And the same thing applied to the rest of your victims. There was too much coincidence."

Rotary grinned.

"So there was too much coincidence. So what?"

"So we were able to beat you at your own game."

"Game?"

"Deceit," Doc Savage said.

"What kind of nutty talk is that you—"

Doc Savage jumped then. He moved with abrupt violence, taking the two men holding him completely by surprise. He was not able to seize a weapon, but he was able to get free, to leap and reach a stairway that seemed to go down into a cellar. A window was near, but he ignored that, hit on his stomach, slid to the stairs, went down them.

Renny, Long Tom and Ham began struggling violently, but with no effect.

Rotary Harrison bellowed, "He's in the cellar! There's no way out! Give me one of those grenades!"

He meant the trick grenades which Doc Savage had so carefully distributed, with explanations about their deadly gas contents, before the raid on the ranch.

Rotary grabbed up one of the grenades. He ran to the cellar opening.

"Get ready to slam the door shut after I throw this egg down there," he snarled.

"Ready," one of his men said, seizing the door.

For the benefit of Doc Savage, down below, Rotary bellowed, "You said wind the key like an alarm clock, didn't you?"

He wound the key.

Instantly, there were explosions all over the room, all through the ranchhouse—wherever the trick grenades happened to be—all coming together. They were not loud reports, but there was a guttural violence about the way they let go, and the gas they spewed was sickening, paralyzing, blinding—if you inhaled it.

Doc Savage came up out of the cellar.

"Let's finish this job," he said.

What Rotary and none of his men knew, and what none of them ever did find out, was that by winding the key on the grenades, you wound a powerful little generator the size of a watch, and the current from this, through vacuum tubes not as large as a peanut, was amplified and put out in an impulse that would effect tiny receivers and these would explode the grenades. Each grenade contained receiver and transmitter, but they were not complicated, because they employed the same circuit. Wind the key in one grenade and they would all explode.

As soon as Rotary Harrison had wound the key, Renny and

Long Tom and Ham, knowing all the grenades would let go now, began to fight.

The gas was not effective unless breathed. So they held their breathing back. Renny and Long Tom did it very successfully. But Ham almost immediately got hit in the stomach.

The blow to Ham's middle was terrific, and it opened up his mouth, and he had gas-charged air into his lungs before he could help himself. He began to yell in pain with the other men, and fell to the floor.

There was nothing deadly about the gas, but it was very painful and brought quick unconsciousness. Not that it did the recipient any benefit.

Doc heard Monk.

Monk's bellowing, even when he was gagged, was distinctive. Doc located the sound, headed for it. Through a door, across a room, through another door. There was a small tight shed stacked high with litter, old camp stools and tent poles mostly. And Monk floundering around in the middle of it.

Monk was doing his bellowing entirely through his nose, which was remarkable. He was making about the same amount of noise as a good trumpet, although it was hardly musical.

Doc stopped, slashed his bindings.

Monk bolted to his feet. Evidently he had been kicking around enough that his muscles were not stiff because he was up and out of the door in a streak. Still making nasal noise of remarkable quantity.

Doc went back into the connecting room, found a window.

He remembered to yell, "Anæsthetic gas!" at Monk by way of warning.

Then Doc smashed open the window, thrust out his head and got fresh air into his lungs. Then he turned and met Rotary Harrison.

In some fashion—astonishment must have stopped the man's breathing until he realized what had happened—Rotary had escaped the gas. His face was purple, bloated, from holding his breath.

Doc tried to belt the wind out of Harrison so he would have to breathe. It was not a success. Rotary piled out into the night.

Doc followed, caught him. They went to the ground. Rotary was strong and desperate. He was not a young man, but the iron of his muscle was astonishing.

Monk Mayfair, entering the big room, saw no one in motion, only men motionless on the floor. He knew there was gas, he could feel the slight sting of the stuff against his eyes. He saw Ham and he was horrified until he discovered Ham merely seemed to be gassed.

Monk went on. He could hear fighting, a few shots, well in the rear of the house. He headed for the spot.

"Hey!" somebody said. "Rotary!"

It was dark in the hall. Monk stopped. He recognized the voice. Butch.

"Yeah?" Monk said.

"This way. We can get to a plane."

"Sure," Monk said.

He moved rapidly and pushed along behind the other man until they came to a lighted room. It was Butch, all right. Butch, slim and pale and delicate-looking. The meekly helpless-looking person.

Monk took Butch by the neck.

"It's a shame to waste time on a spindlin' little guy like you," Monk said. "You oughta—ow! *Ow!*"

Monk's greatest pride was what he could do in a hand-to-hand fight. He liked to brawl, knock-down-drag-out, anything goes, bite-an-ear, gouge-an-eye. He had never confessed to anyone, but he took regular lessons in rough and tumble, in jujitsu, and had even hired an osteopath doctor to teach him how to twist bones so as to hurt the most. He thought he was very good.

He began to get an education. He was hit twice; he didn't know exactly where. But the agony was awful. Stars exploded. Pain made his toes feel as if they were falling off.

He managed, and he thought he was lucky to do that, to fall on Butch.

They went over and over. Bones cracked, muscles popped, joints cracked. "Ow!" Monk bawled. "Ow-w-w-w!" He felt sure he was rapidly being separated from arms, legs, ears, hair, nose.

Somewhere in the back of the house, Renny Renwick yelled, "A gang of them are killing Monk! Come on!"

But when Renny appeared in the door he stopped. He began to grin uncontrollably, then to knot up with laughter. Long Tom joined him. He, too, thought it was funny.

"Get Ham Brooks!" Renny gurgled. "Pour water on Ham or something to wake him up. Ham can't miss this! Ham would give years off his life to see this."

Monk and his tiny opponent went through a convulsion. Monk emitted fresh bellows of pain. He was suddenly not enjoying the fight. He had often, in the past, tackled a dozen men who were fighting men, and howled in glee through the whole fray. Now he was suddenly out of glee.

"Oh! Oh! Oh!" Monk squalled.

"We better stop it," Renny said, "before he eats Monk alive."

He went over and tapped Butch on the head with a revolver barrel. Butch collapsed.

Monk rolled feebly, crawling away from the senseless Butch as if the latter was a tarantula. Monk tried to get to his feet, failed, collapsed, sat there foolishly.

Monk stared at the feeble-looking Butch.

"My, my," Monk said. "And to think there's only one of him."

## Chapter XVI
## TRUTH AND VARNISH

The head of the New York State police and the district attorney from New York City who had been assigned to the case arrived a few hours after daylight.

Explanations and arguments, pro and con, and the taking of statements, occupied about three hours.

The D. A. made the speech of summary:

"Officially," he said, "there has been no proof presented that Mr. Savage maintains any kind of an institution where criminal brains are operated upon. Whatever our personal opinions may be, they probably will remain officially inactive because of lack of such proof. Personally, the idea of treating criminals in that way seems a good idea to me."

Ham Brooks asked, "What about all this stink in the newspapers?"

Doc explained, "When it is proven that the whole thing was simply a cleverly thought-out and executed scheme to pick a bunch of men who had been—ah—amnesia victims in the past, and drug them and force them to commit crimes while drugged, then lay it all on to me—when that is all proven, the newspapers will drop their campaign. And apologize, no doubt."

Ham said, "They better apologize, or there'll be the fattest goblin of a lawsuit after each one of them."

The New York district attorney checked over a list of prisoners.

"We have checked and rechecked the list of prisoners," he said, "and from the statements of the other prisoners, we seem to be one short. The man who was the ringleader. A man by the name of Rotary Harrison."

Doc Savage spoke quietly.

"Rotary Harrison," the bronze man said, "was badly injured. He was sent to a private hospital."

"Can you turn him over to us when he is fit?"

Doc nodded.

"Yes," he said. "But Rotary Harrison will not be proven the criminal leader, I am afraid."

"What do you mean?"

"It will probably develop," Doc Savage said quietly, "that Rotary Harrison was just another one of the list of victims who, like myself, were framed to be the goats."

"But all the stolen money and property is in his name," the D A. pointed out.

Doc shook his head. "Rotary Harrison is turning all the property back to the rightful owners."

The D. A. watched the bronze man for a while. Then he grinned. "Well, that fellow Butch will make a good master mind," he said. "We'll hang it onto him."

He got his papers together and went outside to watch the prisoners being loaded into cars.

The moment Doc was alone with Monk and the others, the bronze man said, "Monk, get to our plane. Get your portable chemical lab."

"What's the idea?"

"Rotary Harrison," Doc explained, "is going to our upstate place for an operation that will wipe out all his memory of the past. I want you to mix an anæsthetic that will keep him unconscious during the trip."

"Yes, I know that," Monk said. "But what was the idea of telling the D. A. that Rotary was just another victim of the plot when you know perfectly well he was the brains behind the whole thing."

"That's right," Doc said. "And that's principally the reason I want to send him to the College. You see, Rotary planned this master crime himself and he hired all the others. He was not only plotting to steal several million dollars but he was going to discredit us and our life work with the public.

"The first thing he did was to get hold of Dr. Nedden and that young fellow, Butch. The two of them traced down some of our graduates, drugged them, stole all the money from the firms they worked for, and when the big blow-up came, they were going to say that we were responsible for the crimes because we had performed brain operations on them. The big scheme behind Rotary's mind was that he would have us trapped and then he could force us to pay blackmail or see the work of our College destroyed."

Monk grunted. "Blackmail, eh? I guess he was figuring to cut himself a big slice of our Central American gold supply."

Doc nodded. "Yes. That was his plan. He was so clever about it that only one man in the organization knew who their leader really was. That man was Butch. He was the one who hired all the others, including Dr. Nedden, and they all got their instructions through that little devil statue which, in reality, was only a tiny transmitting and receiving set."

"Where is Rotary now?" Renny asked.

"Out in the bush, where I hid him," Doc explained.

Monk looked puzzled. "I still don't understand why you're covering Rotary up from the police. I think—"

Renny gave Monk a kick and said, "Come on, you dope."

Monk followed Renny outside. "What's got into Doc?" he said. "Rotary was the leader, and—"

"Possibly," Renny suggested dryly, "Doc is suffering from a slight attack of your chronic trouble."

"Huh?"

"Sis Harrison," Renny said. "In other words, she doesn't know her dad was the kingfish in this affair."

"Oh, oh," Monk grinned. "Now I've run across something I can understand."

## THE TEN TON SNAKES

# I

You ought to know about ribbons. The yellow one with the two red stripes is for China Service. The red ribbon with the pair of triple white stripes—good conduct. Purple with white ends, Purple Heart. Blue, red and white stripes, Distinguished Service Cross. Blue, yellow and red bands, the Yangtze Medal.

The years and the terrors of a man's life worn over his heart.

This boy had all of these ribbons. Except the good-conduct one. He didn't have that one.

He was wearing them, too. They looked like a flag on his chest. Normally he didn't wear them; he carried them in his pocket, in a little teakwood velvet-lined case wonderfully made for him by a Karen in Burma. The boy felt very deeply about them, but he wouldn't have admitted it for anything. However, he wasn't exactly a boy.

He was over twenty-eight. Not old enough for that gray to belong in his hair. He was leathery and rangy and long-nosed and blue-eyed and he looked at you as if he owned you. That is a thing American soldiers are beginning to do, look at you as if they own you. And they do, in a way.

He had a callous like a corn on a finger of his left hand, his 50-calibre trigger finger.

And now they were trying to kill him.

He was walking down Fifth Avenue. Looking. Looking at everything gladly and hungrily, as if he wanted to eat it. Looking at the legs of the girls walking on Fifth Avenue. Ogling the plaster-of-paris legs of the mannikins in the store windows. Going "woo-woo" at the girls walking by him on the street. He wanted to jump over the buildings, you could tell. He would get up on his toes and dance a step or two, and whirl completely around. Like a ballet dancer. As if God had given him wings.

Murder.

It was a very carefully planned thing, this project of sudden death. It was getting the care that a murder deserves. The boy with the ribbons, the boy who was so glad that he was almost sick at his stomach, was going to be slain in cold blood. Cold blood—if anyone knows why they call it that.

It was hard to be sure how many men were going to help do it to him. Thousands of people were on Fifth Avenue, probably no more nor less than are there any days. The murderers were of the crowd, and like the crowd. Pointing them out would have been as difficult as picking four maggots who had had catfish for dinner from a basketful of other maggots who had had sunfish for dinner. Very difficult. They weren't doing anything to get fingers pointed at them.

Keeping track of the boy, was all. Waiting. But waiting has its end. Suspense can draw out just about so far, and then something must happen.

So one of the men walked up behind the boy with a long knife and started to put the blade in between the boy's third and fourth ribs where it would reach the boy's happy heart.

It was a walk-up-and-stab murder, but the sun was shining gaily, making shadows. The sun made the shadow of the man with the knife on the sidewalk, and it looked like exactly what it was, a man with a knife. This the soldier saw.

The soldier did more than dodge. The army had spent a lot in time and patience teaching him what to do when someone tried to shoot, club or stab him. He did it. He did it so fast you could hardly see it.

Slam, slam. Too fast to follow, but the knife was spinning in the air and he who'd held it was on his back with teeth loose in his mouth and an awful feeling where he'd been kicked in the belly. It was an army bellykick, Commando stuff, intended to gut a man if possible. It was no fooling.

The man fell on the sidewalk. He might as well have been dead. He was noisy and he was hurting, but otherwise he might as well have been dead.

The boy looked at the man.

"You blank blank," he said. "I think I know you."

He circled, looking at the man on the sidewalk.

"Why God bless you, I do know you," the soldier said. "What do you know about that. Doggone!"

And he began being un-nice to the man on the sidewalk. What the soldier proceeded to do was sickening, but it didn't sicken. He had been dealing with Japs, and the only safe Jap was one who couldn't be anything else.

He kicked in some of the man's ribs. The man was long and skinny, like a wolf with the sickness wolves get from eating too much carrion, so his ribs were close to the hide and broke easily. The soldier jumped on to the man's belly with both feet. This was guaranteed to rupture, to burst the bladder, etc.

The soldier got off the man's belly and leaned over the man's face and said, "Listen, bub, to what I'm asking you. Is Tucker French, my brother, all right? Is he going to be all right? What do you such-and-such plan to do to Tucker?"

The man on the sidewalk gargled his blood and teeth and pain.

"Come on, boy," the soldier said. "Let's have an answer. Don't be bashful."

No answer.

"Come, come, boy," the soldier said. "What about Tucker? You're not going to hurt Tucker, are you?"

No answer.

"Oh yes, I nearly forgot," the soldier said. "What about the heavy stuff? You boys fixing to do something bad with the heavy stuff?"

The man on the sidewalk finally got his throat sufficiently clear of blood and teeth to form some semicoherent words. When he spoke, he was down to greatest fundamental of all, the thing than which there is nothing much more important. He said, "Please don't kill me."

He said not to kill him in Spanish, because Spanish and not English was his mother tongue.

As if answering his prayer, his friends came to his aid.

The soldier was fooled this time. There were no shadows to warn him. There was only a mild looking man in a blue serge suit who sidled up to the scene with one hand over his mouth as if he was showing horror the way a woman shows it. When he was close enough to the soldier, he slugged the soldier on the side of the face.

The soldier wasn't greatly damaged. He began to fight. He wanted to fight anyway.

Two other men drifted out of the crowd and took a hand, beginning beating the soldier.

"Hey, this guy tried to knife me," the soldier cried. "Cut it out! Call a cop, if you want to help."

This was what he said before he understood that they were part of an organized attempt on his life. When he did realize what they were, he stopped talking. He did everything with his fists and feet that he could.

The men, finding the soldier was extremely tough, began producing knives. These knives did not resemble the knife the first man had tried to use, except in one particular. They were individualized knives. That is, each one was a knife which its owner liked. Which meant that they were men who carried their knives as a habit.

Such men would know how to use knives, so the soldier got away from them as fast as he could.

He escaped by running. He didn't make the mistake of going in either direction along the sidewalk. Instead, he popped into the nearest doorway.

They shot at him. The bullet went past his head and buried itself somewhere in the upper part of the luggage shop in which he found himself.

The soldier was afraid the place wouldn't have a back door. He was right. But it had a basement and a second floor. He took the stairs to the second floor.

There was a bank of elevators and he got in one of them and rode down to the basement, which was also a part of the leathergoods store. He waited around there for a while, looking at suitcases. He had the clerk show him a tan leather case, and faced the stairs and the elevators while he examined it. He saw nor heard nothing alarming. He asked the clerk if there was a back door, and the clerk got such a funny look that the soldier walked off and left him.

The soldier walked out of the front door.

The man who had tried to knife him was no longer on the sidewalk. The man was nowhere in sight. None of the other knife-wielders were to be seen. Nobody recognized the soldier as a participant in the action of a few minutes before. The soldier didn't stick around long enough to give them much chance.

He went to a bar. He had three snorts of rye. He burst out in a sweat and he became sick with the feeling that nerves give to a man's stomach. He was plain scared.

After he felt that he was able to walk down the street without falling on his face (and it took him some time to get back that much control) he got moving.

He went to a phone booth and looked in the phone book for a name: *Renwick, John, civil engr.*

John Renwick, civil engineer, had an office in a ponderous building two blocks from Grand Central station on Fortieth Street. The office was not quite seedy, but it had no floss. The furniture was old, of walnut, and the middle-aged office girl also looked as if she were made of walnut. She listened to the soldier state that he wanted to see Renwick if Renwick was in town.

"He's in town," the office girl said. "Wait a minute."

She went into the inner office, closed the door and put her back against the door.

"A soldier to see you," she said. "Gives his name as Bob French. Says he met you at Yung-shun, wherever that is."

"Yung-shun," Renny Renwick said, "is in China."

You first noticed Renny Renwick's fists. They were too big. He was a big man, more than six feet, more than two hundred pounds, but the fists were still too big.

The fists, as a matter of fact, were the index to the man. They were capable hands, almost ridiculously strong, hands that were not made for soft work or for softness of any kind. Gentleness, yes. But not softness. There were scars on the fists where they had hit things, and the hide was leathery where the sun had beat them, and the palms calloused from handling heavy things.

"Hunan province in China," he said. "That's where we built that intermediate field for the B-29's. Holy cow, was that a place for you! Shoot this soldier in here."

The middle-aged office girl opened the door and told the soldier, "Shoot you in, he says."

The soldier came in holding out his hand and saying, "You remember me?"

Renwick jumped to his feet and roared.

"Hell, yes! Holy cow!" he roared. "What are you doing here? Did they run out of rice whiskey in China? You're the last man I expected to see."

"My time was up and they shipped me home," the soldier said.

"When was that?"

"A week ago."

"Only a week? What are you doing sober? Sit down. What became of Sleepy Wilson? And what about what's-his-name, the flop-eared guy we stole the jeep from that night?"

The soldier didn't answer the questions. He started to, but his words stubbed their toes on his fears and fell flat on their faces.

What he did say was, "Look, I'm in trouble."

Renwick grinned and roared, "Borrowing money from me is getting blood from a turnip. But not for a man from Yung-shun. How much do you need?"

"I don't need money."

"No? You've come to the wrong man, then. I don't know anything about women."

"This isn't a girl."

Renwick examined the soldier intently.

"What's your name?" he asked. "I never did know it, I don't think."

"Bob French."

"All right, Bob French, sit down and see if you can't talk that scared look off your face."

Bob French sat down. "It's a story that has its goofy aspects."

"Shoot."

## II

Renny Renwick's voice was a great rumbling thing developed by bawling at steeljacks on towering skyscraper frameworks and bawling above the clatter of riveting guns. The voice had been rattling the windows, almost. Now that he was silent, listening for the soldier's story, there seemed almost too much stillness in the office.

"It's a shame to drag this in on you," Bob French said. "But you're the only man I could think of that I knew in New York. And I'm scared."

"What are you scared of?"

"Here's the story. I got a brother, see. His name is Tucker. He is younger than me, and he's in South America. Colombia, back in the jungles. He's in the mining business in a small way."

"American citizen?"

Bob French took his eyes off Renwick and put them on the floor and didn't say anything for a moment. "Yes. I don't know why the draft missed him."

"Okay."

Bob French shoved his jaw out and said, "Okay or not, I don't give a damn. I've done enough fighting for all of our family, and I'm glad Tucker kept out of it and I hope to God he continues keeping out of it."

He sounded violent, as if he were taking something out of his heart.

Renny laughed. "Was I picking a fight with you?"

The soldier licked his lips. He looked at the floor some more.

"I got a cable from my brother. That was two days ago. I had cabled Tucker I was back in the States and had a twenty-one-day furlough that was just starting, so that's how he knew I was back and where to find me.

"This cable was funny. It said for me to go see a man named Sir Roger Powell, who would be at the Westland. It said for me to ask

Powell about the heavy stuff. I was to ask Powell what the situation was on the heavy stuff. It said—the cable said—to try to form a judgment about Powell. Well, I did and—"

"What," Renny interrupted, "did the cable mean by asking you to form a judgment?"

"Decide about Powell."

"Decide what?"

"Whether he was a crook or not, I guess."

"What is the heavy stuff?"

"That's all the cable said—heavy stuff."

"You mean it just said to ask about the heavy stuff, and that was all the description it gave?"

"Yes."

"And from that, what did you gather the heavy stuff was?"

"I couldn't figure it out."

"What's your guess?"

"I haven't got any guess."

"Then you have no idea what the heavy stuff could be?"

"None," the soldier said. "I told you this thing had goofy aspects. That's one of them."

"Mind letting me see this cablegram?"

"I'd be glad to show it to you, only I haven't got it."

"What became of it?"

"I destroyed it."

"Why?"

"Habit. I have the habit of destroying all the letters and telegrams I receive when they're not something I have to keep. I've done that for years, I guess."

"What did you do after you got the cablegram from your brother?" Renny asked, settling back to listen again.

Bob French seemed to require a moment to get his mind back on the telling of his story. Then he said, "I went to see Sir Roger Powell. I found him at the hotel, as Tucker's cablegram had said I would. I sent my name up to his room, and he returned word for me to come right up.

"Well, that name of Sir Roger Powell had sure fooled me," the soldier continued. "I expected an old geezer with a monocle and a white goatee. Sir Roger Powell wasn't anything like that. He could have been an insurance agent in Kansas City, for all you could tell."

"Is he a genuine title?" Renny asked.

"Search me. If you're a genuine Sir, don't you have to sit in the House of Lords or in Parliament or something?"

"Search me," Renny said. "I wouldn't know."

"Anyway, Powell didn't admit knowing anything about any heavy stuff. He knew my brother. That was all he would admit."

"You think, then, that he lied to you?" Renny asked.

"Everything he said might not be lies. But he sure lied about the heavy stuff, whatever it is."

"How do you know?"

"I can tell when a man lies to me."

"Always?"

"I could tell this time," Bob French said. "He was lying, all right. There was another guy in the room with him. I didn't like the fellow's looks either. Well, I talked to this Powell fellow, asking him about the heavy stuff, and I didn't get a thing out of him. He just said he knew nothing about any such thing, and that he was very sorry. But I got the feeling he wasn't sorry, and that he knew plenty about the heavy stuff, whatever it is, and that the only thing he was sorry about was seeing me. My showing up that way worried him, all right. Well, I left."

The soldier scowled at the floor for a moment.

"I cabled my brother the results of the interview," he said. "I asked him what he wanted me to do."

"Have you had an answer?"

"Not yet."

Renny said, "You said you were scared. I don't see any reason for your being scared."

"Wait a minute, I haven't told you what happened just before I came up here."

Renny waited patiently. He was interested in the story. He was excited about it, too, and his eyes were bright and intent.

"They tried to kill me on the street," the soldier said. "First, a man tried to knife me. I knocked him down. I was pretty rough. Some other men piled in to help. Too many for me, I figured. So I cut and ran, and here I am."

"How," Renny asked, "did you connect this attack with Sir Roger Powell, the man your brother cabled you to interview about the heavy stuff?"

"This guy with the knife was with Powell when we had our talk."

Renny raised his eyebrows over this piece of information. "That would be a connection, all right. But I don't exactly see what you want me to do."

"Look, you're the only man in New York I know," Bob French said. "I've got some funny trouble on my hands, as you can see.

I'm scared. I've had practice in being scared, because I've killed Japs and had Japs trying to kill me, and I've been scared for a week at a time. And I can still get scared, like when those guys tried to kill me. Right on the street like that, they tried to kill me. I tell you, I never heard of such a damned thing."

"So that's why you came to me?" Renny said.

"That's right," the soldier said. "I got to know you in China, and I figured you would be the man to help me or advise me." The soldier hesitated, then added sheepishly, "Don't get me wrong. I don't expect you to drop your business and grab a gun and rush out to fight my battles for me. Just kick in with some advice, that's what I want. When a man is scared, it helps to have someone around who understands."

"You didn't," Renny said, "come to me because you knew I was associated with Doc Savage?"

"Eh? You're what with who?"

"Associated with Doc Savage."

"Who's he?" Bob French asked.

Renny thought over the answer for a moment, then he laughed. "That's fresh," he said. "That's wonderful."

"What are you laughing at?" Bob French demanded.

Renny chuckled over it for a while. "The idea of you not having heard of Doc Savage, coupled with the coincidence of your popping up with a piece of mysterious trouble like this, strikes me as funny," he explained.

"Who's this Savage?"

"A friend with whom I frequently work," Renny said. Then he frowned, and shook his head quickly. "No, that isn't the way to put it. Let's change that, and say that several years ago I met the most remarkable man I have ever seen. A man with so much ability that it sounds silly when you start telling the truth about him. I'll explain what I mean by silly by saying that his profession is other people's troubles, righting wrongs and punishing evil-doers in the far corners of the earth. See how wild that sounds? Like something out of a book about knighthood. It gives you an idea."

"You work for this fellow, that it?" Bob French demanded.

"I work *with* him, not for him," Renny corrected. "There are five of us who do that. I'm an engineer. I'm the engineering specialist. The others are also specialists. One is an electrician, one a chemist, one a geologist and archaeologist, and the other a lawyer." Renny was silent a moment, grinning. "Here's something else unusual about it. None of us get paid for it."

Bob French stared fixedly at Renny. "When I knew you in China, I figured you were a pretty levelheaded guy."

"And now you don't think so?"

"I don't know what to think. This sure sounds pixyish."

Renny chuckled. "You'll understand it when you meet Doc Savage, the 'man of bronze,' as they call him sometimes."

Bob French gave a visible jump, and said, "The 'man of—' " and didn't finish.

"The newspapers call Doc the 'man of bronze' now and then," Renny said. "Have you heard of him under that description?"

"I guess I have," the soldier said.

Renny watched the soldier curiously. Bob French wasn't a fellow who hid his feelings very well. Renny could tell what was going through French's mind. First, French mentally reviewed what he had heard about Doc Savage. This review, for some reason or other, made French apprehensive. French suddenly decided that he didn't want Doc Savage involved in the affair.

"If you don't mind," French said, "let's you and I work out this thing ourselves."

"You mean you don't want Doc to know about this?"

"I'd rather not."

"Why?"

Bob French didn't reply immediately. He was becoming cautious, stopping to plan his words. "This isn't a very important affair, and Savage is a man who is accustomed to large matters, if what I recall about him is right. I don't think we should bother him with this."

"Didn't someone try to murder you?" Renny demanded.

"Yes, but—"

"Isn't that important?"

"Well—"

"A murder is always important," Renny said. "We'll go to Doc with this thing. Wait'll I get my hat and coat."

Renny went into an adjoining room which, Bob French decided, must serve the big-fisted engineer as living quarters. At least French got a glimpse of a cot and a dresser through the open door.

Now that Renny was out of sight, some of the emotion inside French suddenly appeared on his face. The emotion, a sick apprehension, got the best of him for a moment.

He went to the door leading into the reception room and opened it, not as a man who was in flight, but as a man who was so worried that he felt the need of moving about.

It was when he made the unexpected discovery that the middle-aged office girl was not in the outer office that French's frightened brain hatched a quick plan.

The key in the partition door was on the inside. He had already noticed that. He seized the key and changed it to the other side of the door, stepped through, closed the door quietly, and locked it.

He lifted his voice, yelled, "Renny! Watch out! For God's sake!" He screamed the last part.

He snatched up the office girl's chair and broke it over her desk. He hurled the fragments against the connecting door. He emitted a series of loud grunts and gasps, and shoved the office girl's desk around.

Renny hit the other side of the partition door, rattling the locked doorknob.

"French, what's happening?" Renny yelled.

"They've jumped me!" the soldier howled.

He stamped and slapped the desk. He seized his blouse, deliberately tore it half in two up the back, wrenched off the blouse-half including the sleeve, and threw it on the floor.

Then he ran out into the corridor. He had been afraid someone would have heard the uproar and come into the corridor to investigate. But no one had.

Bob French ran to the door at the end of the corridor which was marked EXIT. This led to the stairs. He went down the stairs in clattering haste.

## III

Half an hour later, Renny Renwick was saying to Doc Savage, "He got a cable from his brother to ask a man named Powell about something called the heavy stuff."

Renny went on with the story, and Doc listened.

Doc Savage was a taller man than Renny Renwick, and probably as heavy, but it was only when he was near Renwick that this was apparent. Standing apart, Doc seemed of slighter stature. Most muscular men and most big men look muscular or big. Doc didn't.

There were two or three startling things about his appearance. His hair was bronze-colored, and only slightly darker than the sun had made his skin. He had golden eyes that were unusual, almost weird. Otherwise he was not particularly handsome. He dressed with an obvious effort to make himself inconspicuous, but with little success. He was a man who would be conspicuous anywhere.

He had received an excited telephone call from Renny. He had hurried to Renwick's office, and now he listened to the story of Bob French's visit.

"They grabbed him," Renny concluded, "when I was in the other room getting my hat and coat. They must have jerked him into the reception room and locked the door between the two offices before he began to fight. The fight must have been a beaut. It only lasted a couple of seconds, because it was over, and everybody was gone, by the time I could find something heavy enough to break down the door."

"You searched for French?" Doc asked. He had a voice which was somewhat startling because of the impression it gave of controlled volume and power. It had a quality which highly trained voices have.

"Sure I looked. I ran into the corridor, yelling for French. I didn't get an answer. I dashed back and telephoned the elevator starter downstairs to keep his eyes open for a man of French's description. But I must have been too late, because French hasn't left since. He might still be in the building, of course."

"Where did this fight take place?"

"The reception room."

Doc said, "Let's have a look."

In the reception room, he picked up the broken pieces of the office girl's chair and examined them.

"Where was your office girl?" he asked.

"Mrs. Carter goes home at four," Renny explained. "It was about four-fifteen when this happened. She had already gone."

The office girl's desk was overturned on the floor.

"Where was the desk placed before?" Doc asked. "Let's put it back where it was."

Renny returned the desk to its original position. "About here, I think," he said.

Doc Savage examined the desk, and thoughtfully compared the parts of the chair to the marks on the top of the desk. He gave more attention to scratches on the side of the desk.

Renny said, "They tore half of his blouse off him. Here it is."

Doc looked at the blouse.

"Would you like to hear some Sherlock Holmes work on this?" he asked.

"What do you mean?" Renny inquired.

"Nobody attacked your man," Doc said. "He staged the thing himself."

Renny scratched his head doubtfully. "I don't see how you figure that."

There was only a narrow space between the desk and the wall, where the office girl's chair would normally have been. Doc stood there.

"From the marks on the desk, the chair was swung by someone standing about here," he said. "You'll notice there is hardly room for anyone to have been in front of the chair when it was swung, indicating French picked up the chair and smashed it down on the desk.

"The marks on the side of the desk indicate it was kicked several times in the same place. That could happen in a fight, but it is hardly likely.

"None of the chair fragments show traces of having hit a man. A chair, or even a chair leg, is a heavy weapon, and if you struck a man with one, some blood or hair or hide should adhere to the weapon."

Renny nodded thoughtfully.

"Of course any one of those freak things could happen in a fight," Doc added. "But it isn't likely that all of them would happen in the same fight."

"Holy cow!" Renny said. "Now that you bring this up, I remember that French didn't seem so happy about bringing you into the case."

"Oh, he showed some reluctance?"

"Yes, he did. At first, he didn't seem to know who you were. Then it dawned on him that he had heard of you, and right away he suggested that we shouldn't bother you with his trouble."

"Did he give any reason?"

"No. He only said that he didn't think we should bother an important man like you with the matter," Renny said. "Doggone it, I should have attached more importance to his reluctance."

"It looks as if he staged a fake attack, then escaped down the stairs."

"That's the way it seems, all right."

Doc asked, "When French first began asking you for help, did he seem sincere?"

"As sincere as anything."

"When did he change?"

"When he realized who you were."

"As I understand it, you first told him that you would bring me into the thing, calling me by name," Doc said. "Was that when French got excited?"

"No. He got excited when it dawned on him who you were. He'd heard of you as the man of bronze. I mentioned that was who you were, and that was when he changed his mind about wanting you in it."

Doc looked thoughtfully at the half portion of Bob French's coat.

"He wanted us to investigate the thing," Doc said. "But he didn't want to appear in it himself any more."

Renny was startled. "How you figure that?"

"He must have staged the fake attack to get us excited," Doc pointed out. "Otherwise he would have merely slipped away from you."

Renny clapped a hand to his forehead. "By God, that's right. What's the matter with my brains, anyway!"

Doc went through the half of Bob French's blouse. In the pockets he found cigarettes, book matches, two Chinese cash coins with square holes in their middles, an English shilling coin, a cigar.

Renny scrutinized the book matches. "None of this stuff means anything. I thought the matches might, but they're from a chain outfit that has branches all over the city."

Doc indicated a small white cloth tab clipped to the blouse collar. It had inked markings.

"Laundry tag," Doc said.

Renny brightened. "By golly, that's as good as an address. Doesn't the New York police have a directory of these laundry marks?"

"I think so," Doc said. "But tracing it down is going to take time. We want to talk to this Sir Roger Powell fellow without delay. So we had better turn the job of tracing down the laundry mark over to Monk."

"Good idea," Renny agreed.

Monk Mayfair was the only other one of their group who was in New York, or in the United States for that matter. Monk was Lieutenant Colonel Andrew Blodgett Mayfair, the chemist of their outfit.

Doc got Monk on the telephone.

"The blouse with the laundry mark will be in Renny's desk in his office," Doc said, after he had told Monk what had happened. "Your job is to get it, check back the laundry mark with the police, and find Bob French if you can. Better not waste any time."

Monk had a small squeaky voice. He wasn't too happy about the assignment.

"You guys wouldn't be shoving off some routine on me, so you can go after the exciting part?" he demanded.

"What makes you think that?"

Monk snorted. "I've had some previous experience."

"If you're not interested—"

"Oh, I'll go after the laundry angle," Monk said hastily. "But it's funny I always get this leg work."

Doc mentioned Monk's reluctance to Renny Renwick while they were riding an elevator down to the street. Renny said, "Monk always finds something to squawk about. But he's worse lately. I think he misses fussing with Ham Brooks since Ham went to Europe to work on that legal tangle the Nazis left."

Doc agreed that Monk certainly missed Ham. He added that it was a relief, though, not to have to listen to the quarrel the two had carried on for years, and not to have to put up with the practical jokes the two liked to pull on each other.

They got a cab.

"The Westland," Renny said.

"That's on Madison, ain't it?" the driver asked.

"Right."

During the ride, Renny told Doc Savage what he knew about Bob French. On the Yung-shun job, on which Renny had been supervising engineer, French had been with the army engineer group assigned to the project. Renny had been assigned the same living quarters as French, a Chinese farmer's house, and they had become friends in the same fashion as any two men would become friends under the same circumstances. French's two-fisted ability had impressed Renny.

It was Renny's opinion that French would have been a Major or a Colonel—French was a buck sergeant—if the man had been more amenable to discipline. French was one of those fellows who didn't regard the war as a career, hadn't the slightest intention of staying in the army a minute longer than was necessary, and got away with anything and everything he could. Some of it he didn't get away with. He had been busted back to private grade several times for just helling around. But there was nothing wrong with Bob French's war-making. He was a guy who was in it to lick the Japs and Nazis, and the hell with the rest of it. Renny had liked him.

None of which shed much light on the matter at hand, Renny admitted.

"Here's the Westland," Doc said, looking out at a radio prowl car, a detective squad car and a police ambulance.

## IV

"Holy cow!" Renny said. "Things don't look too peaceful around here!"

Doc paid off their cab, and entered the Westland. It was a luxury hotel. Modernistic, chrome and black, with surrealist murals on the walls. Not garish, though. And not cheap.

In the cavernous, indirectly lighted lobby, business was proceeding as usual. However, the doorman and another man, evidently the assistant manager, were standing with two detectives. They were okaying people who entered, it was apparent, when one of the plain-clothes sleuths came over and stopped Doc and Renny.

"You are not guests here, I believe," the officer said.

Doc produced a billfold, and leafed through the assortment of permits, licenses, memberships cards and identification cards. He found what he wanted. The detective looked at the document and said, "Huh!" explosively.

Doc said, "If whatever has happened here concerns a man named Powell, we'll want the low-down on it."

The detective glanced from Doc to Renny dubiously, then said, "You'd better wait here a minute." He went to a telephone and spoke over it, reading from the card Doc had given him during part of his conversation.

Coming back, the officer said, "Okay. Sorry to keep you waiting. This is the first time I have had one of these things sprung on me." The card Doc had given him was an honorary commission in the New York City police force.

"What's going on?" Doc asked.

"Fellow named Powell got shot at," the officer explained. "He doesn't know who did it, he says. We're checking people in and out of the hotel in hopes of getting a line on something. No luck yet. Can you help us?"

"I haven't met Powell," Doc said.

"What do you want to see him about?" the detective asked.

"On a private matter," Doc said.

The police detective didn't like the answer. He still held Doc's card of identification. He glanced at it as if wondering how much weight it carried.

"People are generally better off if they give us information when we ask for it," the officer said finally, thinly veiling a threat.

"I'm sure they are," Doc told him. "Where will we find Powell?"

"He's in his suite, eighteen-eleven," the officer said reluctantly.

Riding up in the elevator, Renny said, "The cop was disappointed."

Doc nodded. "Normally I would not advise anyone to withhold information from the police. But, unfortunately, the newspapers have an uncanny facility at finding out what the police are doing, and we can do without any front page splurges."

Sir Roger Powell was a lithe, neat young-acting middle-aged man in a blue pin-stripe suit and white shirt. His black hair stood up like a fresh brush and his moustache was a work of art.

He opened a door which had two holes, bullet holes, in the panel, after they knocked on it.

"Ah, some more police," he said not unpleasantly.

"Not exactly," Doc told him. "You are Powell?"

Powell hesitated, smiled, said, "Well, you must be newspapermen, then. Won't you come in? Yes, I'm Powell."

They entered, and there was a uniformed police patrolman sitting in a chair watching the door intently. He had a revolver on his lap.

Doc went to the policeman and showed him the same identification he had shown the police detective downstairs.

"Mind if we talk to Powell privately?" Doc asked.

The cop knew what the identification meant. He had a better idea than the detective. He said, "Be okay if I wait out in the hall?"

"Sure."

The cop went out.

Powell stared at Doc and Renny. "I say, have a bit of influence, haven't you?"

Renny said, "My name is Renwick. This is Doc Savage, Mr. Powell."

Powell was startled into being very English.

"I'll be damned, really I will," he said. "You know I thought there was something familiar about you."

"We've met before?" Doc asked.

"I've met your reputation a number of times," Powell said amiably. "I never saw you personally before, that I know about. I think I'd have remembered, old boy."

The suite was large, airy and expensive looking. Through a door there was a bedroom, and on the floor and on a rack were two pieces of handsome, monogrammed luggage.

From the looks of the walls, at least five bullets had clouted into the plaster. The floors had not been swept, and some of the plaster had been tracked on the carpet.

"Any idea why we're here?" Doc asked.

Powell gave them his smile again. "Considering that I have lately had a gun emptied at me, that would be a logical guess as to the reason."

"I believe you know a man named Bob French," Doc said.

All amiability, almost all emotion, left Powell's face while he looked at them.

"Oh, that," he said.

"Know him?"

"I met," Powell said, "a man who claimed to be Bob French."

Doc said, "He came to see Renwick here. Renwick knew him in China. He wanted Renny's help. When he found out that I was associated with Renny, he changed his mind about the help. He ducked out."

Powell frowned. He got out a cloth bag of tobacco and a book of papers and went to work on a cigarette. He didn't look like a man who would be rolling his own. It didn't fit him. He took plenty of time to think while he was rolling the cigarette.

He said, "Ordinarily I wouldn't call that a sound reason for your being here."

"That was no reason; it was something to start us talking," Doc explained.

"I could," Powell said, "tell you to go to hell."

"Are you?"

Powell laughed. There was utterly no humor in the laugh.

"Tell Doc Savage that? Naturally not," he said. "Because I have heard of Savage. I have heard that you make a business of helping people out of trouble, provided the trouble is unusual enough to interest you. However, I'm going to ask you one question: Just whom do you think you are helping out of trouble?"

"Bob French," Renny said.

Powell turned to Renny. "Pardon me, but I don't get it. Bob French ran away."

"He's a pal of mine and he was scared," Renny said. "He came to me for help. He's going to get help."

"Perhaps he doesn't want it now."

"He hasn't said so."

"And you're going to help him?"

"If we can."

Powell's laugh came, still without heartiness. "In anyone else, that would be unreasonable, you must admit. You have no actual interest in the matter. The man who asked you for aid apparently doesn't want it now." He examined them and suddenly smiled as if he understood them thoroughly. "But of course I don't consider your interest as unreasonable. I've heard of you, and I know that the things you do which are seemingly without motive really have a very strong motive, which is your love of excitement."

Doc asked patiently, "Do we talk about Bob French or not?"

"Of course we talk," Powell said.

Powell snuffed out his cigarette, then took a stand facing them, his back to the window so that, intentionally or not, the light was in their eyes and they couldn't see his face too well.

"There's much I don't understand. I want to say that first," he told them.

Renny said, "Begin with Bob French's brother. You're supposed to know him."

"With Tucker French? That was where I was going to begin anyway. I got acquainted with Tucker in Colombia, South America. Tucker French is one of those somewhat strange and mysterious white men who take their living, in one way or another, out of the jungle."

Powell wheeled abruptly and went into the bedroom. He came back with one of the neat, monogrammed traveling bags, opened it and showed them the contents.

The bag held two-way airplane radios of the smaller sort, and a salesman's prospectus of larger outfits.

"I sell this stuff," Powell said. "I sell it in South America, and that's how I met Tucker French. He wanted a portable radio for use in the jungle, and I sold him one, and we became acquaintances. I suppose you would call us friends, except for one thing: I never got to know too much about Tucker."

He closed the suitcase. Then he resumed his stance with the light at his back.

"Three weeks ago, I happened to mention to Tucker French that I was coming to New York to brush up on my contacts with manufacturers and new post-war types of radio equipment. He asked me to bring a shipment of snake skins to New York for him. I agreed.

"So I was given a very heavy box of snake skins. Or rather, the box was put aboard the ship which was to bring me to New York, after having been passed by the Colombian officials who, in times like these, examine the things which are exported.

"I came to New York, and the customs officials here passed the box of snake skins, and I had them transferred to the warehouse where I usually store my radios. The case of snake skins was very heavy.

"I was to contact a firm named Blassett and Morris about the snake skins. I did so. Blassett and Morris said they didn't deal in snake skins. They didn't know Tucker French, either, and said they'd never had any dealings with him."

Powell paused and puffed his cigarette.

"You see the thing was beginning to get strange," he said.

Doc Savage asked, "What did you do next?"

"I cabled Tucker French the facts. I have not received an answer. The same day, this man saying he was Bob French called on me and made some mysterious remarks about something he called the heavy stuff. I told him I knew nothing about it."

Powell paused again, this time to get their attention.

"Remember, I'm not sure Tucker French has a brother," he said. "Tucker never mentioned having one."

"What happened after Bob French's visit?" Doc asked.

"Nothing, until today," Powell said. "A little over half an hour ago, there was a knock on the door of this hotel room suite. I opened the door. A man fired a revolver at me. He missed. He fired, in fact, three shots while I was holding the door open. I slammed the door. He fired two more shots, emptying his gun, the bullets going through the door."

Doc Savage said, "The bullets all missed?"

"That's right. The man was very excited. And of course, I did some dodging."

"Did you know the man?"

"No."

"Ever seen him before?"

"Not that I recall."

Doc Savage had been sitting on a straight-backed chair. Now he came to his feet, took a few strides toward the window as if to look out. This brought him in a better position to study Powell's face. The man's countenance was as pale as ivory and coated with nervous perspiration.

"Powell," Doc said, "what do you think is behind the trouble?"

Powell threw out his hands. "I don't know. I told you I didn't know when I began talking."

"You're sweating," Doc said.

Powell blew up.

"By God, of course I'm sweating!" he yelled. "Why wouldn't I be? I've never been shot at before. It was a miracle that fellow didn't kill me when he emptied his gun at me."

"You are sure," Doc asked drily, "that he really tried?"

Powell threw up both clenched hands preparatory to a tirade. But before the words got away from him, he took control of himself. He lowered his hands and straightened his coat by jerking at the sleeves.

"If he didn't," he said, "he gave an imitation that utterly convinced me."

Doc changed to a manner that was friendly and said, "We are not trying to accuse or irritate you. If my questions seem pointless, or too pointed, it's because the affair seems confusing.

"It's confusing enough," Powell agreed.

"Would you," Doc asked, "like to plunge into it and see if we can find out what it's about?"

"You're damned right," Powell said vehemently.

"Then why don't we take a look at the box of snake skins?" Doc suggested.

Powell hesitated barely long enough for it to be evident that he had hesitated. "All right," he agreed. "But I don't see what good that will do."

They went out into the hall, and Doc told the policeman, "Mr. Powell is going with us. Will that be all right?"

The officer nodded, then said, "I think I ought to check on that, to keep myself clear."

"Go ahead."

The cop was back shortly. "It's okay."

They found a cab downstairs. Powell gave the driver an address, then leaned back. Powell looked controlled, smug, righteous.

Doc said, "By the way, I overlooked something."

"Yes?" Powell smiled slightly.

"When Bob French came to see you, were you alone?"

"Yes, I—" Powell hesitated, puckering his forehead thoughtfully. "No, I wasn't, either. Mr. Jessup was there."

"Jessup?"

"D. B. Jessup. He happened to be there when Bob French called, and I think he was present during the interview."

"Who is he? Friend of yours?"

"Not exactly a friend," Powell said. "D. B. Jessup had written me a letter to my Colombian headquarters, saying he had some army surplus radio equipment in which I might be interested. He asked to call on me when I came to New York. So I got in touch with him, and he called."

"Buy any radios from him?" Doc asked.

"No, as a matter of fact I didn't."

"Why not?"

"His prices were too high. I didn't even bother to go look at his stuff. His prices were clear out of reason."

Renny leaned forward. "This D. B. Jessup—was he a long, lean man. Dark hair. Sallow skin. Very skinny, with kind of a wolf face and an unhealthy look?"

"Why, yes—" Powell bolted upright in the seat. He held himself there with arms rigid, fists clenched. He showed utter alarm. "You know him?"

"Is that Jessup?"

"It answers his description."

"That's the man," Renny said, "who tried to stick a knife into Bob French."

The tip of Powell's tongue showed between his teeth for a moment. Then he leaned back, very carefully, as if he was afraid he would fall, and said, "God love us!" in a horrified voice.

"You know where we can find Jessup?" Doc Savage asked.

Powell shook his head slowly. "The man told me he was leaving town, checking out of his hotel. He said he was going to the Coast to see what luck he would have selling his radios."

"Was it after Bob French visited you that Jessup said he was leaving town?"

"Yes, it was." Powell shuddered.

# V

The warehouse was far downtown on the East River, not far from where the South American shipping lines had their docks. It was not a beautiful neighborhood. The wind brought some of the smell from Fulton Fish Market. There was a name, *Powell Export,* over the entrance.

"I use this place for storage," Powell explained. "There are occasions when I have a chance to buy up a good deal of radio equipment at bargain prices, and I need a place to store it. This is a particularly opportune time for that, with the war near its end and the army and navy contracts being cancelled."

He unlocked the door and went inside.

There was some out-of-date radio equipment standing around. Old battery sets. Some newer stuff, but none of recent manufacture.

"Some of my bad investments," Powell said wryly. "The French case is back here."

The case was about three by four by four feet.

Renny was surprised by the heaviness of its construction.

"Looks like a machinery case," he said. "Look at that iron reenforcing."

"There's nothing but snake hides inside," Powell said. "The customs men opened it in my presence."

"Suppose we open it," Doc suggested.

Powell was agreeable. "There is a pinch bar and a wrench somewhere around." He went hunting the items, found them, and they started on the case lid fastenings.

"What kinda snake hides are these supposed to be?" Renny asked. "Something for a museum?"

"Oh, no. They're commercial," Powell explained. "There are several varieties, but most of them are anacondas. You know what anacondas are—anyone who has been to South America does. Sometimes they're called boa constrictors, but they're not true boas. You hear wild native stories down there about anacondas fifty feet long that can swallow a full-grown bull. However, I think they only get to be about thirty feet long, and not very often that."

"What're the hides used for?"

"Women's shoes, purses, or whatever is made out of snake-skin. I think they're sold by the pound, much as any other hides, although I'm not sure."

Renny asked, "Is that part of Tucker French's business, marketing snake hides?"

"So I understood."

They got the lid off finally. It was bolted, not nailed, and as Renny had remarked, it was heavy.

The hides were heavy also, most of them salted. It was a messy job as they unrolled each skin, and inspected it.

They finished the job, then looked at each other foolishly.

"Blank," Renny said. "They're just snake hides, as far as I can tell. What do you say, Doc?"

Doc eyed the hides with no approval. "They seem to be snake hides," he said, with no attempt to be funny. "We'll look at the box itself, then put them back."

Renny climbed onto the edge of the box. He gave it several whacks with the pinch bar, said, "It sounds solid enough. I'll take a look at the bottom."

He jumped to the floor, grasped the box and heaved. Nothing happened.

"Holy cow!" he said.

Doc Savage frowned suddenly. "What's wrong?"

"The dang box weighs a ton," Renny said. "How about you helping me turn it over."

"You should be able to handle a box that size."

"I must be getting weak in the push. Give me a hand," Renny said.

Doc joined him. Together, they heaved at the box. With no result.

Renny, exasperated, said, "The danged thing must be nailed to the floor."

Doc turned to Powell. "You notice this thing being particularly heavy before?"

Powell hesitated. "Well, not—yes, I did. You understand, I haven't handled the thing myself. But it broke the sling when they were loading it off the lighter on to the steamer at Cartagena. But I just supposed that green hides were very heavy."

"No box," Doc said, "should be this heavy."

Powell showed sudden emotion. "You mean the box has a double bottom or something?"

Doc scooped up the pinch bar. "We'll soon find out." He went to work overturning the case.

It became ridiculous. The pinch bar split the flooring, but finally he did get the case pried up about two inches. Renny had found an iron pipe, which he rammed under the case. They pried and grunted and heaved and finally got the box up on its side.

"I'll be danged!" Renny said sheepishly. "Did you ever see the equal of that?"

"How do you account for the empty box being so heavy?" Powell asked.

"The thing's got to have a false bottom," Renny told him. "I'll see in a minute."

The big-fisted engineer, with the end of his gas pipe, gave the box bottom a wallop. The solid sound he got obviously astonished him. He scowled, growled, "Gimme that pinch bar," and went to work.

By the time he had pried a board off the bottom of the case, his long face had a foolish expression.

The case bottom was obviously solid.

"God bless us, what kinda wood is that?" he blurted. He produced a pocket knife and took shavings off different parts of the case.

"Well?" Doc asked.

"Oak," Renny said. "Plain oak."

"An oak box should not be that heavy."

"You're telling me!" Renny picked up the pinch bar again.

"What are you going to do?" Powell demanded.

"I'm going to take this thing to pieces a board at a time," Renny said.

"That seems foolish to me," Powell said. "You can see it's an oak box."

Renny's voice was becoming a rumble, the way it did when he was excited. "Brother, this box weighs three tons if it weighs an ounce. I'm an engineer and I know it's an impossibility for it to weigh that. I want to know why."

Renny began beating at the stout oak planks.

Powell looked contemptuous of the whole thing. He said, "This is getting childish. Here, I'll find you an axe and you can split the boards."

He went away and came back with a fire axe that was sharp.

Renny took the axe. It was large, heavy, made for the sort of thing he wanted it for. He came down on the oaken planks, one after another, splitting them. He split the right side, first, then the left side, then the bottom, which was uppermost. The planks split readily enough. They were, after all, just wood.

Disgusted, puzzled, Renny lowered the fire axe, and rested. The back of the box was unhandy to get at, and after he swung at it a couple of times, he gave the box an angry shove.

The box skidded across the floor.

Renny's eyes popped.

He seized the case and turned it over without much trouble.

"Holy cow!" he blurted.

Doc Savage himself grasped the box. He found that now he could lift it entirely without difficulty, whereas a few moments ago he couldn't have gotten it a quarter of an inch off the floor without leverage. It had taken the utmost strength of Renny and himself combined, exerted on levers and the pinch bar, to lift the case at all. Renny might have exaggerated slightly when he said it weighed three tons, but he could not have been far off.

Three tons was about what thirty heavy men would weigh. At least three tons was thirty times two hundred pounds. Now the box didn't weigh as much as one two-hundred-pound man.

"It's impossible!" Renny rumbled.

Doc turned the box over two or three times more. He made, for a moment, a small trilling noise. It meant the same thing as a whistle of astonishment.

There was some salt on the floor, salt from the snake skins which had stuck to the inside of the box and been dislodged by Renny's pounding. Mixed with the dirty salt were snake skin scales, dirt and small litter.

Doc raked the fire axe through the salt and litter, but it was immediately evident there was nothing of any size in it.

Powell suddenly giggled. It sounded hysterical. "What do you expect a couple of handfuls of salt to weigh, three tons?"

Doc straightened. He felt foolish, and he was angry with himself for being so completely baffled.

He said, "A moment ago, that box weighed as much as a heavy truck. Now it weighs less than I do. How do you account for that?"

Powell tittered wildly. "Maybe there was a three-ton mouse in it."

Doc said violently, "Don't be a fool!"

The silly merriment slid off Powell's face, which became strained. "Will you name one reason why I should stand around and tolerate being called a fool?" he demanded.

Doc got hold of himself. He had lost his temper because he was baffled and confused. He became ashamed of having done so.

"Calling you a fool was uncalled for, and I apologize," he said.

Powell was mollified. "It was my fault. What just happened to that box is so unbelievable that my first impulse was to laugh at it. What do you think made it suddenly lose its weight?"

"I have no idea," Doc told him. "But we are going to find out."

"Well, if I can do anything to help, tell me," Powell said.

A new voice said to them, "Help is what you're going to need —if you make one jittery move!"

The voice was in the warehouse. But where? Doc turned slowly, searching.

"Stand still, damn you!" the voice warned.

Doc froze.

The voice said, "Now turn your head to the right. See it?"

It was a rifle muzzle projecting from a large packing case that looked fragile. The rifle snout waggled to get their attention.

The voice added, "You've probably got guns. All right, don't use them. I've got brick stacked up inside here, and unless you hit this crack first shot, I'll kill you all!"

No one said anything.

There was a stir inside the box. A brick sailed out over the top and hit the floor.

"See, bricks," the voice said. "Now, turn your backs to me."

They turned their backs.

"Okay," the voice said. "Now drop your guns on the floor and kick them off to one side."

Renny carefully produced a pistol from an underarm holster. It was a spike-nosed weapon which would take either a clip or a ram-horn magazine and would fire either single shot or fully automatic.

"All right, Savage!" the voice said.

"I do not carry a gun," Doc said.

"Powell!"

"I am unarmed," Powell said shakily.

There was a silence. The hidden man appeared to be debating the truth of their statements. He cleared his throat noisly.

"Buck, I guess it's safe to come out and frisk them," he said.

Buck proved to be a heavy man with a large courtplaster strip across his nose. The adhesive, about an inch and a half wide, placed diagonally, had been put on so that it pulled the upper part of his face out of shape on one side and the lower part out of shape on the other. It was probably as effective a disguise as a mask, and certainly more efficient.

Buck searched them. He did it as if they were red hot, and he seemed to grit his teeth each time he touched them. He was scared.

Renny asked him sourly, "What would you do if I jumped and said boo!"

Without a word, Buck whipped out a blackjack and laid it against the side of Renny's head, hard. Renny fell, going down in sections, making a heavy noise on the floor. He landed with his face in the salt that had been knocked from the packing case when they were working on it, and hardly moved afterward.

Doc, the violence in his voice poorly controlled, said, "That wasn't necessary."

"Guys who get funny make me nervous," Buck said. "They ain't scared, and when they ain't scared they're liable to do anything."

"I can assure you that I'm scared," Doc said.

"Then get your hands behind you. Both you birds."

They were working to a plan, because Buck had lengths of rope in his pockets, already cut to the length for tying wrists and ankles.

Buck tied them. He knew his knots. He used a highwayman's hitch on their wrists, then made them lie down, carried the rope up around their necks, gave it a twist, carried it down and doubled their legs back and did another highwayman's hitch around their ankles.

It was a vicious tie. If they struggled, they would strangle themselves.

Buck tied Renny.

Then he gagged them all. He had the materials for that, too. Adhesive tape and three large sponges, for stuffing in their mouths.

The man in the box—he was still in the box—said, "If I was you, Buck, I'd scatter them out around the place. Otherwise they might get together and untie each other in a hurry."

Buck said, "Yeah, that's a good idea."

He hauled Renny off to the back of the building, dragged Doc around to the side, and hauled Powell forward and dumped him behind a pile of boxes.

Of the three, Doc was the only one left where he could watch what went on.

The man in the box came out. He was stocky and dark-skinned, as if recently from a climate of heavy sunshine. He had a thin wire of a scar on his chin and a thick cluster of pocks on the left side of the neck.

"Get the jug," he said.

The jug was a glass one, gallon size. It was full of yellowish liquid. The skull-and-crossbones label said sulphuric acid.

The other man dug out a package, and from a spot in the corner of the wareroom took a large pottery crock. He dumped the contents of his package into the crock. Doc knew immediately what it must be—some form of yellow prussiate of potash.

"Dump in the stuff in the jug," the heavy man said.

There was quite a chemical commotion in the crock, which was understandable. The fumes which arose had no great amount of color.

The two men got out in a hurry. There were no words of parting.

They slammed the door and locked it.

Doc stared at the crock. He tried the binding on his wrists. Tight. Very tight. And the sponge in his mouth, taped there, was an effective gag. The chances of making enough noise to bring help from the street were not worth mentioning.

Shots, of course, would have been heard on the street. That was why there hadn't been any shooting. That was why they were being killed this way.

Doc Savage closed his eyes tightly, trying to shut out the vision of poisoning by vapor of hydrocyanic. It would be quick. One breath usually brought oppression and suffering at the temples and the nape of the neck. The eyes grew cloudy, and it would be almost impossible to keep from throwing the head back. In a moment would come vertigo, then prostration, that awful hypertension in the head, the ghastly stiffening of the body, the legs stretched and flexed and the arms flexed and the fingers splayed. Then respiration would cease.

First there would be the odor, of course. The odor of bitter almonds, the scent a peach seed has.

Quick. He remembered, dry-mouthed, the medical aspects of the stuff which he had studied. It acted directly on the nerves, the only objective lesion being a spasm of the respiratory system, the lungs contracting in the lower thoracic cavity would become blood-tinged and—on autopsy—the veins would stand out as clearly as if filled with the brightest red ink.

The bronchial tubes would be affected, too; an autopsy would show them constricted and almost entirely closed.

All of this in a minute or so. Unconsciousness first, and then a stiffness, and then one gigantic awful wrenching inspiration of breath, and then death.

But first the odor of almonds. And he thought he could catch it now.

## VI

The old cop who had charge of laundry marks didn't like being called back to the office after hours.

"You might at least get around here during the day," he said.

Monk laughed at him. "Don't tell me the police never have a laundry mark looked up except between eight and four."

The old man snorted. He took the half of Bob French's blouse from Monk, but before he would do anything about it, he insisted on filling out a lengthy form. "Name?" he growled.

"Monk Mayfair," Monk said.

"That's not your full name."

"Lieutenant Colonel Andrew Blodgett Mayfair," Monk said wearily. "Height five foot four, weight two hundred, occupation chemist, avocation chasing excitement with Doc Savage, favorite hobby blondes preferably over twenty-one—"

"You're as funny as a crutch," the old man said.

He finished filling in the blanks, had Monk sign, then went away with the blouse half.

He was hardly out of sight, it seemed to Monk, before he was back again.

"Bouse was last cleaned or washed by the Univex Laundry, in Jackson Heights," he said.

"Great grief, did you have the information in your hat?" Monk gasped.

The ancient sneered at him. "It's done by television."

Properly impressed and amused, Monk left the police station and got in his car. The car was eye-filling. It was a second-hand job which had belonged to a Balkan dictator who had been chased out of his country by another dictator. The car, a special job from end to end, was but slightly less a spectacle than a Grand Canyon sunset.

In many ways, the car was Monk. It was loud, spectacular, in not too good taste, and unless one liked ultra-modernism, it was as ugly as a sore thumb on an angel. Monk was like that. And he was homely. His looks were something to scare the socks off babies, except that there was a certain gleeful pleasantness about him. The car was efficient; the very best metals and the very finest workmanship were in it. The same with Monk. He was one of the world's best industrial chemists, when he worked at it. His difficulty was not working at it often enough. He liked excitement, and preferred chasing it as a member of Doc Savage's group of five aids to working at his profession. As a result, his habitual financial condition was one to interest the sheriff and the wolf. It certainly wasn't something to interest the incendiary blondes Monk spent his spare time pursuing.

He crossed Queensborough bridge to Roosevelt Boulevard and Jackson Heights. The Univex Laundry was closed. He spent an hour finding the office manager of the laundry and dragging him away from a dinner party.

The laundry was efficient enough to keep a record of their work.

"The blouse was done for a soldier named Robert French," the laundry man said. "Here's the address." He wrote the address out. It was a little farther out in Jackson Heights.

It was a cottage, a private home. There weren't many of those in Jackson Heights which was an apartment house and duplex home development. But this was out toward Flushing, a part of a block where there were small houses. This was a frame house. Frame houses were scarcer than just plain houses.

Monk drove past and looked over the place. The lawn was cut, but he could tell from other signs that the house hadn't been lived in for a long time. The shrubs, for instance, had grown wild and untrimmed. And the place needed painting. It had that look that houses get when they aren't lived in.

Monk wondered if he'd drawn a blank. Wondered if Bob French had given a phony address.

At the corner was a neighborhood drugstore. It was the kind of a drugstore that had pinball machines and a soda fountain and tables on the sidewalk for the customers. A neighborhood loafing place. He parked in front.

Monk went in and asked a middle-aged man with an apron, "Know anybody around here by the name of Bob French? I've got the wrong address, or something."

"Fifth house from the corner, this side of the street," the man said, naming the address Monk had.

"Swell," Monk said enthusiastically. "Now, if he's just home."

"Bob's living there, anyway," the man said. "Just got back from the war. Been in China, where it's tough. Got his hat full of medals. I was talking to him the other day."

"You sound like an old family friend," Monk said.

"I am."

"Where's the brother, Tucker, now?" Monk asked.

The man frowned, hesitated, then said, "I didn't ask."

Monk thought: Why didn't you ask? You're an old family friend. There was something here.

"Tucker been gone quite a while, hasn't he?" Monk said, fishing for more information.

The man said, "I don't know anything about Tucker. If you're from the draft board, I still don't know anything about him."

Monk got it then.

"Draft evader, eh?" he said.

The man tightened up. "I wouldn't know."

Monk laughed and said, "That Bob is a great guy. He's done enough fighting for the whole family. Buddy of mine was with him in China, place called Yung-shun. They built an air field there, and I guess they had themselves a time on the side. I hope Bob is at home. Don't want to miss him."

"Saw Bob around this morning," the man said.

"Any of the rest of the family at home with Bob?" Monk asked.

"Mother and father are dead, didn't you know that?"

"Never heard it," Monk said.

"Car accident two years ago. Tucker was the kid of the family. Just the two boys, Tucker and Bob. House has been closed while they were away. Don't know of any other relatives, so I guess nobody is there with Bob."

"Thanks," Monk said.

He intended to leave then, but didn't. He changed his mind when he saw how the man was looking at him, weighing him.

The man seemed to decide he liked Monk. He leaned over the counter and lowered his voice. "This friend of yours who was with Bob in China. What was his name?"

"Renwick," Monk said. "Renny Renwick."

The man nodded. "Why, sure, Bob was talking about him. Laughing about the time they'd had in China."

"They had the time, I guess," Monk said.

The man dropped his voice even lower. "What I wanted to ask you about—there was a girl in here a little while ago. Asked where Bob French lived. She was a damned good-looking girl, and so I told her where Bob lived, then I wished I hadn't."

"What made you wish you hadn't?"

The man pointed. "You see the black coupe parked yonder?"

Monk said he saw the car.

"She didn't go to Bob's house. She's sitting in that car, watching the house. Kind of a funny way to do."

Monk chuckled and said, "Maybe a disappointed girl friend. I better warn old Bob."

"She ain't no disappointed girlfriend," the man said. "Not her."

"What makes you think so?"

"Nobody would disappoint her," the man said. "You walk past and take a look and you'll see."

Monk had a way with women. Sometimes it got him a poke in the eye, but frequently it didn't. His method included everything but tact.

Monk opened the door of the black coupe and got in.

"Has he come out of the house yet?" he asked.

The girl didn't quite tear the other door of the car off getting out, but it was only because the door flew open instantly.

She looked back into the car at Monk, much as one would look through the zoo bars at a jackal. She didn't say anything.

It was Monk's theory that all women liked to hear you say that they were beautiful. He said, "You're the loveliest thing I've seen, as lovely as the flowers in the valley of Kashmir, which are supposed to be the most glorious sight that man's eyes—oh, brother!"

What ended his speech was the fact that she was more beautiful than he was saying she was.

"Time out while I learn to breathe again," he said weakly.

"Must you?" she asked coldly.

"Now, now, let's keep the conversation in a warm climate," Monk said. "I chill easily. Anyway, you should only look like that at Hitler and Hirohito. Also at all other guys."

She examined him. Apparently she found nothing of which she approved.

"Just who do you think you are?" she demanded.

"Not the same man I was a moment ago," Monk said, grinning. "Rest assured of that, and I doubt if I'll *ever* be the same."

She continued to scrutinize him distastefully.

"What was it you said when you got in the car?" she asked.

"I asked you if Bob French had come out of his house yet," Monk said. "But already I can think of much better subjects to talk about. Your eyes, for instance. And our plans for the next few years. Oh, boy! Some of the things I've got to talk about may have been talked about before, but I'll bet you I can give them a new—"

She astonished him by getting back in the car.

"First things first," she said. "What about Bob French?"

"Really, must we—"

"Is he a friend of yours?"

"I don't know yet, and anyway—"

"Why not?"

"Why not what?"

"This isn't getting us anywhere," the girl said. She took an object out of her purse. "Maybe this will."

The object from her purse was black, made of steel and had a remarkably large hole where the bullets could come out.

"Bless us! Do be careful with that!" Monk gasped.

"Can you drive a car?"

"No."

"You can learn on this one then," she said. "And don't be coy. I saw you drive past a while ago in that combination of a sunset and an earthquake on wheels."

"But I don't want to drive anywhere," Monk protested.

"You're not being asked for an opinion."

"I can't drive. Meeting a vision like you has been too much for me. Look, I'm shaking all over," Monk protested.

"You had better shake." She poked him in the ribs with the gun, rather emphatically. "There is nothing whatever wrong with this gun."

"You wouldn't shoot me!"

"Right in the edge of Jackson Heights, I would," she assured him. "Get going. Go around the block, and we'll pick up Bill."

## VII

Who the hell is Bill? Monk did fast thinking while he drove.

Bob French got into his thoughts, which he shouldn't have. Bob French, according to the version Monk had received from Doc Savage over the telephone, had come to Renny Renwick for aid. Bob French had told Renny that he, Renny, was the only one in New York whom he knew, which was why he'd come to Renny. This seemed to be shaping up as a darned lie.

Who was Bill?

"Your brother?" Monk asked hopefully.

"Who?"

"Bill."

"Watch where you're driving," the girl said. "You run into the curb and blow out one of my tires and I'll probably shoot you anyway."

Monk gave more attention to piloting her car. "This suspense is murdering me," he muttered.

They rounded the block and traveled a short distance and she said, "Pull over and stop."

Monk obeyed. A tall woman leaning against a light pole stepped on the cigarette she had been smoking and came toward them. The lamp post which had been propping her up, it occurred to Monk, commanded a view of the alley behind Bob French's house, and all rear exits to the French house. This could be a good reason for the woman being there.

Monk examined the woman from the lamp post. It was his candid opinion that there must be a carnival around and she was the lady performer who straightened horseshoes with her bare hands.

This female peered into the car at Monk. In a voice reminiscent of a bullfiddle, she said, "My goodness, I thought it was a bearskin rug you had picked up somewhere."

Her own wit apparently struck her as hilarious. Because she upset the whole neighborhood with laughter. Frightened sparrows flew out of trees.

Monk was somewhat hairy, but he didn't feel it called for that much noise.

"Go away, before you lose a friend," he told the thundering female.

"My, my, you've got a nice voice," the big girl said. "Like a frog after something had swallowed him."

Another laugh, and more sparrows flew out of the trees.

"Why didn't I say my prayers," Monk muttered.

The female turned to the beautiful vision and asked, "Who is he, Grace? What tree did you get him out of?"

"He got in the car with me, Bill," Grace said.

"What do you know! They never get in the car with me," Bill said.

Monk pointed at the roaring woman and asked, "Is this Bill?"

"Yes," Grace said.

"I'm not as relieved as I thought I'd be," Monk said dubiously. "Does she bite, too?"

The two girls held a conversation about Monk, but omitted him from participation.

Grace, the gorgeous one, said, "He got in the car and asked if Bob French had come out yet."

"He must be a friend of Bob French's," Bill said.

"I don't know," Grace said. "But at any rate, he's not a friend of ours."

"Who is he?"

Both girls now looked at Monk, and Bill thundered, "Who are you, handsome?"

Monk maintained a peeved silence.

Grace said, "He's a wolf. You should have heard the awful, corny line he pulled on me."

"That was before I got a good look at you and lost my voice," Monk said.

Bill whistled admiringly. "Say now, that wasn't bad. That wasn't bad at all. Maybe he's a higher grade of wolf than you thought he was."

Monk said nothing.

Bill told him, "I do hope you're a medium grade of wolf or better. Because I do some wolfing myself, if offered medium grade or better material."

"God save little Andrew Blodgett Mayfair," Monk mumbled.

"His name is Andy," Bill said. "Little Andypandy. Isn't that sweet?"

Why the hell did I ever get in this car, Monk wondered.

Grace was frowning at Monk. She hadn't at any time shifted the muzzle of her gun away from the most vulnerable part of Monk's anatomy.

"Bob French hasn't come back and I don't think he is going to," she told Bill.

"What makes you think he won't be back?" Bill asked.

"Because, I searched the house, and it looked as if he had closed up the place for quite a while. His army clothes were all gone, and the water was shut off. It looked as if he didn't plan to be back.

"What did the man in the drugstore know? You were going to talk to him."

"Nothing, Grace said. "He knew French, but he didn't know anything else that would help me. I think he became suspicious when I was questioning him, too. I think he told Andypandy that I was watching the house, too."

"Stop calling me that!" Monk pleaded. "My name's Monk Mayfair."

They ignored him.

"I think Bob French has gotten away from us," Grace said.

"Could be," said Bill.

Monk said, "Well, I wish I could say it has been pleasant meeting you." He opened the car door and prepared to get out.

"Where you going?" Grace demanded.

"Away," Monk said. "Away to reflect on the adversities of life. I may become a hermit."

"No, you don't," Bill said.

He swung out of the car.

Then he was back in the car. His midriff felt as if a blockbuster had landed there. He couldn't believe it was only Bill's right jab.

Bill got in the car beside him. The three of them made a tight fit. Bill held Monk's head tenderly. "He hurt his little tummy," she said.

Grace said, "If he tries to get out, swat him again."

She put the coupe in motion.

The lovely girl and the strong-armed character were going to take Monk to their office and have a talk with him. They discussed their plans quite freely. If Monk didn't wish to talk, they were going to get the words out of him anyway. Bill said she knew how. Monk didn't doubt it.

The two girls talked about someone called Benjy. Benjy was an old dear, they agreed, and he was supposed to be doing something for them and they hoped he had been successful. Monk gathered that Benjy was employed by them. He had been employed by them a long time. In fact, Monk rather gathered that old Benjy had been employed by the fathers of the two girls before their time.

The office proved to be on upper Lexington Avenue. It was located in an impressive office building.

It was now getting dark, after hours for office building traffic, and Monk wondered how they were going to get him inside. He couldn't see how they would do it, if he chose to try to prevent them.

It was simple.

Bill said, "Oh look, isn't that a beautiful girl going yonder."

The next thing Monk heard was Grace telling somebody, who proved to be the elevator operator on night duty in the office building, that, "It was something called slivowitz that did it. He got along fine as long as he stayed with gin, rum and bourbon, then he had to try slivowitz."

The elevator operator said he would help them get Monk into the office.

"You hit me again," Monk accused Bill, and Bill patted his shoulder comfortingly.

The elevator operator finished helping with Monk and went back to his work.

There was another man in the office. Benjy. He was a little taller than Monk and between forty and eighty years old, the doubt about his exact age being the result of innumerable wrinkles. He looked like a pleasant old geezer. The faithful old bookkeeper type.

Benjy was worried.

"I'm afraid I've done something awful," he said.

Bill was pleased. She said, "My God, Benjy, don't tell me you finally have a misdeed to your credit."

Benjy squirmed. It was not a light matter to him. He gave both girls a rebuking look. "I'm not at all sure we're doing the right thing, not at all sure."

"Skip the sermon, will you Benjy," the girl said.

Benjy became indignant.

"Listen to me, both of you!" he said seriously. "Your fathers, neither one of them, would approve of what you are doing, and you know it. I promised your father"—he pointed at Grace—"and I promised your father"—he pointed at the herculean Bill—"that I would look after you. That's exactly what I promised them."

The girls had a system on the old boy. They put their arms around him and patted his back and chucked him under the chin and told him he was fine, he was doing a wonderful job, they couldn't get along without him, and they loved him like everything. Old Benjy ate it up. If he'd had a tail, he would have wagged it so hard he would have fallen down.

"Now tell us what happened Benjy," Grace said.

"I followed that fellow, and he didn't see me," Benjy said.

"You mean the one who hung around trying to watch us?" Grace demanded.

"That's him, the short one with the scar on his chin and them pockmarks on his face," Benjy agreed. "Well, here's what happened. This fellow met another one. That one was heavier and meaner looking. The two of them went downtown to a warehouse marked Powell Export."

Bill puckered her lips and whistled. "Then they were working for Powell!"

"That's what I thought, but I think I was wrong," Benjy said. "Because they went in the warehouse and they hid. The back windows of the warehouse were boarded over, but there was a crack in the boards where I could see what went on. There was a shed over the crack, or rather a shed built on the back of the warehouse, and the window that had the crack between the boards was in that so I could—"

"You could watch," Bill said. "What did you see?"

"Well, these two fellows hid themselves in packing boxes in the shed. They waited. They waited three or four hours."

Monk was keeping very still. He was afraid, if he said anything that would draw attention to himself, that they would lock him up somewhere to get him away from the conversation.

Benjy continued, "Three men came. One was Sir Roger Powell. The other two I didn't know at the time, but I thought there was something familiar about one of them. Later, when I found out who they were, I could understand why that one looked familiar. Well, these three men had come to look—"

"What were their names?" Grace interrupted.

Old Benjy grinned at them coyly.

"You'll be surprised," he said. "These three men had come down to look at a box. It was a big, heavy box. It was a box which Sir Roger Powell had brought from South America for Tucker French."

This had an effect on the girls.

"Wow!" Bill said. "Wow! Oh, boy!"

Grace just gasped, but she could gasp very prettily.

Benjy was as proud of himself as Hitler was in 1940. "As soon as they began taking the snake hides out of this box, I knew what it was," he said.

"Snake hides!" Grace said, with another gasp.

"Sure. Them big boa constrictors they grow down in South America."

Bill frowned and demanded, "Where were these other two fellows all this time."

"They were hid, I told you that."

"Oh."

"They got the snake hides out, and then they tried to move the box," Benjy said. "They couldn't."

Both girls said, "Oh!" together. They said it as if they couldn't be more excited.

Monk didn't get it at all.

Benjy hooked his thumbs in the armholes of his vest, like a politician who had just been re-elected. "Wait until you hear the rest," he said. "It gets more exciting as it goes along. After the three men took out the snake hides, they couldn't lift the box. So they got suspicious. They got a fire ax and—"

"You mean," Grace demanded, "that they didn't know what was in the box?"

"Didn't seem to."

"Didn't Powell?"

"Acted as if he didn't."

"Oh, oh," Grace said.

Benjy said, "Well, they cut loose on the packing case with the ax, and chopped and chopped. They found out the case was ordinary wood. Then, all of a sudden, they found they could lift the case. That surprised 'em some."

Benjy paused, grinning.

Grace asked, "Was there loose salt? Were the snake hides packed in salt or something? And did it get scattered over the floor?"

"Sure."

"Then I know what happened," Grace said. "I know what happened to make the box lighter."

Monk wished he knew. The whole story sounded far-fetched to him. He suspected they might be telling a pack of lies in order to confuse him.

Grace asked, "Didn't they find out what made the case lighter?"

"No."

"They must have been pretty dumb."

"Oh, I wouldn't say that Doc Savage is so dumb," Benjy said.

Monk jumped straight up and yelled, "Doc Savage! Was Doc with Powell?"

Bill and Grace were dumfounded as well. For the next few seconds, everyone stared at everyone else, and Benjy teetered with his thumbs in his vest armholes.

Then Grace said, "Doc Savage—you mean that big bronze fellow who is such a mysterious figure when he is mentioned in the newspapers? The one who is so handsome?"

"That's him," Benjy said.

"And he's not so handsome," Monk said.

"What do *you* know about him?" Grace demanded.

"I've never been able to understand this effect Doc has on the wenches," Monk said gloomily. "He doesn't run after them, and in fact he's what you would call inaccessible goods. On the other hand, take me. I'm accessible, and I chase 'em. I don't savvy it."

Bill examined Monk and said, "Oh, I don't know. You sort of interest me, handsome."

Monk shivered.

Grace demanded of Benjy, "Is Doc Savage involved in this affair?"

"Yep." Benjy nodded vehemently. "Don't you want to hear the rest of the story—how they almost killed Doc Savage, his friend Renny Renwick, and Powell?"

# VIII

The remainder of Benjy's story got their close attention. It was worth it.

"Those two fellows hidden in the wareroom came out," Benjy related. "They had guns. They surprised Doc Savage, Renwick and Powell and tied them up. They gagged them, too. And then they did a bad thing."

Old Benjy faltered. He lost his thumbs-in-vest-armholes pride. He became an old man, a timid old man, who had been close to death, to murder.

He mumbled, "They had some kind of chemicals, something in a jug and something else. They put the stuff in the jug in a crock and put the other stuff in it, then they ran out and shut the door."

The old man shuddered.

"I could look at Doc Savage's face and I could see the stuff in the crock was going to kill him," he said.

"What did you do?" Grace asked.

Benjy shuddered. "I ran out of the shed. I ran around to the front of the warehouse. The two killers were there, waiting for the men inside to die, I guess. I yelled, 'Help! Police! Murder!' And the two men ran away. I scared 'em away."

Monk began breathing again. He believed old Benjy's story now. The old man wasn't that good an actor.

Benjy said, "I held my breath and ran into the warehouse. I figured the stuff in the crock was making gas. I got out my pocket knife. I keep it sharp. I cut Doc Savage and Renwick and Powell loose. Maybe I didn't save their lives, because Powell had his hands almost loose. Anyway, Doc Savage and Renwick and Powell ran out of the warehouse, chasing the other two fellows who had tried to kill them. They told me to run out of the warehouse, too, and I did."

Old Benjy winked foxily.

"After they were out of sight, I ran back in the place, though. I picked up the crock and carried it out and dumped it down a storm sewer grating in the street. I held my breath."

Benjy began to look pleased with himself again.

"I left the warehouse door open for the wind to blow in, and I went and got a hand truck and a crowbar. I borrowed the hand truck and crowbar from a place down the street that moves heavy machinery.

"I got what had fallen out of the packing case and was lying in the loose salt, kind of embedded in the floor where they hadn't seen it. I was lucky. I wheeled it down the street. It was almost more than I could manage to move. I sure got tired.

"Finally I hired a truck. I didn't know where to take it. Finally I took it to your apartment, put it on the freight elevator, and wheeled it into your front room. The building super at the place knew me, and let me in. I left it there, and came here."

Benjy let out a long breath.

"That's all there is to it," he finished.

The girls screamed, "Our apartment! Maybe it isn't safe there!" They started for the door.

"Wait for me!" Monk yelled.

They looked at Monk as if they'd forgotten him. Bill said, "Let's take him along. On the way, we may be able to find out who he is."

They didn't take the coupe this time. There were four of them —Benjy was going along—and there wasn't room in the small car. Benjy's car was parked near, so they took that. It was a sedan, one that had been built back during Hoover's administration.

"My feelings are hurt," Monk confided to them. "Or anyway my ego is."

"That's too bad," Grace said with almost no interest.

"My name is Monk Mayfair."

"So you mentioned."

"But haven't you heard of me?"

"Of course not," Grace said.

"Such is fame," Monk complained bitterly. "Anyway, I'll let you in on something. I'm a spear-carrier for Doc Savage."

Grace showed a disgusting amount of interest in this. "You work for Mr. Savage?"

"Uh-huh."

"Is he as handsome as his pictures?" Grace asked.

"Oh, hell!" Monk said, and he wouldn't answer another question.

The girls had an apartment in one of the fashionable buildings close to Radio City. To live there cost plenty. Monk knew, because he had been thrown out of one of the places—not this one, but one much like it—for being unable to pay his rent.

There was nowhere to park directly in front of the building, and they finally had to use the Radio City garage.

The girls hurried on ahead, and Monk and Benjy fell behind.

"They're so excited, aren't they?" Benjy said to Monk.

"Everybody is excited, including me," Monk told him. "What's the matter with that Grace, anyway. I don't get any office there at all. It was my idea that the prettiest girls fall for the homeliest guys."

"They're lovely girls, both of them," Benjy said. "I've known them since they were babies. Both their fathers joined the army, but they didn't do it until I promised them that I would look after the girls. I'm like a second father to them."

"That Bill," said Monk, "scares the socks off me."

"She likes you."

"That's what scares me." Monk frowned at the old fellow. "What's this all about, anyway?"

"It's a little secret the girls have," Benjy said firmly. "If they want you to know, they'll tell you."

The man they thought was dead was lying as if he had tried to crawl under the modernistic lamb-colored couch in the bright living-room. He had one arm and part of his face under the couch. There was considerable blood about.

It was a very gory mess and Bill further dramatized the scene by making a sound like a large mouse and fainting.

Monk looked around for a place to put her, complaining, "She weighs a ton."

Old Benjy levelled both arms at the man on the floor and cried, "A dead man! A dead man!"

Grace, much more practical, pointed at the floor two or three times, at different places each time, then turned to Benjy and demanded, "Benjy, is it gone? It's gone, isn't it?"

Benjy stopped ogling the man on the floor long enough to bleat, "Yes, it's gone."

Monk deposited the cumbersome Bill on the floor.

He didn't like the job, but he picked up the wrist of the man partly under the couch. He found pulse. It was evident that a fairly harmless bump on the head had made the man unconscious, and that the impressive gore was the result of a fist having hit the fellow's nose. Monk hauled him out from under the couch and turned him over.

"Bob French!" Grace cried, pointing at the man.

Monk agreed that it was Bob French, recalling the second-hand description of the soldiering French brother which he had received from Doc Savage.

Monk asked, "Is this your apartment?"

"Yes," Bill admitted.

"What," Monk demanded, "do you mean by having dead men around the place?"

This alarmed Bill sufficiently to give Monk some satisfaction. But Bill fooled him. She went to the door, examined the edge near the lock, and pointed. "See here," she said. "They drove something in between the door and the jamb, forcing the lock. You can see the marks."

"Who did it?" Monk asked.

"I have no idea."

Monk turned to Benjy. "Do you?"

Benjy was calm. He wasn't completely calm, but he was calm enough to surprise Monk. The old man was evidently at his best when the going got tight. It was a rare fine trait, and Monk's opinion of the old man climbed considerably.

"It might," Benjy said, "have been those two bad men who tried to kill Doc Savage, Renwick and Powell. They might have managed to trail me here."

"Thought you said they didn't."

"I didn't think they did. They might have. I don't know for sure."

Monk shook Bob French. "Maybe this guy will tell us if we can wake him up. Can you bring me a pan of ice cubes from your refrigerator?"

Monk's methods were direct. He unbuttoned Bob French's shirt and pushed the ice cubes inside, pan and all. French made some tittering noises, like a silly girl, and came out of it. Monk, in withdrawing the pan of ice cubes, had a slight accident and spilled the contents inside French's shirt, causing some excitement.

"Take it easy," Monk told French.

Bob French got himself organized. Apparently he didn't know

who Monk was. Monk was fairly sure French knew the girls, Grace and Bill. But the acquaintance didn't include old Benjy.

Monk said, "My name's Mayfair. Monk Mayfair."

This didn't click with French.

"Renny is a pal of mine," Monk said. "I'm one of Doc Savage's group of assistants."

Bob French moistened his lips. He was doubtful. "Are you kidding?"

Monk shrugged. "Suit yourself."

Bob French looked around the living-room of the apartment. He became visibly alarmed. "Did they get it?"

"Get what?" Monk asked.

French blinked owlishly. He decided not to confide in Monk. At least, he did not answer.

Old Benjy leaned over Bob French.

"Somebody got it," Benjy said. "Can you tell us who it was?"

"Renny?" French was looking at Monk. "You mean Renny Renwick, the engineer? You're a friend of his?"

"That's right," Monk assured him.

French grasped his shirt front and flapped it vaguely, fanning the wet cloth. He fished around inside and brought out an ice cube which he had missed. "What time is it?" he asked finally.

Monk pointed at the electric clock. It said a quarter until midnight.

Bob French became alarmed.

He said, "Three of them did it. They were watching this place."

Grace demanded, "What did they look like?" And then she described the two Benjy had followed, the pair who had tried to kill Doc Savage, Renny and Powell.

"No," French said. "No, that sounds like the two who were watching this place first."

"My God, who's watching who!" Monk complained. "This is getting confused."

French looked pained.

"All five of them work together. It's simple," he said. "When I first got here—" He hesitated, glancing at Monk. "You apparently know I went to ask Renny Renwick for help?"

"Yeah, I got a telephone call to that effect," Monk told him.

"Well, I was seized at Renny's office, but I escaped from—"

Monk's laugh was loud, bitter, skeptical. "French, are you going to tell us any truth at all?"

French looked uncomfortable.

"Doc figured out that nobody jumped you at Renny's office. You faked it," Monk added.

French's deeply tanned neck got darker. He shook his wet shirt some more. He got out a handkerchief and dabbed at the bloodstains on his chin.

Suddenly he said, "Okay, that was a phony. I was so scared I didn't know what to do, so I scrammed out."

Monk opened his mouth, then closed it. He'd been about to ask Bob French why he'd been terrified when he learned Doc Savage was going to be involved. That was what had happened.

But French was tough guy, he had just barely decided to talk to them at all, and calling him a liar would probably shut him up. Better let him go, Monk decided, and try to pick the truth out of whatever he had to say.

"Go ahead," Monk muttered.

Bob French scowled and spoke emphatically. He had some truth to tell now, Monk decided, and he wanted them to know that it was the truth.

"I didn't know what to do, but I knew where the girls lived, so I came here to see them," French said. "I was going to walk right in and talk to them. That was what I planned. But outside, down the street a ways, I happened to see a mug who looked familiar. He hadn't seen me, so I kept out of his sight. I looked him over, and pretty soon I realized I had seen him three or four times the last couple of days. You know what that meant?"

"He'd been following you?" Monk suggested.

"That's right. Part of the push that was following me around before they tried to put that knife into me."

"Then what'd you do?"

"I camped around. This guy had some pals. Four of them. They were hanging around with their eyes big. Watching the apartment."

French indicated Benjy. "Pretty soon this old gaffer slipped out and followed two of them off. He did a pretty slick job. I almost didn't catch him doing it. I stayed here and watched the other three. I was here about four hours. Then this old fellow came back, wheeling something on one of those heavy hand trucks. He took it in the apartment house. The three guys watched him. Pretty soon the old fellow came out and left."

Benjy looked sick. "The three men saw me?"

"Yep."

Benjy's shame was pitiful. He had been stupid, and he was bitterly discouraged with himself.

"Well, I could tell the three guys who had been lousing around were excited about what they'd seen the old fellow wheel in on the truck," Bob French said. "They were gonna come up to investigate, I guessed. So I decided to beat 'em to it."

French got up and essayed a step or two, then reached out quickly and grabbed a table for support. "Wow! My head sure whirls! Two of them were sapping me at once, the last I remember."

Frowning, Monk asked, "Didn't you leave out a little in between?"

"Oh, you mean how did I get in? Back way. I didn't lose any time. But, damn the luck, when I got up here, those guys were already here. They had one posted around a corner in the hall. While I had my ear to the keyhole, he came up behind, cut loose on me, and knocked me through the door into the apartment. Well, they swarmed over me with saps, and that's where I took a blackout."

He indicated the floor.

"The freight hand-truck was sitting right there, I remember."

Bill planted her hands on her hips angrily. "We're sunk! We don't know what to do next!"

Bob French grinned without much pleasure.

"I got a little climax," he said.

"What do you mean?"

"I woke up before the three guys left," French said. "I heard them talking. They're going to scram out for South America. They're going after my brother."

Monk asked suspiciously, "If you regained consciousness and overheard that, how come—"

"How come I was asleep again when you got here?" French grimaced. "They popped me one for the money before they left. It's a wonder they didn't mash my skull."

"You know where they're going in South America?"

"Better than that," French said, "I know where we may be able to head 'em off before they go."

Monk yelled, "Why wait until now to tell—"

"If you had my head, you'd know why!" French snarled dizzily. "But let's go."

He named an airport in New Jersey.

"Let's head for there," he said.

They decided riding down in the elevator that they would use Benjy's old sedan for the New Jersey trip. Benjy seemed confident it would hold together for the journey. Everyone else was dubious. They were arguing about it, striding down the sidewalk, when Bob French let out his yell.

His squawl was hair-lifting. It was about the most arresting sound Monk had ever heard. It was formed of words, not noise, and it was a practiced thing. It was a warning, one he'd used before.

While he was still making the sound, French had scooped up both Grace and Bill, one in the crook of either arm, and yanked them across the sidewalk and behind a parked car.

Monk realized by now what had alarmed French.

A black object, small and round, that had skipped across the sidewalk and under one of the cars.

A grenade? Bob French seemed to think it was. Monk reasoned that soldier Bob French had seen enough grenades to know what one was. So he grabbed for Benjy—Benjy wasn't there, though —and got going. Old Benjy didn't need urging. He was ahead of Monk.

They joined French and the two girls.

French yelled, "Grenade! Get going! Run!"

Monk had a second thought. He said, "I don't think that was a grenade."

French and the two girls were running. Old Benjy told Monk, "It was a hand grenade, brother."

Benjy joined the flight. If it was a grenade, there was no point in getting blown up to prove it, so Monk legged it after the others.

"It wasn't," Monk puffed.

"I know one when I see it," Benjy said. "I was in the other war."

They reached Benjy's car, which was fortunately pointed the way they were going. Benjy landed behind the wheel. The two girls, Bob French and Monk piled in the back. Monk, scrambling to get inside, yelled, "It hasn't gone off, so it wasn't any grenade."

"Sometimes they miss fire," French said.

Benjy was twisting and stamping on gadgets. The old car began moving.

French, on his knees on the rear seat, looked back through the window. He yelled, "Watch out! The guy's out on the sidewalk, ready to throw another!"

Monk raised up to look. He got a glimpse of a man standing on the sidewalk, whirling one arm above his head in what looked like a pitcher's windup. "Godamighty!" Monk croaked, and hauled the girls down on the floorboards.

The car took the first corner with a noise like canvas tearing. There was no grenade explosion.

"Decided he couldn't throw it that far," Bob French said. He looked at Monk. He was sweating. He said, "I vote for that airport. I don't want any part of guys with grenades. Not when I'm empty-handed."

"That's two of us," Monk agreed shakily.

"Three," old Benjy said. He settled down to his driving.

## IX

Renny Renwick was not normally a man of many cusswords.

But after the car carrying Monk, Grace, Bill and old Benjy vanished, Renny spoke for approximately two minutes without using a word that could be found in a dictionary.

Sir Roger Powell took it, but his face got gray with rage.

"No man has talked to me like that!" he said finally.

"I should do more than talk to you!" Renny yelled. "What the blue-blaze-coated edge of hell were you trying to do?"

"Get their attention after they came out of the apartment house!" Powell snapped.

"Why not just call to Monk?"

"I wanted to get their eye furtively. I thought someone might be watching. I didn't want to create a disturbance."

"No disturbance! Holy cow!"

"It didn't turn out like I expected," Powell muttered. "That Bob French is war-simple. He thought I had tossed a hand grenade and he went crazy."

"What did you toss?"

Powell went to the curbing, got down on hands and knees and fished something out from under an automobile parked there. He brought it back. "This," he said.

It was a wad of paper. Dark brown paper. Renny unrolled it. The wrappers off a couple of candy bars, loosely wadded.

Powell explained, "We haven't had a chance to eat dinner, as you well know. So I bought a couple of large candy bars to fill in. These are the wrappers."

Doc Savage arrived. He had been farther up the block, parking their car.

"What caused the uproar?" Doc asked.

Renny explained the mishap, omitting the cussing. "I wasn't close enough to get Monk's attention," he said. "That ball of paper looked like a grenade to Bob French, I suppose, and he started a stampede."

Powell said, "What kind of a fool would think a grenade would be thrown at him on a New York street!"

"Look, Bob French is a soldier and he's been where it's hot. Where he's been, any unexpected thing the size and color of that wad of candy-wrapper could be a grenade," Renny said. "I know. I was in China with him for a while."

"I didn't intend to frighten him."

Renny complained, "Did you have to wave your arm like you were getting ready to throw another one?"

"I was trying to get their attention." Powell pushed his jaw out wrathfully. "What's the matter? Can't anyone but you make mistakes?"

"Where have I made a mistake?" Renny rumbled. "Listen, brother, if you want—"

Doc Savage said, "Oh, stop it! A mistake is a mistake."

Powell said, "Yes, and a loud-mouthed fool is a loud-mouthed fool."

"Meaning me?" Renny asked ominously.

Powell examined Renny deliberately. He examined Renny's fists with the most care. He moistened his lips. "I don't think I could lick you," he said. "Anyway it would be foolish to try, wouldn't it? I mean, what would be the purpose?"

"You figure I'm a fool?"

Powell grinned slightly. "I figure we all probably feel like fools right now," he said. "You want an apology?"

Renny finally grinned himself. "Ah, not right now," he said.

Doc Savage said, "We might as well take up where we left off, now that you've stopped acting like kids."

They walked to the apartment house from which Monk and the others had come.

This, Doc reflected, is like getting all set for the ball game, and the other team not showing up. He was suddenly tired, hungry, baffled.

The most baffling thing was that box in the warehouse which had been so unbelievably heavy—and as unbelievably become light again. He wished that he had examined the thing more closely.

For the last three hours, they had been running their heads off. The progress they had made hadn't been easy. Luck had been with them, or they wouldn't have gotten as far as they had.

Luck had been with them when they discovered the trucking establishment where old Benjy had rented the hand truck. They'd been looking for the hand truck. Doc had found marks in the spilled salt, elsewhere on the warehouse floor—marks obviously made by a hand truck.

A hand truck had suggested something heavy to be moved, and that had started them hunting for a trucking concern that might have done the job. They had found it eventually. Old Benjy and his hand truck—and something remarkably heavy on the hand truck, in a small box—had been brought to this apartment house. One of the men with the truck knew the apartment number to which the box had been taken. He'd been impressed with the building, and remembered the apartment number because he supposed it was the living-place of some big shot.

When one looked back, their finding the apartment seemed simple and direct. But it had been hard work.

They got the apartment house superintendent because they wished to enter the apartment at least half-way legally. They noted the evidences of violence—the traces of the door being forced, and the bloodstains on the living-room rug.

Doc's quick search of the place turned up nothing of value. It was just a rather fine apartment occupied by two girls.

The apartment superintendent answered questions. Grace Blassett and Willa Morris were the occupants. Two fine girls. Very fine. Paid their rent on time. No wild parties.

The two girls operated the firm of Blassett and Morris. Their fathers had gone to war, enlisting in the army about a year previously, and the two girls had taken over the firm. Yes, the super had some idea of what sort of a firm Blassett and Morris was. They were purchasing specialists, industrial supply. If you had a factory, for instance, and needed a special machine, a supply of steel, or any hard-to-get raw material, you employed Blassett and Morris. They went out and bought it for you at the lowest possible price.

Sir Roger Powell listened to this. He smiled thinly, and got out his cloth sack of tobacco and papers and made a limp cigarette.

Doc said, "We might as well go back to headquarters. Monk will contact us as soon as he can, and he will call us there."

They rode back in Doc's car.

"All right," Doc said to Powell. "What about Blassett and Morris?"

"Eh?"

"You mentioned them before," Doc said.

Powell contemplated Doc and Renny. Powell still looked well-tailored, neat, although his pinstripe suit and white shirt were a mess. It was the man's manner which gave him that prim quality. He had combed his black hair and given his moustache a twisting with his fingers, getting it back in shape. The hand-made cigarettes still seemed incongruous for him.

"Oh, yes," Powell said finally. "When Tucker French in South America gave me the mysteriously heavy box of snake skins to bring to New York, I was to get in touch with the firm of Blassett and Morris. That's what I told you."

"Was it the truth?"

Powell flushed. "Certainly."

"You said you contacted Blassett and Morris, didn't you?"

"I did. They didn't deal in snake skins. They didn't know Tucker French."

"How did you contact the firm?"

"Telephone. I talked to a woman. I presume one of the young ladies whose apartment we just left."

"Know anything more about them?"

Powell said violently, "Dammit, I wish I did."

They reached headquarters. There was no message from Monk. There was a gadget which would have recorded one, had Monk telephoned in. Doc liked gadgets, and he had developed this recorder affair, an automatic gimmick which told a caller, with a recorded voice, that no one was in the office, but that if the caller would speak his or her message, it would be put on record. The recording was done magnetically, on a wire.

They ordered up food from an all-night restaurant. While he was eating, Powell told them more about himself. He got to talking about his birthplace, which he said was Epping Forest, near London. The pleasant memories of his youth and early manhood there, he said, were good to have with him. He talked about the deer in the forest, the herons and the kingfishers and the many small songbirds. He understood, he said, that the Germans had bombed nearby High Beech, where Tennyson was living when he wrote "The Talking Oak" and "Locksley Hall."

Doc said, "High Beech is five miles south of Epping Forest, isn't it?"

Powell drew slowly on another hand-made cigarette. "That's about right."

Doc looked at Powell intently. "It wasn't when I was there."

Powell froze. He picked up his fork, then put it down again slowly. He muttered, "You've been there."

Doc nodded. "And you haven't."

Powell grimaced sheepishly. "Believe it or not, this is the first time I've been caught. Dammit, I should have remembered High Beech is part of Epping Forest. I've read enough about the place that I should have remembered that."

"Are you an Englishman at all?" Doc asked.

"No," Powell confessed.

Renny put down his own knife and fork. He stared at Powell, then at Doc. "Is this important?"

"I don't see why it should be important!" Powell said instantly. "I've been telling that lie for years. If you want to know the truth, I was born on the wrong side of the tracks in Kirksville, Missouri. My name is Roger Powell, all right. I put the Sir on to it back in the days after the other war, when titles were all the rage. It helped me, so I kept on doing it."

No one said anything. Powell sat there looking sulkily at his plate. He didn't seem ashamed particularly. Just disgusted that they had found him out.

The telephone rang. The outside wire.

Monk.

"Santa Isabel," Monk said. "It's on the Rio Negro River, Brazil. Back in the godforsaken jungle. You can find it on the map."

"All right," Doc said. "What about it?"

"Get down there," Monk said. "That's where I'm going."

"Why?"

"That's where everybody we're chasing seems to be headed. Listen, I can't give details. Just get down there. I'll leave a message at the biggest store in town, if I get there first. Okay?"

"If you know what you're doing," Doc agreed.

"I hope I do."

"All right."

"And, Doc, will you talk to a guy here. I'm renting a six-place plane from him. You know me, always broke. I want you to tell him you'll pay for it. And hold your hat. He wants plenty for rental."

"We have planes of our own," Doc said.

"No time to get one."

"Put the man on," Doc said.

The man wasn't particularly suspicious. He just wanted to be sure he got his money. He was trying to overcharge, and they had an argument about that, but came to terms. By this time it developed that Monk had gone. He had taken off in the rented plane.

"Just what happened out there?" Doc demanded.

The man—he was the operator at an airport about forty miles out in New Jersey—talked freely. He was somewhat alarmed, and wondering if he shouldn't make a report to the CAA or the Army.

Four days ago, a two-motored plane had arrived at his field and been hangared there, which was not unusual. About half an hour ago, several men, he didn't know exactly how many, had arrived in a hurry and piled into the plane and taken off. They had signed out for Miami.

"Did they load anything heavy into the plane?" Doc asked.

No, they hadn't, the man said. He added, "But during the four days the ship was hangared here, one of the men brought out stuff in boxes or suitcases at various times and put it in the plane."

"Are they gone?"

"They're taking off. So is the ship your friend rented from me. What shall I do about this? Is there something wrong?"

"Give me the NC numbers of both planes," Doc said. "And their types, cruising range, and radio equipment, if you have it."

"Sure, I've got that. Wait'll I get the register." The man soon supplied the information. He asked again, "What'll I do?"

"Let us handle it," Doc said.

He hung up.

Renny had cut in an amplifier-speaker gadget on the telephone, so that he and Powell had heard both ends of the conversation.

"South America!" Powell blurted. "This is fantastic!"

"Know anything about Santa Isabel, in Brazil, where they're going?" Doc asked.

Powell nodded. "I've been there. It's not too bad. But the country around there is really something. It's probably the least-known stretch of country left on the face of the earth."

Doc nodded, watching Powell. Whatever the trail Monk was following, it must be hot and important. Monk was no fool. So Doc intended to go to South America. He intended also to take

Powell, because Powell was part of the queer affair. It would be simpler if Powell agreed to go willingly.

"Going along?" Doc asked.

"You're damned right!" Powell said instantly. "And if you wonder why, I'll tell you. It's because two attempts have been made to murder me, and I'm mad."

"That's reason enough," Doc said, glad there was not going to be an argument over Powell's going. He added, "Say, I made a dumb mistake. I didn't ask who went with Monk in the rented plane."

He called the New Jersey airport operator again.

Five people had left in the plane, including Monk. The operator described the other four. The descriptions fitted Grace Blassett, Willa Morris, old Benjy and Bob French.

Doc told Renny, "Let's get some equipment ready in a hurry. Jungle stuff. Quinine, insect repellent, machetes, weapons, some trade stuff for natives. We'd better work fast."

Powell was getting doubtful. "My God, that's thousands of miles down there. How do we know we'll find anything when we get there?"

"We'll keep track of those two planes," Doc said.

"How on earth can you do that?"

"The Army and Navy interceptor network," Doc said dryly, "has a setup which they think can track a mallard duck from Cuba to Canada."

"Will they cooperate?"

"We'll see. I'll do some telephoning while you and Renny get equipment together."

The Army and Navy would cooperate. It took some telephoning to Washington to get it done.

Powell was impressed. He told Renny. "You fellows get things done."

Renny said sourly, "It sure looks it, don't it? Here we are busting our necks to get to South America, and we haven't the least idea why."

"How," Powell asked, "do you suppose Monk Mayfair found out that we should go to Santa Isabel?"

"I wish I knew," Renny said.

# X

They began the southward flight. Renny flew. Doc began fishing with the radio, prowling the wavelengths which Monk might use to call him.

Finally he got Monk. Monk spoke Mayan, an almost unknown dialect, as far as the civilized world was concerned, which Doc and the others had learned in Central America a long time ago.

Monk said his plane had a standardized wavelength radio transmitter. He didn't dare use it much. But he could receive on any of the aeronautical frequencies. Would Doc use two hundred eighty-five, a little above the standard control tower frequency, and keep him posted about the whereabouts of the plane they were trailing? He said he presumed that Doc had the Army and Navy interceptor service at work tracing the ship.

Doc said he would.

After that, they got half-hour reports from the Army in code. Renny had brought one of the little portable decoders used by the military. He made the settings, and keyed off the translations.

Powell was skeptical.

"They won't be able to keep track of the plane," he said.

"Watch them," Renny told him.

"What makes you so damned sure?"

With some indignation and pride, Renny said, "I helped the Army and Navy set up their interceptor alarm system. It was primarily an engineering job in communications."

Powell raised his eyebrows. "Didn't mean to hurt your feelings."

"You didn't," Renny rumbled. "Ignorance never does."

As the pair sat scowling at each other, Doc wondered if they were going to have a fight after all. But they took it out in unpleasant looks for the time being.

Doc relayed the army reports to Monk from time to time, speaking Mayan on the two-eight-five waveband. Monk's ship immediately dropped back about forty miles in order not to be sighted by the other ship. So Monk was receiving the information, although he wasn't acknowledging it for fear that the ship they were following would pick up his signal and recognize his voice.

"How long," Powell asked, "is this easy stuff going to last?"

"Until we get well across the northern coast of South America," Renny told him.

Powell whistled. Later he asked, "Where do you suppose they'll refuel?"

That had been bothering him, Monk said.

But the refueling turned out to be a simple matter. The ship simply doubled right a hundred miles, set down at a designated civilian field in Florida, took on a load of gasoline, signed out for Atlanta, Georgia—which was a lie—and took off. Ten minutes later Doc knew exactly how many gallons of gas and oil they had taken aboard.

Spotter reports showed the ship was heading out across the gulf stream.

Doc Savage refueled in Miami. His plane was an amphibian, two-motored, not particularly large, and not the fastest thing in the air. But it was stable, capable of long range, and with the flaps cracked, could set down in any field capable of handling a lightplane.

Powell expressed an interest in learning to fly. Renny killed time by letting him play with the duals, first switching on the auto pilot and not telling Powell about it, so that Powell thought he was handling the ship. Renny thought it was very funny. But Powell eventually became suspicious, and they came near having another fight.

It was monotonous.

Doc Savage finally talked a little about himself. It was the first time Renny had heard him do that.

Doc talked about the strangeness of his early life, the different outlook it had given him. He said that he had never known just what had happened to his father to cause him to put his small son, Doc, in the hands of scientists for training. It was a weird upbringing, aimed entirely at making Doc into a combination of mental marvel and physical giant—if science could do it. The elder Savage had not lived to see the final outcome of his plans for the boy.

"It was effective, but probably not as effective as he hoped," Doc said slowly. "Looking back on the fantastic business, I feel lucky as anything, because it seems to me that what I got was a psychological course guaranteed to make a freak." The bronze man grinned slightly. "I find myself doing, or on the verge of doing, many queer things as a result of the training."

He fell silent, then started again and explained that what he had missed most was a normal youth, the thrills and the heartbreaks and the excitement of devilment, which boys have. He had not missed these at the time he was not getting them, because he hadn't known about them, but he missed them now.

He frequently suspected that being a juvenile was something a man had to work out of his system, like getting rid of his baby teeth, he said. He still had the kid stuff in him. He'd never had a chance to work it off. As a result, he spent his time chasing excitement now, whereas if his youth had been a normal one, his adult life would have been normal. In other words, he would now be a young settled family man with a wife who dragged him out to bridge parties.

Renny laughed at that. The idea of Doc being dragged out to bridge by a henpecking wife struck him as funny.

Doc shut up, made somewhat uncomfortable by the levity.

"We all look back," Powell said, "and wish that our lives had been different. I don't think there breathes a man who doesn't do that."

For four hours they flew above an overcast that ended at twelve thousand. Renny got busy with an astral sextant, the Maggie, and stuck his head up in the astro dome. He tinkered with the computer and chart.

"South American coast should be below," he said.

Doc nodded, pointed. Far ahead were snow-capped coastal Andean peaks, like muddy froth on the vast whiteness of the cloud floor.

"From here on, there'll be no spotter network to keep track of Monk and the plane we're following," Doc said. "The thing for us to do is refuel somewhere and head straight for the Rio Negros country."

Renny dug around in his navigation stuff.

"There's open weather at Fernando, on the Orinoco," he said. "According to my dope, we can get ninety octane gas there. That should do us for a round trip, in case we can't get gas in the Amazon headwater country."

"Give me a course and ETA for Fernando," Doc said.

Flying down out of the rather open mountain country into the Amazon basin was an experience that somehow discouraged talk. They were going into one of the most untouched places in the world.

Doc flew fairly low; there was no sense in flying high. There were no places to land, because now they were traversing the immense expanses of jungle where there were many small streams, but no rivers large enough to show through the overcoating of green growth.

The world was a green carpet, not smooth, but knobby and limitless. Certainly a drab thing to the eye. But when the plane flew low, the hobgóblin nature of the jungle was evident. Occasionally through the umbrella of foliage, they could see the undermass of the jungle, the fallen and decayed trunks everywhere, over and about them the thickets, the vines that draped from trees a hundred and fifty feet high, the incredible tangle of lianas everywhere, and the gaudy sick-bright colors of the flowers.

Renny knew something of this jungle country. He had been into it before. But for the sake of devilment, he pretended complete ignorance and got Powell talking.

Powell took the bait. He knew the jungle, and wanted to tell about it.

"The small blue birds you see occasionally in flocks are *uirapuru,* or charmer bird," Powell said. "They're called charmer birds because of their beautiful singing, and the weird effect it has on other birds. You'll see flocks of different kinds of birds being led through the forest, and the leader will be a charmer bird."

"No kidding!" Renny said.

Powell nodded. "Some of the natives make no-devil charms out of the charmer bird skins. Other natives buy them for very high prices, the price varying according to whether the charm is a woman charm or made for a man. It's very fascinating. But of course the funny thing is the way the charmer bird can lead all the other birds through the jungle."

"I'll be darned." Renny tried to keep a straight face.

Renny caught Doc's eye, and his glee cooled. Doc knew, of course, that Renny was almost as familiar with charmer birds as he was with blackbirds or sparrows.

"How about doing some navigating?" Doc asked Renny dryly.

Renny went back and prepared to get another astral fix. There was a foxing of cirrus clouds in front of the sun, and he decided to wait until they were out of the way.

He cut in the radio directional loop, intending to get a fix on one of the broadcasting stations at Caracas, Venezuela, and perhaps at Bogota, Colombia. As a matter of course, he had the receiver tuned to the frequency which Monk had last used to communicate with them. He changed to broadcast wavelength, and fished for the Bogota station, getting mostly static.

That Powell, Renny thought sourly, talks too much. Probably that's because he's a salesman. And he's got that damned superior way which high pressure salesmen get.

A shout from Doc Savage blew Renny out of his reverie.

"The loop!" Doc yelled. "Cut the loop in on Monk's frequency!"

Renny grew cold. He'd left Monk's wavelength unguarded, the first moment they'd done that since leaving New York. But Doc, with the other receiver tuned from the cockpit, had covered the wavelength when he'd noticed Renny fiddling with the loop.

"Hurry up!" Doc shouted.

Renny got the loop set tuned to Monk's frequency.

Monk's voice, weak, gorged with horror, was saying, "—I wasn't expecting the right one to turn out to be a crook." There was considerable garbled by static. Then Monk's voice saying, "—right-hand gear up through the wing, so we groundlooped. One motor is out of the mounts and the gasoline tank in that wing split over everything." More garbled, then, "—I'm pretending to be unconscious so I can talk. Hope you get a radio fix. The men are coming into the plane now. This was all rigged, I can see that. For God's sake, be careful. I think—" What he thought they didn't learn. That was the last of Monk's voice.

Renny sat there with both hands on the loop knob, afraid to take them off lest he disturb the pointer setting. Seventy-three degrees, he thought, ogling the pointer. Holy cow, I hope I really had the null before Monk got shut down.

He took his hands away from the pointer. He stumbled forward to the cockpit.

"What happened to Monk?" he gasped.

"Did you get a null?" Doc shouted.

"Seventy-three," Renny said "What went wrong?"

"Static," Doc said. "So much static we missed just what did go wrong. Monk's plane was forced down. Evidently one of the group in the plane caused it."

"Which one?"

"If Monk said, it was garbled by the static."

"Seventy-three," Renny said hoarsely. "The pointer was on seventy-three. The bearing has got to be that, or two-fifty-three degrees, which would be the opposite."

Doc considered for a moment. "We will try the two-fifty-three bearing."

He brought the plane around to correct for the mile or two they had covered since getting the bearing. He leaned back to look at Renny's loop, on the chance Renny had misread the dial. It said seventy-three degrees, after correction for deviation and variation.

"Break out equipment," Doc said. "It may not be long."

"Doc, you heard Monk's signal," Renny said. "Did it sound close?"

"Fairly close. Not over fifty miles," Doc said.

They could discern streams below, most of them black, as black as the Rio Negro into which they fed. Doc climbed the ship. He cut in the engine mufflers and reduced speed somewhat to decrease the prop roar.

"Use binoculars," Doc said. "If we can spot them from high enough that they don't see or hear us, we might come down in the sun and accomplish more."

Renny rumbled, "Who the devil do you suppose doublecrossed Monk?"

Powell scowled. "That Bob French fellow, probably. He struck me as a shifty sort."

"Nuts!" Renny said.

Renny was angered. He had been through a good deal of rough stuff with young Bob French in China, and he was inclined to trust French. Bob wasn't shifty, not in Renny's opinion.

Then suddenly his wrath froze. For an instant he thought: No man should ever get mad! Because his rage had almost caused him to miss Monk's plane.

"There!" he yelled at Doc. "About two hundred degrees, five miles away! Monk's plane!"

Doc put the big plane in a glide. He cut the switches. He didn't quite close the throttles. Powell's hair seemed to visibly stand on end.

"My God, you'll need motors to land!" he screamed.

Renny said, "They've got starters."

The sun was low. Not quite on the horizon. But there wasn't more than an hour of daylight left.

They came down to three thousand before they could tell much about Monk's plane.

It was Monk's plane, all right. They could distinguish the NC number on the upper wing panel.

"That's a landing field, isn't it?" Doc demanded suddenly.

The same idea had hit Renny. A landing field. Not a paved runway, but a fairly clear landing strip.

Monk's plane was piled up at the midway point of the runway.

A ground loop had obviously taken it to the left, and it was jammed among the small trees at the edge of the runway.

A figure appeared in the open, waving both arms.

"Who's that?" Powell demanded.

Doc said he couldn't tell. "We've been seen, so we might as well start the motors," he added.

Shutting plane motors off in the air, then getting them going again with the electric starters was always ticklish business. The starters wailed, and the props went over jerkily. Then the stacks coughed blue smoke, the engines got going and Doc resumed breathing.

Doc said, "Keep your eyes open for funny stuff."

He sent the ship down in a spiral, watching the ground.

Powell muttered, "A runway! The way this jungle grows, it would take a young army to keep a runway like that cleared."

"It's not such a mystery," Renny told him. "I think it's an old lake bed, a dried mud flat that is so impregnated with minerals, —possibly salt—that the vegetation won't grow on it."

"Watch for trouble!" Doc warned.

They were getting down low enough now to make a stab at identifying the figure which was gesturing at them. It was broad, not tall.

"Monk!" Renny yelled. "That's Monk! That's the suit Monk was wearing in New York. He always wears the same suit a week at a time." He scowled. "Wait a minute. His face doesn't look right."

They were around six hundred feet, so identifying a face, even Monk's face, was mostly guessing. Doc sent the ship lower.

"Seems to be blood on his face," Doc said.

"Uh-huh," Renny muttered. "Could be red berry juice, if it wasn't Monk, too."

The figure below solved their doubts by suddenly dashing into the jungle, and reappearing dragging a limp man. He waved his arms triumphantly, jumped around, went back and came out dragging another figure.

Renny roared, "Holy cow! It's Monk! He cleaned up on them after he radioed us! That explains the blood on his face. They had a fight, and Monk licked the pack of them."

This struck Doc as a natural conclusion. Monk was phenomenal in a hand to hand fight.

Doc put the plane across the field at a hundred and fifty feet, then banked back explaining, "We will drag the field at about ten feet altitude to be sure it's all right."

He arched back, adjusting flaps and props and getting down the gear. He could see the landing strip clear ahead. It seemed okay. The only moving figure in sight was the one they had identified as Monk.

He was thinking how fine everything was when the trip-rope of vines flew up in front of the plane. He hardly saw the thing before he hit it.

Things began coming off the plane, the first thing being the right-side motor.

## XI

There were probably no tougher vines in the world than those which grew in the Amazon basin jungle. They were the greatest obstruction to movement. Some were three or four inches thick, and from that they shaded down to fine threads that were as tough as buckskin. The trip-rope was made of vines.

It was no five-minute job. The main rope was a braided cable effect, with stringers hanging down. There must be, over at the side in the jungle, a devil of an efficient weight and pulley gadget to yank it up so quickly.

The starboard motor went out of its mount because the bent propblades threw it off balance. It just tore itself loose.

The shock was not too terrific. The plane was heavy, and it snapped the vine cable.

The vines were tangled in the left motor, which was still running. The vines beat and flailed and knocked the glass out of the cabin windows on that side, tore the wing covering. The noise was of many bullwhips.

Doc cut the motor-switches. He whirled the control wheel and did a fandango on the rudder bars. He didn't get the ship quite level. But he did get it mushed out in landing attitude. The only trouble was that they weren't going straight down the runway any longer. The jungle was puffing up in front of them.

The plane fuselage dived into the jungle, leaving both wings behind. It shed wheels, fuselage-skin and other things including anything resembling its former streamlined shape. The uproar was as if several sacks of very big cans were being dragged over rocky ground. Early in the uproar, Doc hit the safety catches and the cabin doors and escape hatches flew off the plane, propelled by the jettisoning devices.

The first thing to do after any plane crackup was get out. Get free. Because nothing burns quite as vigorously as an airplane. Doc twisted about, said, "Renny, are you—"

"Hell, yes," Renny said.

Powell was fighting with his safety belt. He couldn't get the fastener unhooked. He seemed all right otherwise. Doc reached up —the plane was on its nose—and twisted Powell's belt fastener open. Powell was merely confused.

They piled out of the ship.

"Get away from here!" Doc said. "Move fast!"

Powell lost his confusion. He bored into the jungle with the practice of an expert and the vigor of a man with death blowing on his heels.

Renny said, "Holy cow!" and charged after Powell. Renny would keep track of Powell, Doc knew.

Doc himself moved rapidly for a few yards, or as rapidly as the tangle of the jungle would permit, then gave all his attention to being silent. He went back to a spot where he could see the landing strip.

The man they had thought was Monk was gone. He hadn't been Monk, of course.

The "unconscious men," who the pretended Monk had hauled out into the clearing, were gone. Doc surmised they had arisen and fled under their own power.

You mutt, he thought. What did you use for brains a minute ago?

He went back to his wrecked plane. It had not burned. He scouted the vicinity carefully, decided it was safe to enter the ship, and did so swiftly. The stuff he wanted was the medical kit and portable radio. He got them. He left the plane quickly.

His plain white shirt was nothing to be wearing in the jungle if one wanted to escape discovery. He stripped it off. To help against the heat, he used his pocket knife to make his trousers into shorts. All the time, he was listening.

Nothing seemed to be stirring in the jungle. That puzzled him.

As protection against insects, he rubbed some chemical repeller into his skin. The jungle mosquitoes could be a fright, so bad you carried a sack and sat with your legs in that whenever you rested. There were *puim*, the little lice with wings and the *maquim*, which had the habits of chiggers, but considerably more voracity, and others as bad.

After a while, he caught a sound. He heard it again. He began moving, stalking the noise.

It was a native. An unlovely, insect-welted little jungle man. He had a pot belly and muscles like wires and a gee-string and a blowgun as long as he was. He had the tiny arrows for the blowgun tucked in his frizzled hair.

He was stalking the plane.

Shortly he put an arrow into the blowgun, raised the long tube to his lips, and blew out his cheeks, held them a moment, let the air go. Actually, the little arrow's *tink!* on the metal flank of the plane was louder than the blowgun sound.

The small native waited a while, warily. Then he took another shot at the plane, as if he thought it was some great wounded bird that he was going to dispatch with his arrows.

Doc waited, watching. He kept his ears open, lest other natives approach and surround him before he knew it. They could move silently in the jungle. Their stealth could surprise you. But they weren't superghosts. He was not afraid of being taken unawares.

Now the one native was advancing.

The little jungle ruffian held both hands up, palms out, an accepted gesture of peace, and walked to the plane.

He stood beside the plane, listening.

"Anybody home?" he asked.

Doc came near starting violently enough to betray his hiding-place. The native's English wasn't good. But it was plainly understandable, with a slightly slangy swing. And it was so utterly the last thing Doc expected the little imp to say that he was dumfounded.

The pot-bellied little man looked into the plane. He stepped up on the wing stub, opened the cabin door, which had swung shut, and looked inside. He scratched his head, puzzled.

He knew what planes were, Doc decided. When he'd fired those arrows, he hadn't thought he was attacking a big bird.

Doc watched the fellow prowl around the ship. The man found the tracks made by Doc, Renny and Powell. As soon as he found the tracks, he whirled and dashed for the landing strip.

Out on to the landing strip, head back, stomach out, he sped toward the southern end of the strip.

He vanished into the jungle.

There was time to second-count to about twenty.

Then shots. First one rifle bang. Then three more, scattered. A shotgun crashed, evidently a double-barreled gun because it went off twice.

Someone swore in good New York English and said, "The little son-of-a-gun got away!"

Another voice called, "You see the plane?"

Monk's voice!

The first speaker said, "I can see where it crashed into the jungle down yonder."

Now men came out on the landing strip. The first was a very tall young man with stooped shoulders. Then, in a group, there were Monk Mayfair, Bob French, old Benjy, and the two girls, Grace Blassett and Willa Morris.

There were about a dozen natives with them. These natives looked better fed and were wearing different articles of European clothing in the individualistic fashion which natives like. One man had two neckties tied around each forearm.

The tall, stooped young man was the leader. He shouted, "There's their plane!"

The group raced down the landing strip.

Doc remained where he was. Not far from the plane. But hidden among the vines.

Monk, he saw, seemed to be in fair shape. Monk looked somewhat confused, however, as if things had been moving too fast for him.

Bob French and old Benjy he identified without trouble. He had their descriptions—Renny had described French, and they'd learned about old Benjy at the New York apartment house of the two girls.

He found it interesting to identify Grace Blassett. Monk had been acting somewhat queerly in the course of recent events. Doc began to see what was probably causing Monk's deviations.

The racing group reached the plane. They searched it. Monk scrambled inside the fuselage.

"They're not here!" Monk yelled angrily. "Dammit, those natives must have packed them off!"

The tall, stooped young man turned to one of the natives, happening to choose the unorthodox wearer of the neckties. He grunted and gurgled at the native. The native looked at the ground for a while, then did some grunting himself.

"He says," the tall, hunched young man translated, "that there are not enough native tracks for the natives to have carried them off."

Monk scratched his head. He examined the ground himself, and evidently decided it was logical.

Monk lifted his voice.

"Doc!" he bellowed. "Oh, Doc! Are you all right?"

Doc kept silent. He wasn't sure what was going on. It struck him there was something queer.

"Doc!" Monk was howling. "Renny! Hey, this is Monk. Come here, before the gooks find you!"

His roar shook the jungle. Obviously Renny and Powell heard it.

Shortly Renny called, "What gives, Monk?"

"Come on outa there," Monk shouted at the jungle.

Renny appeared then. Powell was with him.

Doc Savage watched Monk and Renny pound each other on the back. The situation seemed to be all right. And yet in the back of Doc's mind there was a specter of doubt, a black threatening uncertainty. It sat there like a dangerous beast.

Monk was yelling, "Where's Doc? Good God, do you suppose they got Doc?"

His concern got the best of Doc's better judgment, of his vague conviction that he shouldn't be doing this.

He walked out of the jungle, joining them.


The tall, stooped young man was Tucker French. Bob French —who was still in his army uniform—made the introduction.

"This is Tucker, my kid brother," Bob said.

There were family resemblances. Both had long noses and blue eyes and a gangling length that was almost awkwardness.

Tucker French put out his hand.

"Savage? Doc Savage?" he said, as if puzzled. "Well, I've never heard of you, but apparently my brother has. And he seems impressed."

Monk had a story to tell.

"Doc," he said excitedly, "Doc, when we came down to land in that clearing, a vine rope tripped us—"

"Just how," Doc asked, "did you know about the landing strip?"

Monk indicated Bob French. "He knew."

"Naturally I knew the location of the strip," Bob French said.

Tucker French, his brother, put in—too quickly, it could have been,—saying, "Bob should know. I've written him about it often enough, and it's easy to find, in the fork of two rivers the way it is."

"That's right," Bob said.

Their glibness gave Doc Savage a queer feeling, and the reason for the queerness he didn't exactly understand. He said, "Let's go back farther than that. Monk, how did your party happen to head for here in the first place?"

"For South America, you mean?"

Monk scratched his head. "Well, back in New York after Bob French called on Renny asking for help, then skipped out so mysteriously, you assigned me the job of tracing Bob French through the laundry mark on his blouse. Well, I traced it to his address in Long Island City, where I met these two girls who were also hunting French. We joined up with Benjy, here, who works for the girls, and then we found Bob French in the girls' apartment."

Monk deviated to explain about the mysterious, very heavy something which old Benjy had moved from the downtown warehouse to the girls' apartment—the stuff having been stolen by the men who had knocked out Bob French.

"Bob French had regained consciousness after they kayoed him and heard them say they were headed for South America, and what airport they were leaving from," Monk continued. "We figured we could tear out there and head them off. Well, we tried, but they were already taking off. So I rented a plane in a hell of a hurry, telephoned you, and we followed them.

"You didn't exactly follow them," Doc reminded him. "You had Santa Isabel on your mind. You said you thought that was where they were heading."

"Sure."

"What put Santa Isabel in your head?"

Monk pointed at Bob French. "Him."

Bob nodded. "That's right. I remembered hearing them say they would fly a straight course from Caracas to Santa Isabel on the Negros river in Brazil."

Doc said patiently, "Now, what put this particular landing field in your head."

"Him again." Monk indicated Bob French.

Bob French scowled slightly. "I got that idea no more than an hour ago, when it suddenly dawned on me that this flight course would put us over brother's landing strip."

"So," Monk said, "we thought we'd sit down and ask brother Tucker what it was all about."

"You made a queer landing," Doc reminded him.

Now Tucker French entered the conversation. "If you don't mind," he said, "I think we had better get the more important material you wish to salvage out of the plane, and head for the safety of my trading post."

One of the natives had been grunting uneasily, and now he burst out in a series of vocal sounds, interspersed with grunting and snorting, to express himself. Tucker French evidently understood the primitive language, because he showed some concern.

"There are hostile natives nearby in the jungle," Tucker French told Doc.

Doc made no comment. Could be, he thought. But if there were, the grunting and snorting native hadn't heard them. Doc had been listening himself. He was willing to bet that there hadn't been any sounds in the jungle which were man-made.

Monk said, "The natives wrecked my plane. They seized us as soon as we crashed. They were carrying us off."

Tucker French said, "Fortunately, I heard the plane come down, and so I rushed to the spot, surmising what might have happened. With my men, I was fortunate enough to overhaul the war party which had your friends, and rescue them."

Monk grinned. "That was nice timing, too."

"Much of a fight?" Doc asked.

"Not much. There was some dart blowing, then the little devils who had us just faded away into the jungle."

Tucker French said, "They're not anxious for a pitched fight with me. They're marauders, more cunning than violent." He grimaced. "However, they did surprise me, when they wrecked your plane."

"My plane, you mean?" Doc said. "They wrecked it?"

"Of course."

"They're persistent."

Tucker French laughed grimly. "That's right. They're after me, of course. But they've been after me for a year or so."

"They've tried this plane-wrecking gag with a vine rope before?" Doc asked curiously.

"Oh, yes. Matter of fact, that's why I no longer use the strip. They nearly got me."

"What," Doc asked, "is the trouble between you and these natives?"

Tucker French shrugged. "Why did my grandfather have to fight Indians in Dakota? Much the same sort of thing."

He glanced about uneasily at the jungle. And one of the natives grunted excitedly, pointing.

Tucker French walked over to the object which was exciting the grunter, and plucked it from a thick leaf in which it was embedded. It was one of the tiny blowgun darts.

"I don't believe we should stand around here any longer," he said. He opened his shirt and showed them that he wore a metallic mesh undershirt of the type often worn by explorers in the poison-arrow country. "Even with one of these, I don't feel safe."

They got going.

## XII

The walk was not long. About half an hour. Powell dropped back with Doc Savage, and talked glibly about the jungle. It sounded to Doc as if Powell was talking from nervousness. Some of what he told them was trite stuff.

The *piranha*, for instance. The *piranha* were the small flat fish with the ferocious expressions and teeth that could cut like razors, the fish which suddenly appeared in a stream by the thousands at the trace of blood, and in a moment or two would leave nothing but the skeleton of a man.

Doc listened patiently. Everybody, he supposed, had heard of *piranha*.

Another thing Powell talked about was the difference between the black *jacare* and the brown one. The black one frequently reached a length of twenty-five feet, and was the most dangerous of the caiman family. You could guess the mind of a light-colored *jacare*, he warned, but for God's sake be careful about the black ones.

Powell was scared, Doc finally decided. Whether Powell was frightened of the natives or not, Doc couldn't tell.

The going was not hard. They were on a path, a well-trimmed one, and they went fast.

Tucker French dropped back and told Doc Savage, "The path we're on now is my main road to the river. We use it frequently. My place isn't far."

Doc said nothing. He was wondering why nobody had said a word about the pink elephant in the affair—the cause of all the scuffling. The "heavy stuff," whatever it was.

It seemed that everyone was avoiding it.

They reached Tucker French's place.

Anywhere but in the jungle, it wouldn't have been impressive. In the jungle, it was. It was in a stretch of country which an explorer would have called palmy. Which meant simply that it was higher ground, well-drained, that there were tall *babassu* palms, the fronds of which met overhead to form a cathedral-like effect with the last of the evening sunlight streaming down.

There was an outer cultivated fence of thorn trees, something like the "hedge" fences found in Iowa and Missouri. But thicker, more rank. Nothing larger than a mouse could pass through the fence readily.

The trading post was in the center of the fenced circle, the fence being far enough away that no blowgun arrow could reach it.

There were four buildings, none of them large, connected with a low wall so that the effect was somewhat that of a fort, but not too much so. Stone was the building material used. The stone had been dug up on the site, and laid with a mortar of local siliceous sand and lime made by burning limestone on the spot.

There was nothing extraordinary about the spot, except that Tucker French's personal quarters were air-conditioned. The air-conditioning was not too good, but it was better than the jungle heat. Tucker French was obviously proud of it.

"I have some good *maté,*" he said. "How about a highball?"

Doc said grimly, "You might also serve up a little more information."

This sounded, he realized, more angry and suspicious than he intended.

Tucker French's innocence was almost baby-like. "I don't understand."

"The box of snake-skins," Doc said. "What about it?"

Tucker French looked vaguely dumfounded, as if he didn't in the least know what a box of snake-skins was.

Sir Roger Powell said, "He means the box of snake hides you gave me to take to New York."

"Oh, those," said Tucker French vaguely. "Why, I ship a few snake hides now and then. What about them?"

"The box seems to be behind this trouble," Doc told him.

Tucker French smiled. "Oh, you must be mistaken. They were just snake skins."

Doc said, "You gave them to Powell to give to Blassett and Morris."

"Yes, that's right."

"Blassett and Morris had never heard of you and they don't deal in snake hides," Doc countered sharply.

"We discussed that before your plane landed," Tucker French said easily. "I'm afraid I made an error."

"Error?"

"I understood Blassett and Morris were snake-skin dealers. I was wrong." Tucker French smiled again, but it wasn't very genuine.

Doc could feel tension growing in the room. There wasn't anything visible. It was just a feeling.

"The box was pretty heavy," he said.

No one said anything. Grace Blassett wasn't looking at anyone. Her face, Doc thought, was getting a little gray with fright.

"It was a pretty heavy box," Doc said. "Three of us could barely lift it with levers. Then it suddenly became as light as a normal box should be."

Tucker French smiled. "Is this a ghost story?"

Doc was silent. It was a difficult silence, because he was trying to hold down a growing impulse to smash things. He was, he saw, being roundly lied to.

He turned slowly to old Benjy. "What was it that you took from that downtown warehouse in New York to the girls' apartment?" he asked the old man.

Benjy looked him in the eye.

"Nothing," Benjy said. "I didn't take anything. You can't prove I did."

Doc looked intently at the ceiling.

"Does anyone have the least idea why we're down here?" he asked wearily.

"To have a drink with me, I hope," Tucker French said, laughing again. It was a queer laugh.

Suddenly Doc was sure that Tucker French was a very dangerous fellow.

"I don't drink," Doc said shortly.

The night came on slowly. Now and then a native would come to consult with Tucker French to the effect that there was no sign of the other natives, the bad ones, the marauders.

Doc gave no inkling that he could understand the grunts and snorts and cackling that was the native language. He understood it fairly well. Well enough to know that the natives were saying what Tucker French said they were saying.

Also he understood the lingo well enough to know that the natives were mouthing exactly what they had been told to say. The natives were poor actors. They had poker faces, but they didn't get the necessary conviction into their grunts and other sounds.

Doc began to find cold sweat on the backs of his hands. He knew it was along his backbone, too. He was frightened.

The outward appearance of things was as social as any cocktail hour would have been in the jungle. It shouldn't have been. It was unnatural.

Monk and Renny felt the same way. He could tell. Monk was fascinated by pretty Grace Blassett, but fear was beginning to get the better of Monk's prowling instincts. Renny's long face was more composed, but his big hands were gripping various things, the arms of his chair for instance, very tightly.

A native announced dinner.

"Perhaps you would like to clean up," Tucker French said easily.

Doc managed to get Monk and Renny alone in the modern bathroom.

"How do you feel about this?" Doc asked them.

Monk said, "I'm beginning to sweat icicles."

"We're being ganged up on," Doc said.

Renny nodded. He thought so, too.

Doc said, "Back there in the jungle, during this capture and rescue thing you fellows went through—did Tucker French have a chance to talk to Benjy, the two girls and Bob French without you hearing?"

Renny scowled. "Yes, he did."

"Notice any change after that?"

"Come to think of it, yes."

"All right," Doc said. "It's the three of us against the rest of them."

Monk asked, "What do you think they're planning to do with us?"

"I don't want to scare myself by wondering," Doc told him. "Keep your eyes open."

He went back to the living room. He found Powell and Tucker French holding a lips-to-ear conversation. They didn't quite spring apart guiltily. At least, Powell was the only one who sprang.

"Powell was just telling me the latest war news," Tucker French said. "I'm a few months behind on it."

They hadn't been discussing any war news, Doc knew. Powell looked too relieved. He looked like a man who wanted to giggle, like a man who had just won the sweepstakes.

"Don't you have a radio?" Doc asked idly.

"It's out of order," Tucker French said. "One of the fool natives broke the tubes."

Doc said, "Your brother Bob says he received a cablegram from you."

Tucker French smiled his worst smile.

"That's quite a mystery, isn't it?" he said. "I wonder who could have sent it?"

"Quite a mystery," Doc agreed, trying to use the same man-eating cheerful tone Tucker French was using.

Dinner was uneventful, but it was also as false as the gaiety of medical school students eating dinner on a dissecting table as a gag. Doc himself ate nothing which Tucker French did not sample first. He noticed that Monk and Renny didn't either.

Throughout the meal, Tucker French kept up a running fire of questions at his brother. Bob, what kind of action did you see in the army? Was China very interesting? How many times were you shot at?

They weren't the questions, somehow, that a brother would ask another brother. And the answers weren't right, either. They were forced.

Doc formed a fairly certain conviction that Bob French didn't like what was going on, but for some reason or other felt that he couldn't do anything about it.

After dinner, Doc said, "I have a portable radio. We might tune in some news."

He went to get the little portable outfit—a transmitter-receiver combination affair which under favorable conditions could reach some other station, probably one at Manaos or Bogota.

He found the radio smashed.

"These damned dumb natives!" Tucker French said with anger which must be feigned. "One of them smashed it, I'm afraid."

Doc nodded.

"And the radio transmitters in both planes were doubtless ruined in the crash," he said.

"I'm afraid so," Tucker French said.

"That's too bad."

"Indeed it is," Tucker French agreed. "Do you and your two friends mind sharing the same bedroom?"

"Not at all."

"I'll show you where it is."

The bedroom was large and had several very small windows which Doc was particular to note were not large enough to permit a man to escape by crawling through them.

Tucker French, in the course of looking over the room, emitted a startled cry and sprang forward. He bent over a small object on the floor.

"For God's sake, keep away from this!" he cried.

The insect on the floor was an ant.

It was a peculiar ant, however. It was about an inch and a quarter long, with a velvety appearance and an enormous head.

Doc had a near malaria chill for a moment. An *iste* ant. The bites of the things were deadly poison.

Tucker French told them what it was. He dressed it up a little, making it sound as if the *iste* bite was worse than that of a cobra.

"It's the work of those infernal natives who were shooting poisoned arrows at us," Tucker French told them emphatically. "Now and then they catch some *iste* ants and let them loose near my stockade fence. This one must have worked its way into the house. I'll help you search your bedclothing for more of them."

They didn't find any more *iste*.

"I don't believe it is safe for you to walk around the place during the night," Tucker French told them.

"Yes, that seems to be fairly obvious," Doc agreed, using the man-eating cheerful tone.

When they were alone in the bedroom, Monk whispered, "Say, are we gonna stay in here tonight?"

"We are not!" Doc said vehemently.

"Then what—"

"We are going to the bathroom together again," Doc said.

They strolled to the bathroom. They met Tucker French enroute, and told him they were going to the bathroom.

The bathroom had a window a man could crawl through.

"Crawl out," Doc said. "Hide. Don't move around and get yourselves seen. In an hour or so, or when everyone is asleep, come and get me out of that bedroom, because I have a hunch the door will be locked by then."

Renny, having difficulty keeping his whisper from being a roar like his voice, whispered, "And I've got a hunch nobody plans to sleep in this house tonight."

"Out of the window," Doc said.

"How you going to cover when they check up to make sure we're all in our little beds?"

"I'll try to sound like all three of us," Doc said. "Get going."

Renny went out of the window. Monk followed. Monk whispered, "If those jungle natives hanging around—"

"You can forget the jungle natives hanging around," Doc said.

"Yes, but will they forget me?"

"They aren't."

"Eh?"

"Those jungle natives," Doc said, "are the figments of Tucker Powell's imagination, I hope."

Monk shivered before he disappeared and said, "I hope so, too."

Doc went back to the bedroom. He didn't meet anyone. He closed the door and locked it on the inside, after noting that there was a padlock hasp on the outside. It was a very strong door.

He took off his shoes and lay down on one bed and turned out the light, then waited for the check-up.

A knock on the door.

"Yes?"

"Thought you might like some cold beer as a nightcap," Tucker French's voice said.

Doc said, "Monk, do you want some cold beer?"

Imitating Monk's voice as closely as he could, Doc said, "No, my feet are cold enough as it is."

"Renny?"

"No, thanks." Using Renny's voice.

"I guess not," Doc said using his own voice again.

"Well, sleep tight," Tucker French said.

He sounded as if he had been fooled.

Surmising that the fellow might listen outside the door, Doc proceeded to carry on a three-sided conversation using the voices of Renny, Monk and Himself. He did that for a while. Then he had his voices agree that they might as well get some sleep.

Lying there after he had finished, he felt silly. He was pretty good at voice mimicry. He had practiced it a lot, and he had used it before. But he felt silly anyway.

He was somewhat pleased, too. It was a crazy sort of a thing to do. He liked such things.

He thought back, lying there in the darkness, of the monologue he had given, while flying south in the plane with Renny and Powell, about his strange youth. About the lack of a normal boy's devilment and small adventures which had featured his youth. Of how he was convinced that having missed such things as a kid accounted for his present interest in the fantastic and the adventurous and the quixotic.

The self-analysis was accurate, he hoped. It was a sensible explanation of the elation with which he seized upon a goofy way of accomplishing something instead of using a more normal and probably more sensible method. Like the trick he was trying to pull now.

Such methods probably meant he needed psychoanalysis, he reflected.

# XIII

A couple of hours later, Monk Mayfair clubbed someone over the head outside the door. It didn't make much noise.

Doc whispered, "Watch the door, it squeaks." They eased the panel open carefully.

"Lucky they didn't have it padlocked," Monk breathed. "Just stuck a bolt in the staple."

"Who did you hit?"

"One of the local boys," Monk explained. "He was standing here with a rifle, but he turned his back."

They carried the native into the bedroom. Monk had used his fist on the fellow, so he would probably revive in time.

"Tie him and gag him," Doc said.

They ran into difficulty. The native had some kind of adenoidal difficulty which rendered him unable to breathe through his nose. If they gagged him, he would suffocate.

Renny said, "I've got an idea." He went away and came back with the carafe of *maté* which had been served earlier in the night. He began pouring it down the native.

Monk started to giggle. He finally had to collapse on the edge of the bed and hold his mouth.

"What the hell's the matter with you?" Renny demanded.

"What you trying to do to that native?"

"Make him drunk so he can't talk for a while."

"With *maté*?"

"Sure."

"*Maté* is a form of tea. It has no alcoholic content, and contains less caffeine than ordinary tea or coffee."

Renny stared at the carafe intently. Without a word, he put it down on the floor and walked out. Doc kept a straight face with some difficulty.

Renny came back with a square-sided bottle. He said, "At least I know what gin is." He began pouring gin down the native who had been on guard.

Doc shook a little with silent laughter, entertained by Renny's sheepish disgust. It was good, he suddenly realized, to be able to laugh. The mirth, like a clean shower, washed away some of the slime that continual fear was beginning to deposit on his nerves.

While Renny was funneling gin down the native, Doc asked Monk, "Anything been going on?"

"Plenty big pow-wow in the main storeroom," Monk said.

"What about?"

"No idea. Renny and I couldn't get near enough to overhear."

"Who attended?"

"Everyone."

"The two girls?"

"Uh-huh," Monk said sourly. "I can't feature Grace Blassett being mixed in something shady, but I guess she is."

Renny straightened.

"Let's go see what the pow-wow has developed into," the big-fisted engineer suggested.

They moved warily through the house, stepping cautiously, stopping to listen. Doc found an outer door, moved it carefully and got it open without enough sound to worry them. They stepped out into the night.

Something seemed to be going on around at the front of the place.

"Careful," Doc breathed.

A moment later, they could see what was happening. Renny's, "Holy cow! They're all going into the jungle!" wasn't necessary.

It was a grim-faced group in front of the trading post. They were all there, except Tucker French. And he appeared shortly, with an electric lantern, dragging a two-wheeled iron cart. The cart was small, with wide-tread wheels. It was something like a wheelbarrow, except that it was two-wheeled.

Tucker French told Benjy, "You bring this." Benjy took the cart.

They walked toward the gate in the hedge. Tucker French unfastened the gate. He did not close it. The gate was unguarded.

Monk growled, "Say, they're not much scared of the boys with the blowguns!"

"There aren't any boys with blowguns besieging the place," Doc said.

"But that arrow Tucker French found sticking in a leaf—"

"He probably stuck it there himself," Doc said. "Then found it later for our benefit. Come on."

The jungle darkness was thick because of the canopy of palms overhead. Nothing happened when they passed through the gate.

Doc went ahead, feeling the way. There was a path, not hard to follow. The iron cart Benjy was dragging had taken to squeaking. The sound was a help.

The way led sharply upward. There was a hill which they had not noticed particularly from the air. Hills in the jungle were difficult to locate, because frequently the trees in the damper jungle grew a hundred feet taller than those on drier high ground.

This hill was rocky, too. The trees on it became not much more than rank bushes. The path was not wide, but it was solid, easily followed. The canopy of foliage above shut off less light now, so they could see where they were going, discern the path easily.

The cluster of lights ahead came to a stop.

"Take your time getting up on them," Doc warned. "And separate. When we meet, it will be on the west side, toward the moon."

He parted from Monk and Renny, silently.

Because it was obvious the group ahead did not expect to be followed, he went ahead boldly, only using care not to make any noise.

Powell, Tucker French, Bob French and all the others were gathered together. Benjy was leaning on the iron cart, mopping perspiration.

Doc frowned. Evidently they were where they were going. But the spot did not look interesting. There was just rock. Hard stone, which could be some sort of quartz.

Tucker French made a speech.

He said, "Like every explorer, I was always taking rock samples when I traveled. This rock here is quartz, and you find minerals in quartz veins frequently. So I prospected the place as a matter of course."

Powell said, "Your finding it was an accident, then?"

"Not entirely," Tucker French told him. "My compass was acting funny as anything, and that aroused my curiosity. It led me to the exact spot."

"Right here?"

"Yes."

"I don't see anything."

Tucker French laughed. "I hope not, all the trouble I took to hide it."

He began kicking brush aside, exposing an expanse of loose stone.

"Help me toss the loose rock aside," he said.

"How far down is it?" Powell demanded eagerly.

"Right on top, almost."

Doc watched them remove the loose stone from a small pit. All of them worked but the two girls and Bob French. These three stood back, white-faced, and watched.

Once Tucker French said to his brother, "Get in here and help, Bob."

Bob French said nothing, did not help.

They cleared the hole and climbed out.

Tucker French said, "Let's get our breath." He mopped his face, then continued, "Maybe it hit in the form of a meteor centuries ago. I don't know."

"What makes you think a meteor?" Powell asked.

"Well, the only thing that science has ever heard of that is anything like it is the substance of which one of the stars is composed. Astronomers found a star made of something like it."

Old Benjy snorted. "How the hell can they tell what a star is made of?"

"They can, don't kid yourself," Tucker French told him. "They analyze the light from the star, somehow. I can't give you the exact procedure. But they get what they call a spectra by breaking up the light. If the body is hot they get what they call an emission spectra, and it's fairly easy to make a spectrum analysis with a gadget made of flint and crown glass prisms, I think."

"That's enough to confuse me," Benjy said. "I'll take your word."

Tucker French said, "All right. Let's get a chunk out. We'll have to use crowbars and tongs."

He got down in the pit with Powell. For the next ten minutes the men alternately struggled, cursed, and perspired.

It took four of them to lift out what they were after.

The object they had, as nearly as Doc could make out, was not much larger than a marble.

"Hell, this is a light piece," Tucker French said.

"You kidding?" Benjy said.

Tucker French said they had better rest a while before trying to put it into the cart.

"This is lighter than the one I sent to New York embedded in the bottom of the box which held the snake skins," Tucker French said. "That one was not much larger than the eraser off a pencil."

Bob French frowned at his brother. "How'd you get the other piece out?"

"By stripping the inside of my cargo plane," Tucker told hi
"Then I reinforced the ship so that it would carry it. I flew it as f
as Cartagena, made up the special box, got enough snake hid
locally to fill it, and turned it over to Powell to take north."

Bob French wheeled to Powell. "So you knew what it was
along?"

Powell hesitated. "Yes."

"And you were going to steal the sample?"

Tucker French laughed unpleasantly. "He was going to steal n
only the sample, but the whole deposit. He got in touch wi
Blassett and Morris, told them what he had, and found out it wa
valuable. So he got a gang together intending to come back dow
here and do me in."

Powell said coldly, "I wasn't going to kill anybody."

"I can imagine," Tucker said bitterly.

Bob French growled, "Now wait a minute! Don't start a figh
Let me get this straight. Powell, I can see why you lied to me ar
said you didn't know anything about any heavy stuff. You didn
want to give away the secret. But what about that attack on you
the New York hotel?"

"Fake. Arranged it myself." Powell sounded pleased wit
himself. "That was to fool Doc Savage, make him think I didn
know anything about anything—to make him think I was
danger and needed his protection. As long as he was protectin
me, I would know what he was doing."

"At the warehouse, it was your men who tried to kill him?"

"Yes."

"You were with them. Why wouldn't the gas have killed you?

"Because I would have got the hell out of there before it did.
wasn't tied like the others. My men just pretended to tie me. B
old Benjy came busting in and ruined the plan."

Bob French shook his head strangely. He turned to the tw
girls, said, "And you were in on it too, murder and all?"

Grace gasped, shook her head mutely. Her companion, Bil
said, "No, no, we didn't have any part in that!"

"It looks to me as if you did."

Bill looked ill. She said, "Powell came to us and told us abou
the heavy stuff, and we knew it was valuable. But we didn't tru
Powell, and began watching him. We saw he was up to somethin
crooked. So we began trying to get the heavy stuff ourselves."

"Oh, you were going to steal it yourself."

Bill shook her head. "We were protecting your brother'

nterests. We wanted to handle the heavy stuff, but not if there
vas crooked work connected with it."

Bob French spat violently. "Just sheep in the wolf den!" he
aid.

His brother said, "Cut it out, Bob."

Bob French stared at his brother. He did not say anything more.

Old Benjy, leaning on the cart again, said, "To put it all in a
nutshell: Tucker French found this stuff. Tucker French couldn't
go to New York to sell it himself on account of he is a
draft-dodger. So Tucker gave a sample to Powell to take to New
York and arrange a sale. Powell tried to steal the whole thing.
Blassett and Morris tried to prevent it. Bob French tried to prevent
it. Doc Savage tried to prevent it. We all wound up here."

"One big happy family!" said Bob French bitterly.

"Why not?" his brother shouted at him. "We decided there was
no need for violence, that there was enough money in it for all of
us. So we would all drop our schemes and work together. Isn't
that sensible?"

"Doc Savage," Bob French said.

"Eh?"

"What do you plan to do with Savage and his two friends?"

"Let him cool off," Tucker French said. "Then tell him the
truth. If he wants to be contrary, there is nothing he can do. At the
worst, we may have to make him walk to civilization, which will
take him a couple of months."

Grace Blassett said anxiously, "You mean that? You're not
going to kill him?"

"Good God, no!" Tucker French exclaimed. "Let's get this
piece loaded and get back to the post."

They heaved and grunted some more, and finally got the small
fragment of whatever it was loaded into the cart.

Tucker French flopped down on the ground, puffing.

"I'm exhausted!" he gasped. "Bob, you and Benjy and the girls
go ahead with the cart. Powell and I will be along as soon as we
catch our breath."

Powell puffed, "Golly, that's an idea." He flopped down beside
Tucker French.

Old Benjy began wrestling with the cart. He and Bob French
pulled. The two girls pushed.

They struggled down the trail with the unwieldly load.

Doc remained where he was. Tucker French and Powell, he
was sure, had remained behind for some good reason.

Tucker French did nothing but breathe heavily for a whil
Then he growled, "Well, you know where it is now."

"How much is in there?" Powell asked.

"Piece the size of a small house, nearly as I can tell."

Powell whistled softly. "That's plenty."

Tucker French asked anxiously, "You're sure it's worth a lot
money?"

"Hell, yes!" Powell exclaimed instantly. "I think the be
market is to sell it in tiny bits to scientists and scientif
institutions and museums. Divided up like that, it'll be worth a
much as gold. More. There's nothing else like it on earth. Ever
scientific research laboratory will want a piece."

Tucker French nodded. "I hoped it would have some specif
value immediately. It's a new element."

"You don't seem to realize the curiosity value of the stu
alone," Powell told him. "We would divide it up in pieces the siz
of a pea and get a million bucks peddling it to people who ju
wanted a chunk for a curiosity."

"You reckon that's the only value it's got?"

"I don't know. Probably not. We'll have to find out."

The two were silent for a while. The iron cart was squeaking i
the distance.

Powell laughed suddenly. It wasn't pleasant.

"What's the matter with you?" Tucker French demande
nervously. "What are you laughing at?"

"At Doc Savage," Powell said.

"What do you mean?"

"You know what we've got to do with Savage, don't you?"

"Eh?"

"Kill him. Kill Monk Mayfair and Renny Renwick, too."

## XIV

The two men sat there. Tucker French stared sickly at th
ground. He didn't say anything.

"The two girls and that Benjy had better be gotten out of th
way, too," Powell said.

Tucker French shuddered. "I—I can't stand for that."

"You won't have to."

French stared at him. "What do you mean?"

Powell said, "You know my boys in the first airplane? The one in the plane which Savage's plane, and the other ship with Monk and Benjy and the girls and your brother, followed down here?"

Tucker French shook his head. "What have they got to do with it."

"Plenty."

"But Doc Savage doesn't know they're here. He doesn't know that the plane bringing them landed ahead of everyone else, let them out, and then the pilot took the plane on to Santa Isabel to make a false trail if one was necessary."

"No, he doesn't know that."

Tucker French said uneasily, "I don't like your tone. What the hell are you driving at?"

"My boys are hiding out in the jungle near here."

"All right, let them stay out of sight! Pay them whatever you agreed to pay them, and don't tell them anything and—"

"You don't get the idea," Powell said coldly. "You're slow, brother."

Tucker French started to get to his feet. He acted like a man half-frozen.

Powell took a gun out of his clothing, said, "Sit down, sucker."

Tucker French sat down slowly.

"You get it now, don't you?" Powell said.

"You—you're not—"

"Uh-huh. You bet I am." Powell cocked his gun. It was a revolver. "I'm going to take over. Savage and his two friends have to go. Why not you? Your brother, old Benjy, the two girls, too?"

"My God, you're insane!" Tucker French's voice was hoarse.

"Don't move," Powell said.

Powell put two fingers between his lips and whistled shrilly. Three times.

"That's the signal to bring my men," he said. "I told them to stick around and follow us when we left the stockade. Follow our lights, I told them."

Doc Savage came to his feet. He had, for the few brief seconds that he was given to have it, the ghastly certainty that he and Monk and Renny had walked into a devilish predicament. He was right.

From nearby, a voice, one of Powell's men, yelled, "Watch out, boss! Savage and two of his men are around here!"

Tucker French jumped at Powell then. And Powell shot French twice, putting both bullets in Tucker French's face.

The weird part of what followed was the part played by the flashlight which Tucker French was holding when he died. The convulsion which came when the bullets hit him caused him to throw the flashlight. It spun in the air for a moment, splattering light over the jungle as if there was a series of lightning flashes. And when it landed, it did not go out, but rested in a bush with the beam planted on Tucker French's body. It remained there, blazing light on the body.

Powell backed into the jungle after he shot Tucker French, backed slowly, holding his gun ready.

Doc moved silently, stalking him.

Powell called, "You say Savage and his men are here?"

"Yeah."

"How do you know?"

"They followed you up here. Ahead of us. We've been hoping to find—"

A fight broke out in the nearby jungle. Two blows, a shot, scuffling, brush snapping.

Monk, Doc knew. It had to be Monk. Anyone else would have had better sense than start a fight against odds in the jungle night.

Doc lunged for Powell. It was too far, and moreover he tripped. The best he could do was slam his shoulder against Powell violently. Powell didn't fall. He just received a hard push, and kept going. Doc went down, tangled in vines.

Powell whirled. His gun made thunder and winking red glare. Doc rolled, got behind a tree trunk.

Powell screamed, "Get together! Don't try to fight them here! Get together! We'll go to the trading post—"

Where Monk was fighting, sudden silence came.

Then Monk's voice said, "I got two."

Gunsound crashed in the jungle again. A revolver made five splitting roars, emptying itself.

Then silence. Suddenly footsteps were pounding madly from the direction of the post. Up the trail.

It was Bob French. He stopped when he saw his brother. Doc couldn't distinguish him in the darkness, but he heard Bob French's breathing stop.

"Who did that to Tuck?" Bob French asked hollowly.

"Powell," Doc said. "This is Savage. Monk and Renny are around. So are Powell's men and Powell. Be careful."

"How many?"

"Shut up," Doc said.

"How many?"

A gun cracked as someone fired at Bob French's voice.

Bob French shot back instantly. He killed a man. The man he killed didn't scream, but began breathing his life away with awful, labored sounds that were somewhat like snoring.

"I was hoping they'd shoot at my voice," Bob French said. "That's one."

Then they heard from Renny. He rumbled, "Here they are! The rest of them!" And his roar merged with the frantic splatter of gunfire.

Doc charged the sound. He heard Monk going for it, too. But Bob French was ahead of them both. Bob French, with fury, violence, jungle-fighting experience, and a gun.

For the next few seconds, it was one of those things you don't exactly remember afterward. Not that things moved too fast to remember. It was more the fear, the frenzy of trying not to be killed, and to kill, maim, mangle, do anything to save your life.

Doc himself had a throat when silence fell. He had to force himself, making quite an effort, to relinquish his grip before the man he was holding should die.

"How many?" Bob French's voice asked.

Monk said, "Six. Seven including Powell."

Bob French said, "Renny?"

"I'm okay," Renny's voice said.

"A little like the Burma jungles, wasn't it?"

"Uh-huh. Is this all?" Renny asked.

"That's all," Bob French said.

"Providing," Doc Savage corrected, "the natives don't give us trouble."

The natives didn't give them trouble. It made no difference to them, their spokesman explained to Doc, what the white men did to each other. They hadn't been enthusiastic about what was going on, anyway.

The natives would dig graves for those who had been killed, though.

Bob French insisted that his brother not be buried with Powell. Bob said he had no particular regret at having killed Powell.

"I blame Powell more than my brother," Bob explained grimly. "Tucker was a coward at heart, and I knew it and I never blamed him. Something like that, a man has or he hasn't."

Doc said, "Tucker did not start out trying to be crooked."

"I don't think so," Bob agreed. "Tucker was a draft dodger,

though. I knew that. That's why, back in New York, when I went to Renwick for help, I acted so queer when I found out you would get into the affair. I knew you wouldn't have much sympathy for a draft dodger. So I tried to back out. I didn't want to see Tucker in the penitentiary. He was my brother. And I've fought enough of this war for our whole damned family."

"I'll tell the natives about the graves."

"Thanks," Bob French said quietly. His eyes were wet when he turned away.

The next two days were uneventful. Doc Savage was trying to get enough radio parts together to make a transmitter. He did not have much luck.

Renny spent most of his time fooling with the heavy stuff. It was a new element of some sort. New as far as anyone having actually gotten hands on any, although astronomers had discovered the stuff on a star.*

The stuff intrigued Renny. He began coming up with all kinds of ideas about how they would dispose of it.

Monk was also having ideas, some of them fairly desperate.

His prize idea was that Doc, Renny and Bob French take the two-fisted girl, Bill, along with them on the jungle trek to civilization. He, Monk, would stay behind with Grace and old Benjy. Benjy could be chaperone.

"Benjy is getting down with malaria, so he'd be an ideal chaperone," Monk said hopefully.

"What's the matter with you and Bill?" Doc asked.

Monk shivered. "She scares me."

"You don't scare her, I've noticed," Doc told him. "She gives you quite a bit of her time."

"Yeah, so damned much of it that I haven't been able to make any hay with Grace," Monk complained. "You know what that Bill reminds me of?"

"What?"

"You know that big gangling bug around here they call a praying mantis? The female mantis marries the male, then eats him for her wedding breakfast. That's the way Bill affects me."

Doc kept his face straight and said, "Renny and Bob French and I were talking, and we thought we might leave you and Bill here with Benjy while the rest of us made the trip out."

"God help me!" Monk said.

In the end, none of them had to walk out. The man who had

---

* The existence of this extremely heavy matter is not imagination. Scientists have discovered a star in the sky composed of extremely heavy matter. As a writer on scientific oddities recently put it, a piece of it the size of a golf ball would weigh one thousand four hundred and sixty tons. Not pounds. Tons.—*The Author*

gone on to Santa Isabel with the plane came back. Evidently the arrangement had been for him to return with the plane in three days. He made a nice landing, and they did an equally nice job of taking him and the plane back intact.

To the world at large, Doc Savage is a strange, mysterious figure of glistening bronze skin and golden eyes. To his fans he is the greatest adventure hero of all time, whose fantastic exploits are unequaled for hair-raising thrills, breathtaking escapes, blood-curdling excitement!

| | | | |
|---|---|---|---|
| ☐ | 20934 | SECRET OF THE SKY #20 and COLD DEATH #21 | $2.50 |
| ☐ | 22619 | THE CZAR OF FEAR #22 & THE FORTRESS OF SOLITUDE #23 | $2.50 |
| ☐ | 14901 | JIU SAN #107 and BLACK BLACK WITCH #108 | $1.95 |
| ☐ | 20573 | THE SHAPE OF TERROR #109 and DEATH HAD YELLOW EYES #110 | $1.95 |
| ☐ | 22610 | ONE-EYED MYSTIC #111 and MAN WHO FELL UP #112 | $2.50 |
| ☐ | 22755 | THE TALKING DEVIL #113 & THE TEN TON SNAKES #114 | $2.75 |

# OUT OF THIS WORLD!

That's the only way to describe Bantam's great series of science fiction classics. These space-age thrillers are filled with terror, fancy and adventure and written by America's most renowned writers of science fiction. Welcome to outer space and have a good trip!